DOW

We hope you enjoy this book.
Please return or renew it by the due date.
You can renew it at **www.norfolk.gov.uk/libraries**
or by using our free library app. Otherwise you can
phone **0344 800 8020** - please have your library
card and pin ready.
You can sign up for email reminders too.

5/23

NORFOLK COUNTY COUNCIL
LIBRARY AND INFORMATION SERVICE

D1425471

ALSO BY TIM SULLIVAN

The Dentist

THE CYCLIST

TIM SULLIVAN

First published in the UK in 2020 by Pacific Press
This edition first published in the UK in 2021 by Head of Zeus Ltd

Copyright © Tim Sullivan, 2020

The moral right of Tim Sullivan to be identified as the author of this work has
been asserted in accordance with the Copyright, Designs and Patents Act of
1988. All rights reserved.

No part of this publication may be reproduced, stored in a retrieval system, or
transmitted in any form or by any means, electronic, mechanical, photocopying,
recording, or otherwise, without the prior permission of both the copyright
owner and the above publisher of this book.

This is a work of fiction. All characters, organizations, and events portrayed in
this novel are either products of the author's imagination or are used fictitiously.

9 7 5 3 1 2 4 6 8

A catalogue record for this book is available from the British Library.

ISBN (PB): 9781801107686
ISBN (E): 9781801107662

Head of Zeus Ltd
First Floor East
5–8 Hardwick Street
London EC1R 4RG
www.headofzeus.com

Print editions of this book are printed and bound by CPI Group (UK) Ltd,
Croydon, CR0 4YY, on FSC paper

MIX
Paper from
responsible sources
FSC® C020471

For Bella and Sophia

1

'Excuse me? How long before my men can get back to work?' Cross didn't answer but instead looked away at the green, bloated face of the young man in the bucket of the nearby JCB digger. Wrapped in a sheet of builders' polythene, he had been stored in a row of garages that were in the process of being demolished. Blood and bodily fluids, released post mortem, were pooling in the creases of the polythene. It looked like a vacu-packed piece of meat on a supermarket shelf. The man's eyes had the dull, lifeless look of a fish that had been on ice at a fishmonger's for too long. The garages were behind a set of 1950s high-rise council flats in Barton Hill. Full of the promise of a better life back then, they now were a depressing blight on the landscape.

Cross turned back to the contractor and studied him for a couple of seconds. He was a ruddy-faced man in a waxed Barbour coat. He looked like he spent a lot of time outdoors, when he wasn't shining the backside of his trousers on a bar stool at his local pub. Cross noted the use of "my men", designed to give himself some sort of elevated status.

'There's a dead man over there. A young man. Murdered

would not be a too far-fetched deduction, even at this early stage,' Cross said.

'I know and I'm sorry about that, but I need to get on,' the man replied.

'We'll need a statement from you and all the workers who were on site this morning. Then they can go home,' Cross said.

'Go home? What are you talking about?' the man spluttered.

'There's been a murder. What *was* your building site has, by the very presence of a corpse wrapped in polythene in the bucket of one of your diggers, become a crime scene. So unless your workforce has an interest in police procedures and forensics, I would be grateful if they could vacate the scene, as soon as they have given their statements. If they are interested, they could stay and observe from behind the tape,' Cross said.

George Cross, that is Detective Sergeant Cross of the Somerset and Avon police force, to give him his full title, wasn't in the least bit surprised by the man's apparent insensitivity to the young man's recent demise. His bizarre belief that work could go on as normal, as if nothing out of the ordinary had happened, was not uncommon with people in such situations.

What the contractor was struggling with was the fact that the policeman's offer to stay behind and observe didn't come across as the least bit ironic. It was as if he genuinely believed some of his workers might have a secret fascination for the workings of the police in a murder case. Which, he wasn't to know, Cross actually did. He was attempting to behave politely and normally with this man, along the lines his partner DS Ottey had been trying to teach him. Cross was incapable of irony and sarcasm. The contractor turned to DS Ottey, who was standing nearby, for help.

'Let's start by getting your statement down,' she said, pre-empting anything further he might say.

Cross walked back over to the corpse. He was more interested in the environment around it than the corpse itself. He'd have a closer look at that in the morgue.

2

'Mr Morgan, how long have these garages been out of use?' he asked.

'Officially just over a year. But people have been using them illegally; some for storage, some for fly-tipping. We even had a couple of junkies living in one of them. Pain in the bloody arse. No respect for private property,' Morgan complained.

'You brought the date of the demolition forward,' Cross stated.

'Yes, permissions came through five days earlier than expected. How did you know?' Morgan asked.

'I checked the Council Planning Notice before I came. Any particular reason for changing the date?'

'I just wanted to get on with it, that's all,' Morgan replied.

DCI Carson, Cross and Ottey's direct boss, had assigned the, by now customary, minimal number of resources to the investigation. This wasn't so much because murder was no longer considered to be a serious crime, but was due to the fact that continual cuts had meant that there weren't enough people around to man a murder investigation properly. Cross couldn't understand why Ottey remonstrated with Carson every time this happened. It seemed pointless to him. Cross would secretly have preferred to conduct these murder enquiries on his own, even though he knew this was completely impractical. It was useful to have people available to pursue any lines of enquiry he came up with. But essentially he liked to work in a solitary fashion. He didn't have to be constantly monitoring his own behaviour to others when he was on his own.

He certainly couldn't be entrusted with leading a team. It had been tried once, with catastrophic results which almost led to his resignation – such was the pressure of having to deal with other people reporting to him. He was best-placed to come up with a plan of action for them all to follow. His partner Josie Ottey, a black single mother of two, would then lead the team and implement his plan. Exactly, and to the letter – which was, she found out early on, the only way it could work. She had been partnered with him despite much protest on her part. Now she found herself constantly being his apologist and interface with the rest of the department. Being his interpreter was not why she'd joined the police. Cross was at best socially awkward, at worst bloody rude. But the fact of the matter was that he was an exceptional detective. So obsessed was he with the minutiae of every case, stuff that others, including herself, would often ignore; such was his rigour about detail, and obsession with logic, routines, patterns of behaviour and any anomalies within them, that he had the highest conviction rate in the area. His social awkwardness and lack of empathy were also particularly useful tools in the interview room, she had begun to learn. That, together with the fact that it seemed to be a place where he felt completely comfortable. Suspects were unnerved by his demeanour and often made the mistake of letting it encourage them to underestimate him. It was a mistake they would invariably come to regret.

Carson addressed the "garage murder" team, as he had labelled it, in the open area. He had a predilection for giving the cases they worked on some sort of colloquial title, as if it gave them an air of notoriety.

'So, the first thing we need to do is identify the victim,' he said, unnecessarily in Ottey's opinion. 'He had no ID on him, no wallet, no phone, driving licence, engraved watch. Absolutely nada. Obviously we'll try fingerprints and DNA, but unless he's in the system, or served in the military, that will probably lead us nowhere.'

Ottey found these meetings both patronising and infuriating. Aside from stating the obvious, it was as if Carson was convincing himself, as well as the others, that he was in charge and had a purpose in the investigation. But he was repeating the information to the very people who had given him that information in the first place. Cross, on the other hand, didn't mind this so much. He thought it useful to remind the team of their tasks and the fundamentals needed in solving any murder. He had no problem with the mundane nature of it all. Besides, it gave him time to think, as the facts were laid out verbally in front of him.

'Josie, what does George think?'

He asked this as if Cross wasn't in the room. Alice Mackenzie was a trainee Police Staff Investigator. She had found this type of thing strange when she first joined the unit six months before. But she saw that everyone else took it in their stride. She learnt that Cross didn't like to talk in front of several people, if he didn't have to. So Ottey would relay to everyone what he was thinking; he'd informed her of this before the meeting – she was no mind reader. As things went, when working with Cross, Mackenzie soon discovered it was one of the less odd things she had to deal with. She was still finding her way round working with him. Trying to interpret what he wanted – although to be fair he was so precise and literal in his instructions that "interpretation" was maybe stretching it a bit – and possibly most important of all, not taking offence at his manner and tone.

'I have no thoughts as yet,' said Cross, answering for himself.

'Should we be looking at the contractor?' Carson asked.

'It seems highly unlikely that he would hide a body in a place he was about to demolish and therefore uncover,' Ottey answered.

'Unless he thought that was a way of getting rid of it,' Carson replied.

'He didn't strike me as being that obtuse,' said Cross.

'He also called it in,' added Ottey.

'Double-bluff? Thinking we would think that?'

Cross didn't answer. This wasn't because he thought, as did

everyone else in the room, that it wasn't worthy of an answer. It was because a question hadn't actually been asked and, therefore, an answer wasn't required.

'Right then, let's do this!' Carson proclaimed.

This annoyed Ottey for two reasons. Firstly, they had been "doing it" before Carson had interrupted and insisted on an unnecessary meeting. Secondly, he said it at the beginning of every investigation, without fail. It was as if he thought he was the desk Sergeant in *Hill Street Blues*, who repeated, at the end of roll call every morning, "Oh, and let's be careful out there". As a kind of afterthought. Carson was obviously trying to give himself some sort of weird slogan. She could swear he'd actually said it in an American accent on more than one occasion. So she often did this – to make herself feel better. Pathetic really, she knew, but anyway, she stopped his authoritative exit by saying, 'One more thing, sir.'

'What?'

'How did it get there? The body. Who put it there? When and where?'

'Sure. We should check past ownership of those garages.'

'We'll get Alice onto it,' she said.

Cross had been back to the crime scene a couple of times. Once, that afternoon, and then again later, after sunset. He wasn't looking for clues. He was just taking the whole thing in. Observing. He often spent time observing people. Sometimes from Tony's café, where he would have breakfast every morning. He was a bit of a student of human behaviour. Not because of his work but because he learnt from it. He tried to observe, to understand the way people worked, in an attempt to fit in himself a little more easily. It had mixed results, but as he was fully aware he didn't have an innate, natural understanding of people and their behaviour, he thought this was possibly the best way to learn.

He was particularly interested in the block of council flats that overlooked the partially demolished garages. There were rows of balconies leading to people's front doors. Some were house-proud and had changed their front doors for something different – to make them stand out from their neighbours. Some used the balcony immediately outside their flat to have plant pots, hanging baskets and window boxes – although as they weren't on actual windows, he thought they should be more accurately described as "planters". There were several comings and goings. Children playing football, and when the inevitable happened and it was kicked over the balcony, arguing as to who should retrieve it. Quite a lot of deliveries. That was something that had changed over the years. Internet shopping meant that there was a constant flow of delivery vans pulling up outside. Deliveroo riders bringing takeaway pizza. Carers and district nurses dropping in on their clients.

A woman smoked outside her front door at regular intervals, occasionally talking to neighbours above and below her. She smoked, watched and thought. Cross wondered whether it was a self-imposed "no-smoking-indoors" ban. She had an impressive array of healthy plants clustered around her part of the balcony. He thought this implied a sense of house pride and purpose. To make the best of what she had. But maybe the plants were the work of a partner or husband who was actually the one who couldn't abide smoking in the flat. His father, Raymond, had kept a collection of house plants when Cross was younger. He was fairly sure they were still there, buried under the avalanche of hoarded possessions Raymond had built up over the years. He had a distinct memory of his father painting the leaves of a rubber plant with nail varnish to make them shine. Cross was disappointed as a young boy that, no matter how long he waited, however much he carefully watered and nurtured the plant, there was no evidence of any rubber ever being produced. It was only years later that he learnt a rubber tree was something entirely different.

He came to the conclusion that this woman liked to get out on the balcony periodically – maybe for a break from her domestic situation indoors. But there was something about the way she looked around that made him think she enjoyed seeing what was going on. Having a natter. Keeping abreast of things, elbows on the balcony. It was a routine, something that kept her going. Kept her sane. He was fairly sure she made mental notes of absolutely everything she saw, no matter how trivial. Nothing happened around that housing estate without her knowledge.

'How long have you lived here?' asked Cross from the end of the balcony, as he approached.

'Shh…,' she said. 'I have some really annoying neighbours. They'll use any excuse for a row.'

'I apologise,' said Cross. She actually looked a little older, close up. Maybe late forties. She'd started forming those thin vertical lines on her top lip, from years of smoking.

'Sorry, what did you say?' she asked.

'I asked how long you'd lived here.'

'You're the detective,' she said. So she'd spotted him earlier.

'I am.'

'I've lived in the area all my life. In these flats coming up for twenty years.'

'Have those garages always been disused in your time here?'

'Yeah.'

'Do you remember them from when you were a child?'

'Sure, they were used a lot then. Mostly for storage, but a couple had been knocked together and a couple of car mechanics worked out of them,' she said.

'Really?'

'Yeah, they had all the gear. Did MOTs and that.'

'They seem a little small for that,' Cross observed.

'I guess so, but they were always busy. Had loads of cars

8

parked up outside. They had an inspection pit and lift, can you believe? In the end they wanted to build a paint shop in another of them, but the council wouldn't let them. So they moved. Shame really. They added a bit of character to the place.'

2

'You don't have to show me that every time you come in here,' said the pathologist as Cross waved his warrant card at her, for about the hundredth time. He looked at the plastic sheeting which had been removed from the body and put to one side.

'Plastic sheeting commonly used by builders, decorators, that kind of thing,' said the pathologist. 'But then you already knew that.'

Cross didn't contradict her, but instead turned to the body on the slab and looked closely at the face. There was a large bruise and cut on the left side, across the jaw.

'Broken?' he asked.

'Clean. Could be a fist from a large male, or an object. Can't tell you precisely yet.'

Cross liked this about Clare. She was not one for making assumptions. She needed hard evidence before making a pronouncement. Some pathologists were far too willing to suggest a theory which could send detectives off on the wrong track for days.

'But it was the injury to the back of the head that killed him,' she went on.

'Any idea what caused it?'

'Probably something he fell onto. Something pretty hard. With an edge.'

'So he's hit... with a fist – or something – then he falls and cracks his skull.'

'In all likelihood, yes, but I will need to confirm.'

'An accident?'

She didn't answer; just gave him a look. It was one he was familiar with from her. It said "You should know better than to ask theoretical questions. I deal in hard medical evidence, not hypothetical fantasy".

'Anything else?' he asked.

'Nothing of note. Except he has some scars on his forearms.'

Cross looks at the scars for a moment.

'Burns?' he asked.

'Could be.'

'May I?'

She sighed. He always did this, without fail. She didn't know why he bothered to ask. As he asked, he was looking in the direction of her box of latex gloves, which meant that he wanted to have a closer look at the body. She always felt it was an implicit criticism of her work.

'Of course.'

Cross examined the body carefully, his face quite close to it, not at all squeamish, taking in every detail. Then he stood, took his notebook out of his pocket and started scribbling.

'Did I miss something?' the pathologist asked wearily.

'As a matter of fact, you did,' he replied. It was not meant to be critical, but she could be forgiven for thinking it was. 'He has very low body fat, disproportionately muscular thighs, distinct tan lines on his upper arms and on his thighs just above the knee. No calluses on his hands though. And he's a regular sunglasses-wearer.'

The pathologist looked at him blankly. Cross was slightly

surprised that he needed to elaborate any further. 'Our John Doe is a cyclist. Possibly professional.'

She laughed involuntarily, as she was, despite herself, quite impressed. 'Do you actually need me?'

'Yes of course,' he replied, without a hint of irony. 'I'm not qualified to perform autopsies, and even if I was I wouldn't have the time.'

And with that he left.

Cross was always busy at work. He was obsessed with how he utilised his time there, bearing in mind how limited their resources were. He felt it incumbent on him to be as productive as possible, at all times. He spent the afternoon putting the final touches to a stack of paperwork for a case that was going to court. For many a detective this was a chore – something that had to be done which they took no joy in doing. For Cross, though, it was almost the best part of his work. For a start it was something he could do on his own, with no involvement from anyone else. But it was more than that. It was the fact that this was when you put your case together. When you provided and constructed a narrative from the evidence and your carefully conducted interview. Cross was a master at the "no comment" interview. He could go on for hours asking questions, which the suspect thought he or she was evading cleverly, on the advice of their lawyer, by replying "no comment". Then he would produce a piece of evidence that would stop them in their tracks and require an answer. These "no comments", once placed in the context of the interview overall, often produced a damning picture of the accused, their credibility and their story. He also had an innate sense of how to manage the limited time in these interviews. He could go on for hours, seemingly directionless, and then suddenly deliver his killer blow and wrap it up in minutes. Cross revelled in finding the most mundane, tiny detail which would completely undermine their case. On occasion other detectives asked him for help in the preparation of their cases for court. If he had time he was more than willing to give them a hand. Ottey often felt he was like the school swot, with other pupils going to him for help with their homework.

He also regularly popped into the CCTV department – although he thought that was a misnomer, if ever there was one. It was a spare office with a couple of computer screens on desks, with the lights dimmed. The occupants were sallow-faced and looked like they could do with a bit of fresh air, or sun. But maybe that was just the silver reflection of the screens in front of them. The officer in charge was Catherine. She was a quiet woman in her late thirties with grey streaks in her hair which she did nothing to disguise. She looked more like a blue-stocking academic or librarian than a serving police officer. Perhaps that was why she found herself in this department.

Not for them the CCTV department of TV fiction, with dozens of screens on one side of a vast spaceship-type room with the ability – at the push of a button – to come up with whatever they were looking for in a matter of seconds. It took days of laborious, tedious scanning of the screens just to come up with a fuzzy frame-grab of suspect vehicles. But there was a sense of calm in the room which Cross appreciated. Secretly he'd love to work in this department. But there weren't enough puzzles in CCTV analysis to satisfy him. The repetitive routine appealed to him. It was also a paper-free zone, he'd noticed. Desks were completely free of piles of paper. He hated that in the incident room. Paper everywhere. Piles upon piles. How could people possibly work in an efficient manner like that? How could they think clearly?

They were looking at CCTV footage from the streets leading into the council block. Those in the block had been vandalised years before. As yet, nothing had been found. They also didn't have particularly specific time parameters to work around, which didn't help.

There was a knock at his door. Cross was the only one in the department, other than Carson, to have his own office. It wasn't a privilege so much as a necessity. He couldn't work in an open area. There were too many things that put him on edge. Mackenzie waited till he summoned her. She had learnt that he didn't keep people waiting unnecessarily, or out of some sense of self-importance, but because he needed to finish whatever he was working on, or complete whatever train of thought he was pursuing, without interruption. She walked in after he had signalled her to enter. She waited till he'd finished typing on his computer and looked up. This was her cue.

'I called British Cycling. According to them, all professional cyclists are accounted for in the UK,' she said.

'And how would they know that, exactly?' he asked.

'Well, what they actually said was that none of them have been reported missing,' she replied.

'Which is an entirely different thing, wouldn't you say?'

'I suppose so.'

'Europe.'

'Excuse me?'

'Of course, but...' He stopped himself as he realised she wasn't asking permission to leave. She often said this as a way of asking him to repeat himself or, as in this case, protesting about whatever he'd just said. 'Is there a problem?' he asked.

'Europe?' she repeated.

Ottey then came into the office and immediately interrupted.

'I think I may have found our man. Avon Cycling Club,' she said.

'An amateur?' Cross said, thinking out loud. Obviously a very determined and dedicated one, he thought.

'So it would seem,' she replied.

'So no need to do Europe then?' Mackenzie asked hopefully.

'Why would you say that?' said Cross.

Mackenzie looked over at Ottey and said 'Because...' but Cross quickly interrupted her.

'DS Ottey merely thinks she may have identified our corpse, but until she knows definitively we should exhaust every possible avenue of enquiry.'

'Okay...' she replied.

'What would happen if we all stopped doing what we were doing every time someone thought they had a lead?' he went on, fully believing that he was fulfilling Ottey's instruction that he should be helping and training Mackenzie; not realising that he was, in reality, sounding dismissive and critical.

'We'd get nowhere fast,' volunteered Ottey. Cross sighed, but he couldn't help himself.

'No, DS Ottey, we wouldn't get anywhere at all,' he said, displaying, yet again, his difficulty with the vernacular and immediate recourse to the literal. 'As soon as we've confirmed the deceased as being part of the Avon Cycling Club we'll let you know and task you with something else.'

Ottey and Mackenzie left. Ottey knew that Mackenzie was still being thrown by her partner, despite having worked with him for months.

'Like I keep saying, Alice. Don't worry about him. Just do everything he asks, exactly as he asks and precisely when he asks and you'll be just fine. Probably.'

She left Mackenzie at her desk, wondering whether she could actually cope with this. She understood he was on the spectrum – she actually had a younger autistic brother – but at times it was easy to forget when he came across as a deliberately rude, objectionable, older white man. She had to remind herself it wasn't personal. It wasn't his intention to be difficult or unpleasant; it just came out that way at times.

3

The man Ottey had spoken to was the Secretary of the Avon Cycling Club, and so he was their first port of call. He was a chemist working out of Clifton village. This was the most upmarket area of Bristol. It contained one of Cross' favourite pieces of architecture, Royal York Crescent. Over two hundred years old, it was once the longest terrace in Europe. Built over vaulted cellars, it still had the grandeur the architect had desired for it two centuries earlier. Cross could imagine Brunel walking down it approvingly when he was dreaming up the Suspension Bridge nearby. He had once heard someone refer to Clifton as "gentrified" and he had corrected them, saying it had always been well-to-do and in no need of gentrification. They parked up outside. Cross looked out of the car window.

'This is annoying. I had a prescription I could've brought,' he said.

He remembered a chemist in this area from when he was young. He was quite a poorly child, due to his asthma, so he had a recollection of a fair few chemists or pharmacies in the Bristol area. He hated that word "pharmacy". What was wrong with "chemist"? When had people in England started calling them "pharmacies"? Was it an American thing? Or European? He made a mental note to check. Things like that would irritate him, like a tune you can't get out of your head, till he'd found the answer. He remembered this particular chemist, because back in the 1970s it was still Victorian in essence. It had ornate wooden-framed windows, a magnificent bank of dispensary drawers, but most memorable of all, a collection of giant coloured dispensing jars in the window. Glass, they were the most vibrant colours: red, blue and green. He would stand looking at his distorted reflection in them, moving around so the distortions changed. Like a hall of mirrors in a funfair.

Mr Ajjay Patel was a fit-looking man in his forties with muscular forearms and calves. He was wearing shorts. They had started by asking about the club in general, before they got to talking about the missing cyclist.

'Alex Paphides. He's training for this year's L'Étape,' said Patel.

'L'Étape?' Ottey asked.

'It's a bike race, over one of the actual stages of the Tour de France. Takes place after it's finished, obviously. Difficult stage this year,' said Cross.

'Yes it is,' said the chemist, impressed by Cross' knowledge.

'Megève to Morzine, 146 kilometres, four climbs including the Col de Joux Plane – 11.6 kilometres with a climb of 1,691 metres and an average gradient of 8.5 to 12 percent,' Cross went on.

'Wow, you know your cycling,' said Patel.

'Not particularly,' said Cross.

'So go on,' said Ottey, bringing them back to the matter in hand.

'The six of them were due to go on a training fortnight in Tenerife. Alex texted Matthew to say he was injured.'

'When?' asked Cross.

'That morning, I believe,' said Patel.

'Who is Matthew?' Ottey asked.

'He's the captain of the team.'

'What about Alex's family?'

'He runs a restaurant. With his brother. In Redland. Greek. Used to be his father's. Family business.'

'Name?' Ottey asked.

'The Adelphi,' said the chemist. 'Do you think something's happened to him?'

'We're not sure. Thanks for your time,' she replied.

As they got in the car Cross turned to her. 'He didn't have a phone on him. Alex.'

'That's true,' she replied.

'We need to find that phone.'

'Restaurant next?'

'Yes.'

They drove to Redland, just ten minutes away. Cross was fairly sure now that Alexander Paphides was their victim. He was a cyclist, and Cross was pretty sure they'd discover some of the food at the Adelphi was cooked over a charcoal pit. Scars on forearms were often a consequence of burns for any chef. But a spitting charcoal pit made it seem all the more likely to Cross. He looked over at Ottey driving. She always drove. Cross didn't have a car, although he was perfectly capable of driving. He preferred to spend his time thinking through the case they were working. This had elicited a comment from Ottey one day – that she often felt like his chauffeur, as they spent so much time in silence with his penchant for non-communication. She had even joked that maybe he should sit in the back of the car. He'd replied that that wouldn't work, as he wouldn't be able to hear what she was saying.

He had become acutely aware of his annoying habits of late – that is, annoying to others – as he had been trying to be a better person in the workplace and a better partner for Ottey. This was all at her instigation, of course, and at his insistence she had given him a kind of crib-sheet to work from. Things he needed to improve and change. Communication was one of them.

'Is this one of those times when you'd like to have a conversation?' he enquired politely.

'No, I'm good, thanks,' she said. He was secretly pleased with himself, though, and crossed that question off his list for the day. He had figured out that asking this question was a once-a-day thing and shouldn't be overdone. And yes, he did have an actual list on his computer. Daily things, weekly things and things of a general nature to do, or say, that might help him get along with people at work.

The Adelphi Palace was a long, narrow restaurant that stretched well back into the bowels of the building it occupied. It was on the end of an undistinguished row of shops. Obviously a popular restaurant, it was heaving for a midweek lunch service. Cross thought they must have a very attractively priced set-lunch menu as well as a high standard of food. He and Ottey waited at the front desk – well, it was more of a lectern with a well-used reservations book on it. The pages were curled up at the edges, and when it was turned over it made that crinkly sound paper makes when it has been assaulted by several biros and pencils over time. A lectern struck Cross as the wrong word for this particular piece of furniture in a restaurant, but he couldn't think of any other way of describing it. A Maître D's station or post perhaps?

A young waitress came up to them.

'Table for two?'

'No thank you,' said Ottey, showing the young woman her warrant card. 'We'd like to speak to the owner.'

'This way,' she said, and disappeared into the restaurant. They navigated their way past waiters in the narrow space between the tables and finally found themselves at a large charcoal pit, where two men were cooking a variety of meats and kebabs. Next to the grill was a tall doner stand and a large refrigerated display cabinet, filled with marinated meats and salads. The waitress introduced them to one of the men.

'Thanks, Debbie,' he said as he came out from behind the grill. He ripped some paper towel off a roll and wiped the sweat off his brow. Cross immediately noticed the scars on his forearms. He looked at Ottey. She'd seen them too. Alex had to be their victim. 'My name's Kostas. How can I help?' said the chef.

'Your arms,' Cross observed.

'Oh yes. Occupational hazard. Mind you, I'm much more careful now. Bit crazy when we start, isn't that right Chris?' They looked over at the other, younger man behind the grill. He held up an arm with a dressing on it. 'He's still learning.'

'Your brother. Do you know where he is?' Cross continued.

'Cycling trip. Tenerife. Back last night,' Kostas answered.

'Have you heard from him since he went?' asked Cross.

'No, but I'm expecting him any minute,' said Kostas.

An unshaven man in his seventies, dressed in a vest, appeared from the back of the restaurant. An absurd amount of chest hair trimmed in a straight line, almost like a hedge, protruded below his chin. He also had a plaster cast on one of his arms. He spoke to Kostas in Greek. There was something about their interaction that told Cross they were father and son. He decided to interrupt.

'Mr Paphides... Alex didn't go on the cycling trip.'

'How d'you mean?' asked Kostas.

'He told the team he was injured. Hamstring.'

'What? So where is he?' asked Kostas.

'That's what we're trying to ascertain. When was the last time you saw him?' asked Ottey.

'The night before he left.'

'Was he driving?' asked Cross.

'No, he was on his bike.'

'Where does he live?' asked Ottey.

'Mangotsfield.'

'Would you mind taking us there?'

'Can it wait till service is finished?' He regretted it as soon as he'd said it. His brother was missing. 'No, of course I will.' He then spoke to his father, again in Greek, presumably asking him to finish the lunch service for him. But his dad was way ahead of him and already behind the charcoal grill. As they left with Kostas, Debbie asked him if everything was all right. Cross noticed that he was about to answer, when he seemed to change his mind and just said, 'Yeah, everything's fine. I'll be back in a bit.'

Kostas led the way in his car: a sleek black BMW M5 with low-profile tyres and a matt-black wrap. He obviously liked his cars. They got to a house in Mangotsfield that had been divided into two flats. Alex lived in the top one. They followed Kostas in as he unlocked his brother's flat with his key. He instinctively called out, 'Alex?' He wasn't to know what Cross was by now sure of – that this was a pointless exercise. In the hall was the travel case for Alex's bike. Like a musical instrument case, but with a large round shape for the wheel. Cross opened it. There was a bike inside. It looked brand new.

'That's an expensive-looking bike,' he said.

'He spent a fortune on cycling. Seemed to change his bikes every few months or when a new model came out,' Kostas said.

'Could we see his bedroom?' asked Ottey.

On the bed was an open walk-on suitcase with Alex's clothes and cycling kit packed for the journey. Kostas took it in for a moment then said hopefully, 'Maybe he left them there when he got back?' but Ottey's expression told him all he needed to know. This was then confirmed by her next question.

'Would you mind if I looked for his toothbrush or a hairbrush?'

'Sure,' he said, without giving it much thought. Then, real-ising the implication of what she was saying, he sank down onto the bed and put his head in his hands. 'Oh no, oh shit...' They were looking for a DNA sample. Cross had watched his reaction, as per his usual methodology, and was convinced that he had nothing to do with his brother's death. He continued his search. Everything was well-ordered. In a wardrobe drawer he found what looked like Alex's "technical stuff I don't know what to do with" stash of wires and old phones with their chargers wrapped around them. People, he had noticed, were reluctant to throw out old laptops and phones, pieces of technology they'd paid a fortune for when they were new and so were now loath to dispose of. It was pointless. Even the cables in this drawer were out of date. The idea of buying something and making it last was no longer a viable option, with the speed at which technology moved on. People had bought into the old sales theory of obsolescence under modern electronics' guise of constant evolution and improvement.

Kostas identified the body of his brother later that day. A terrible thing for a relative to have to do, obviously. Some of them had never even seen a dead body before, and the subtle changes that death brings to a familiar face can be shocking. Also, there, right in front of them is the incontrovertible confirmation of what they were secretly, desperately hoping might have been a mistake.

So they had their victim but weren't particularly any closer to understanding why he'd been murdered. They were sure it was murder because of the way the body had been concealed. Also a fragment of glass had been found in the wound on Alex's jaw.

The team started posing theories. Something Cross never did, because he found it essentially a waste of time. For him it was little more than office gossip, albeit of a morbid nature. Ottey, however, fully indulged in this, mostly because she found it a relief from sitting in silence opposite her partner in his office.

He often reached a time in an investigation where he just wanted to think. She'd challenged him on this, telling him that he was theorising, just to himself. Which was, effectively, the same as everyone else was doing – except he did it in private. He completely refuted this, though he knew there was an element of truth to it. What he was doing was endlessly rerunning the facts at any stage of the investigation, over and over again in his mind. His belief was that something would eventually pop out of the ordinary as unusual, and that this might be of use.

As Ottey was having coffee in the central area with some of the team, Cross was thinking about Alex and trying to build a picture of him. Look in any criminology text book and it will say that he was doing his victimology. This was often where Cross started. More often than not the character of the victim, his habits, friends, family would lead them in an initial direction, which might prove to be useful. Alex was obviously fanatical about his cycling. Cycling at that level had to be time-consuming. So Cross thought his social circle would have been fairly limited and mainly focused around the cycling club. His initial thoughts were to concentrate on the club and the family. If the answer lay elsewhere they would soon find out.

But he had to be cycling miles and miles a day and week. What with working in the restaurant trade, surely he didn't have time for much else.

4

Mackenzie knocked on Cross' office door and waited patiently. He didn't ask her to come in. A detective walked past and smiled. She looked at her uncertainly.

'Oh, he heard you,' she said.

'Right. I'll come back,' Mackenzie replied.

'I wouldn't waste your time. He'll find you when he's good and ready.'

'He didn't even look up; how will he know it's me?'

'Because he's George Cross!' came the reply over the departing detective's shoulder.

She went back to her desk and busied herself in some more logging Carson had given her. She'd made the mistake in the first few weeks of being there, when he'd asked how she was getting on, of saying that she really didn't feel she had enough to do and was sure that she could be a lot more useful. Since then he'd made it his mission to make sure she was completely occupied, every hour of every working day, with mostly mundane and repetitive work. So she was really happy, if a little startled, when Cross appeared at her desk half an hour later.

'What do you want?' he inquired.

'Oh, you didn't say anything about a girlfriend,' she said.

He said nothing. She had learnt that his silence, after a statement had been made, meant he needed further clarification.

'Alex's girlfriend,' she explained.

'He had a girlfriend?' Cross repeated. Ottey had now wandered over. He turned to her. 'Alice thinks Alex had a girlfriend,' he said. It was still strange for Alice when he spoke like this. In truth he was trying to be polite and encouraging, but sometimes, as in this case, it came across as if he was taking the piss. Maybe because he was overstating and giving it more import than he meant, thereby making it sound possibly ironic.

'Kostas didn't say anything about that. I'm sure I asked,' Ottey said.

'You did,' Cross reassured her, 'after we'd discussed his parents' immigration history and Kostas' and Alex's education.'

'There was no sign of anyone else living at his flat,' Ottey said.

'Maybe they didn't live together,' Mackenzie volunteered.

'How do you know this, Alice?' Cross asked.

'I don't *know* it. I just think it might be the case from his social media,' she said, opening a laptop on her desk. 'This is Alex's laptop.'

'I know that,' said Cross. She ignored him and opened up Alex's photo album. Cross and Ottey looked and saw a bunch of fairly typical photographs of a young couple. Cross marvelled at how often young people photographed themselves these days. Everything they did, they recorded. It was almost as if it was evidence that they were having a wonderful and enviable life. Proof for any doubters. Here were dozens of selfies of Alex and a young woman, in various places around the South West and on a trip to London. Alex in full lycra cycling gear, leaning, covered in sweat, against his bike as she stood next to him, holding a trophy. At a table in a restaurant with Alex's family. Probably the Adelphi. It was looking at that photograph that made Cross realise they'd met her before.

'It's the waitress,' he said. Ottey didn't reply. 'The one who took us through to meet Kostas.'

'Are you sure?' she said.

'Definitely.'

'Then why didn't he say anything about her?'

'Maybe they'd broken up?' suggested Cross.

'I don't think so. The last photo was taken the week before he died and they definitely don't look like they've broken up,' said Mackenzie, pointing to a selfie of the couple kissing.

'Good night?' Ottey asked Cross as she drove them back to the restaurant. He looked puzzled.

'I don't understand.'

'Last night. After work? Did you have a good night?'

'Oh, I see. Yes. I did. Thank you.' He looked back out of the passenger window, having navigated this exchange successfully, in his opinion. She looked at him quickly. No, nothing more was going to be forthcoming.

'This is when you ask me... if I had a good night,' she said.

'Yes, of course. Did you have a good night?'

'I did, thank you,' she said. But no follow-up from Cross. 'The girls were asking about you,' she said, referring to her two daughters. He just nodded, acknowledging that he'd heard her. 'They love the bagatelle your father gave them. He did such a great job restoring it.'

'Yes.'

'It makes a welcome change from them being glued to their iPads all the time. A bit noisier and causes more arguments, but at least I know what they're doing.'

'Indeed.'

They arrived at the restaurant. Kostas was waiting for them. Mackenzie had phoned ahead and warned him they were on their way. The restaurant had that "morning after" smell. What were inviting and appetising smells the night before, had now morphed into a stale, listless odour. Kostas made them coffee at the machine behind the bar. An older woman, Kostas' mother, Cross assumed, appeared with a plastic bowl and a couple of bags of vegetables, which she started to prepare at a table in the back. She had been doing this for so many years she was now able to do it without taking her eyes off Cross and Ottey. Cross assumed she also had acute hearing for someone of her age. Kostas brought their coffees over.

'Sugar?'

'No thank you,' the detectives said, almost in unison.

'Kostas, do you know anyone who would want to hurt your brother?' Ottey asked.

'No,' he replied, quite surprised by the question.

'No trouble with competitors? I know the restaurant business can be quite cut-throat at times,' she went on.

'No.'

'Any bad habits – gambling, drinking, womanising?'

'No!' he said, almost laughing at the idea. 'He was obsessed with his cycling. That was it. He didn't drink. He didn't have time for anything else. He was always on that bloody bike.'

'It annoyed you,' Cross stated.

'Only now and then, when he'd leave me on my own here, because he had some big race or training ride with the club. And he could bore for Britain talking about it. But it kept him fit and out of trouble.'

'Did he need keeping out of trouble?' Cross asked.

'No, wait a minute. Do I need to be careful about what I say here?'

'No,' said Ottey. 'Please don't feel that way. You might be aware of something which could be really useful, vital even, for us,' she reassured him. 'Had his behaviour changed at all recently?'

'Yeah, it had. He seemed really uptight, quite aggressive. He'd become really obsessed with this race...' he said.

'Would you describe him as obsessive generally?' Cross asked.

'He hated failing. Always did from when we were kids. At school, even in sports he was crap at, he hated losing,'

'A kakorrhaphiophobic,' commented Cross.

'What?' said Ottey.

'Someone who has a fear of failure. People often think it's an obsession with winning, when it has more to do with a morbid fear of losing, of failure. An important distinction,' Cross said, which left Ottey wondering how many people were actually aware of the word in the first place, to be able to make such a terrible mistake.

'They came in phases, his obsessions. The race was the latest. He'd bulked up a lot and he'd become a real moody bugger,' Kostas continued.

'In what way?' Ottey asked.

'He started getting into arguments with everyone: me, Dad, even customers. Stuff that had never happened before. Then it was quickly over. He could never keep a row going like me and Dad. We can keep them going for days. Him, he has to apologise at the first opportunity. A sign of weakness – I always used to tease him.' Then Kostas lost it momentarily. He cried into his hands silently. Cross just looked at him. Ottey moved forward and put an arm round him.

'You're younger than Alex,' said Cross.

'Only by two years.'

'"Only"? So he was the dominant one. The one in charge,' said Cross.

'He liked to think so,' said Kostas.

'Did you resent that?' Cross asked.

'No,' he said, maybe a little too quickly. Cross just looked at him. Kostas looked away to Ottey and then back to Cross, who was still looking straight at him rather unnervingly.

'That's the first lie you've told us, Kostas,' he said.

'I loved him.' His dad came over and took their cups.

'They always argue, yes...' he said.

'Dad...' Kostas protested.

'Alexander wanted to go to London. Fight, fight, fight. But they love each other. Of course they do. Families fight because they love each other.'

'London?' Cross asked.

'He wanted to open up a restaurant in London. On his own. Wanted Kostas to buy him out of this place,' he continued.

'Which presumably would've meant you going to the bank for a loan,' Cross said.

'Yep. I thought the whole thing was nuts. I couldn't prove it, but I was sure there was some bloody bike club up there he wanted to join. I bet you any money that was what it was about. And that velodrome. He went up there a couple of weekends. Used to say, "Can you imagine if I lived there – in Stratford? I could train every night." Not if you had a bloody restaurant you couldn't, I told him. He just hadn't thought any of it through.'

'Big plans – he had big plans,' said his dad from behind the counter.

'Yeah, yeah,' Kostas agreed and smiled good naturedly. 'He was the "perfect son". As you can probably tell.'

'Obviously the favourite,' said Ottey.

'Oh yes...' he said slowly.

'What happened to your father's arm?' Cross asked, referring to the cast on the older man's wrist.

'He broke his wrist.'

'When?'

'Couple of weeks ago. He has osteoporosis. It's happening more and more often,' he said.

'So this plan of Alex's to go to London. Where had you left it?' Cross asked.

'Well, that's kind of what we did – left it. He was good at

29

numbers, Alex. He was the brains, well, the logistics one, in the business. He did the numbers and saw that I couldn't make the business work if I had a loan, the size I needed,' he said.

'Couldn't you raise the restaurant prices a little?' asked Cross. 'I had a look at the menu the other day. It's very reasonable, cheap even, for such good food.'

'We know our market. It was well and truly tested by our mother and father. Alex would explain it really well. We're just this side of the "tipping-point". If we raised our prices beyond a certain point we would lose customers. To the extent that profits would drop.'

'Interesting.'

'But you know what Alex's genius move was?'

'No.'

'It sounds like nothing, but it had amazing results. It started with water. We carbonate our own, charge people £1.50 and then refill limitlessly without charge. People really liked it, and then Alex said, "Let's make the pitta bread free". Free pitta bread? My father thought it was insane. Not because it'd lose money but because it would fill people up and they wouldn't order enough food.'

'It was true at the beginning,' his father said, as if to prove his point.

'Not for long. People like a bargain. They like to get their money's worth, not feel they are being ripped off,' Kostas went on. 'They like nice gestures.'

'They like free stuff,' his father chimed in, as if he was still really against the whole idea, despite the apparent success of it. For him, there was something fundamentally wrong in giving it away.

'They were a little greedy at first, but then when they got used to it, they ordered only as much as they needed.'

'Except for the man with the carrier bag. You're forgetting about him,' said his father. 'Tell him about the man with the carrier bag.'

'That's true. We did have one customer who took the piss. He brought a carrier bag with him and asked for bread at the end of the meal.'

'What did you do?' asked Ottey.

'It was Alex. He filled the man's bag up to the top with pitta breads.'

'You're kidding,' said Ottey.

'He said he didn't do it for the man asking for the bread. He did it for all the customers watching. They knew the guy was a dick, but then they saw the manager giving him the bread, without batting an eyelid. They felt for him. Were impressed. Would come back, and they did. Some customers still even bring it up. It's like a famous little story,' said Kostas, smiling at the memory.

'Did Alex have a girlfriend?' Cross asked, quickly changing the subject.

'No. Like I said, he didn't have time.' Cross noticed Kostas' mother look up quickly at her son. She had wanted to hear the answer. She was, as usual, preparing vegetables in the back of the restaurant, keeping a weather eye on them.

'What about Debbie? The waitress?' said Cross.

'She's not a waitress,' he replied, looking nervous. He turned to look over at his mother again. Cross had thought earlier that she was there just to listen in on their conversation with Kostas, but he realised it was her vantage point to see and know everything that went on in this place. The men thought they were in charge, but Cross knew this was where the real power lay.

'What about her?' Kostas said finally.

'We'd like to speak with her. Is she here?' Cross went on.

'She's upstairs,' Kostas replied.

'Why the secrecy?' asked Ottey.

'My mother didn't want her involved. She's upset enough as it is. Her relationship with Alex was... private.'

'There's nothing private when it comes to a murder investigation,' said Cross.

'Well it's not like she had anything to do with it. She was working that night.'

'She may not have had anything to do with it, but she may well know something which she won't think is useful, but to us could be important,' Cross went on.

'Kostas, we're only trying to find out the truth here. Find out who killed your brother. No-one's in trouble here,' said Ottey.

'Except for the killer, of course,' added Cross. Kostas looked at him, a little shocked. He couldn't tell whether the detective was making a joke. Kostas stood up to go and get her but saw that his mother had already gone.

'My mother's gone to get her. Can I make you coffee?' he asked.

'That would be nice, thank you,' Ottey replied, as she and Cross sat.

Debbie arrived at the table a few minutes later. They exchanged the usual pleasantries – well, Ottey did. Cross noticed that Debbie had been crying that morning. She was also a lot younger than he expected. What was she? Eighteen maybe? Whatever, quite a lot younger than Alex, who'd been thirty-two.

'So, Debbie, how long have you worked here?' asked Ottey.

'I don't work here,' she replied quietly.

'But weren't you waiting tables the other day?' he said.

'I was just helping out. Nicole called in sick,' she explained.

'How did you meet Alex?' Cross asked.

'Here. We came to eat one night. He looked after us. I was with friends. A birthday.'

'But how...?' Ottey asked.

'Oh, I saw him on his bike a few days later. He stopped. We got talking.'

'Do you know of anyone who would want to hurt Alex?' Ottey went on. Debbie just shook her head quickly, as if implying it was completely out of the question. 'No arguments, no fights with anyone recently?' Ottey continued. Again, just a shake of the head.

'Why were you upstairs if you don't work here?' Cross asked.

'I live here.'

'I see,' said Cross.

'Things were a little difficult at home,' Kostas explained.

'At home? Were you living with your parents?' said Cross.

'Yes. Till I moved here,' she said.

'When Kostas says things were difficult there – is he right?' Ottey asked.

'Yes,' she said, almost in a whisper.

'In what way?' Ottey asked.

'Just usual stuff. I needed a break,' said Debbie.

'What did you think about Alex's plans for London?' Cross asked. He noticed that she was about to answer but gave the slightest of looks towards Kostas and then decided against it. 'Did you discuss it with him? Were you going to go with him?' Again, a look to Kostas.

'It wasn't happening any more. He wasn't doing it.'

Ottey was about to ask another question when Cross, who had been watching Debbie closely, stopped her.

'Actually, I think we have all we need. Josie, perhaps you could give Debbie your card. Call us if you think of anything. Or tell your family liaison officer,' he said.

'Alison?' Debbie asked.

'Yeah, Alison,' said Ottey, who was trying to figure out why Cross had brought the interview to an abrupt close. When they got into the car, Cross turned to her.

'Debbie living with Alex's family? Is that normal?' he asked.

'Not exactly normal, no. But not unheard of. Depends on the circumstances at home. Single mother. New stepfather. Could be anything. Why did you stop me back there?'

'She didn't want to talk in front of Kostas. Actually, to be more accurate, she didn't want to talk in front of the mother.

The woman had obviously said something to her. That's why she went upstairs to get her so quickly.' He thought for a moment. 'Whatever it is, she'll be in touch. She seemed very young. How old do you think she is?'

'I don't know. Eighteen, twenty. Parents?' she said.

'I've no idea. They could be any age.'

'I meant shall we pay them a visit?'

'Oh, I see. Yes, that would be the logical next step.'

5

They pulled up at a house in Eastville. It was on a small, narrow street, on a slight hill. A series of semi-detached houses that each had a lane to the backyard along one side. Ottey turned to Cross and said, 'Remember, they probably don't know anything about this.'

'So don't blurt it out,' he said, repeating what she'd told him before. They rang the doorbell. After a few moments, a woman in her thirties answered the door. She looked tired, with big black bags under her eyes. She was wearing a pink towelling tracksuit and was smoking a cigarette. Ottey showed her warrant card, as did Cross, standing behind her.

'DS Ottey and DS Cross. May we come in?'

A man now appeared behind the woman, slightly older, early forties. His hair was cropped short, as he was obviously going bald.

'What's this about?' he said.

'You are Debbie Swinton's parents, yes?'

'Oh my God, has something happened to her?' the woman asked.

'No, no, not at all,' Ottey replied.

'You'd better come in,' said the man.

The front room was clean, if a little vulgarly furnished. The tops of the walls, where they met the ceiling, were brown from smoking. There was a large glass of white wine on the table in the middle of the room. Cross couldn't help but notice it as he walked in.

'What are you looking at?' the woman said aggressively.

'Your wine glass,' Cross replied, not in the least bit embarrassed.

'What about it?'

'I was just thinking how early it was to be drinking. Then I thought that this probably wasn't unusual for you,' he said. She was about to reply when the man stepped in.

'Perhaps you can tell us how we can help you,' he said.

'We're investigating the mur...' Cross started before Ottey interrupted him.

'Cross...' He stopped immediately.

'I'm afraid we have some bad news, about Alex Paphides. You do know Alex?' Ottey said.

'Yes,' replied the woman.

'I'm sorry to inform you that he's dead.'

'Oh my God,' the woman sat down on the sofa as she took this in.

'Murdered,' said Cross. Ottey looked at him. He just didn't get it. She knew, for him, it was just a piece of information that they needed to impart so that they could get on. He never thought about the feelings of whomever he was talking to. It just didn't occur to him.

'When?' asked the man.

'About two weeks ago,' Ottey replied.

'He was our Debbie's...' said the woman. But she couldn't finish the sentence.

'So we understand.'

'Could you please tell me your names and your relationship to Debbie?' said Cross, getting out his notebook.

'Murder?' the man asked.

'Yes,' said Cross.

'I'm Andy, her stepfather, and this is Jean, her mum.'

'When was the last time you saw him?' Cross asked.

'Couple of months ago?' Andy replied.

'You're sure?' Cross asked.

'Yes,' he answered.

'What about Debbie? When did you last see her?' Cross went on.

'Same,' said Jean.

'I see... So you didn't approve,' Cross stated.

'How d'you mean?' Jean asked defensively.

'Of the relationship,' Cross said.

'Well would you?' she said, stabbing her cigarette out with some force into an ashtray, as if to reinforce her point.

'I have no idea,' he said truthfully.

'He's over thirty,' she said, as if pointing out the obvious to someone who was being a bit dense.

'He's Greek,' said Cross, as if this maybe had more to do with it.

'That's got nothing to do with it,' said Andy.

'You calling us fucking racist?' said Jean.

'He's not calling you anything of the kind,' said Ottey, interceding before this got out of hand. Jean reached for her wine glass and took a large swig. She then lit another cigarette. She did this without thinking, on autopilot. Like it was something she did dozens of times a day.

'She's sixteen,' said Jean. This came as a surprise to both detectives. They certainly hadn't thought she was that young when they met her.

'I see. She looks older,' said Cross.

'She does,' said Andy, agreeing with him. 'I think it makes her think she's a lot more grown-up than she really is.'

'Is that why she moved out?' asked Ottey.

'Yeah, she said we made her feel like everything she did was wrong,' he explained.

'A criticism,' said Jean.

'Does she know about Alex?' asked Andy.

'Yes,' Ottey replied.

'Is she okay?' he went on.

'Upset, obviously,' she said.

Andy sat down opposite his wife. 'We should...' he began.

'She knows where we are,' Jean said bitterly. Andy looked at her. This obviously wasn't the time to have this conversation. Her reaction hadn't surprised or shocked him in the least. He looked up at the detectives.

'Could you tell her we're here for her? Maybe she needs us now,' he said.

'Of course,' replied Ottey. She turned to Cross, indicating that they should leave. But his attention had been taken by a large incomplete jigsaw on the table behind them.

'A jigsaw. Quite a difficult one with all that sky. Not much detail there to help you.' Everyone was looking at him, slightly puzzled, which he took as his cue to go on. 'Invented around 1760, in London, by the cartographer John Spilsbury. To teach geography, interestingly.'

'Is that a fact? I didn't know that,' said Andy politely.

'Yes. They used to mount maps on wood, then cut them up along the countries' borders. They were known as "dissected maps" before they became jigsaws,' said Cross.

'That is interesting,' said Andy.

'I think so,' said Cross.

'He seemed much more concerned about the girl than she did,' said Cross when they were back in the car.

'I can understand that. She's her mother. He's her stepfather,' Ottey said.

'So you would assume she should be the more worried, wouldn't you?' he said.

'She is. It's just hidden. By her anger.' He thought about this for a moment and then shook his head, slightly.

'This is one of those moments where I consider myself fortunate to be childless. If I had any children, I would be in a state of permanent confusion,' he said.

'Which would make you no different to any other parent on the planet,' replied Ottey.

'Really? Gosh. No wonder parents look permanently exhausted,' he said. They drove on for a bit. He had decided not to go back into the office. When they arrived back at the Major Crime Unit he went straight over to the bike shed. She parked and caught up with him just before he was about to leave.

'You going to Raymond's tonight?' she asked. He looked at her inquiringly. 'It's Thursday night. You always go to your dad's on a Thursday,' she explained.

'Yes, I am,' Cross replied.

'Please give him my best,' she said.

'I will,' he said and cycled off.

'See you tomorrow!' she called after him. He didn't reply.

6

C ross arrived at his father's flat a little later, carrying their regular Chinese takeaway with him. He left his bike in the cluttered hallway and found his father typing on an old portable typewriter. It wasn't so much that he didn't use modern technology – indeed he had several laptops of varying age and condition in his vast collection of stuff, populating every inch of space in the flat – he just said that he thought more clearly when he typed. You had to think before you typed, he said. Before you committed to paper. With a computer, erasing was so easy and autocorrect had made people lazy, in his opinion. If they actually had to get out a bottle of Tippex (for younger readers, a white liquid you painted over your errors, like nail varnish, and then typed back over), wipe off the gunk that always accumulated round the top of the bottle, despite all your best efforts to keep it clean, then apply it carefully and wait for it to dry – people might be a lot more careful.

They ate their meal in customary silence while they watched *Mastermind* on the TV. Raymond recorded it for his son, under the illusion that it was his favourite TV show. He was wrong. George had no favourite shows, although if he did, it would doubtless have been some form of quiz. After George had cleared up and was preparing to leave, his father dropped what was, for Cross, a bombshell.

'I won't be able to do this Thursday, or the next for the foreseeable future.'

Now for anyone else, this would just be a small matter. But not for Cross. He didn't like change, and this was, for him, a change of seismic proportions.

'What do you mean? We always have dinner on Thursday nights.'

'I know, but I thought maybe we could change it.'

'Why?'

'Because I have another commitment now. At Aerospace Bristol late afternoon, so I won't be back in time.'

'What are you doing at the museum?'

'I'm doing a tour and giving a short talk. It's what I was writing when you arrived.'

Cross thought for a moment, then said, 'You'll have to ask them to do it on another night. Thursday isn't possible.'

'I did. It was my first thought. Well, maybe not my first. But I knew you wouldn't like it, so I asked. But it's the only evening of the week that works for them. They have a very busy schedule,' his father said.

'Then you'll have to say no.'

'I would really like to do this, George. It's something for me to look forward to.'

'You don't look forward to seeing me?'

'You know I do. But you always say I should get out more. This'll engage my brain. I'd really like to do it, son. We could meet on Wednesday for a while.'

'I have organ practice on Wednesday. We meet on Thursday because it's a midpoint between our spending Sundays together. We worked it out. It's the optimum point in the week. Tuesday will be too early, Friday too late. No, you can't do it.'

To anyone else, Cross would've just sounded like a spoilt

child, rather than a mature man in his fifties. But it had nothing to do with him wanting to get his own way. It was more that he relied on this routine. Raymond knew that once Cross thought it through he would, albeit reluctantly, agree. He didn't like things sprung on him, that was all. He needed notice, time to process how he would cope with this new disruption.

'But we *could* see each other next Thursday.'

'Good.' Cross turned to leave, thinking that he'd made his point and that they would have dinner as usual the next week.

'You could come and see me give the talk and we could get dinner on the way home. It'd be a bit later than usual, but I thought maybe you'd like to do that. Come along and give the old man some encouragement. Maybe give me a few notes and pointers after.'

'No. I don't think so,' said George, and left. As ever, Raymond wasn't upset. He'd known in advance that this would be his son's reaction. As with everything with George, it would take time. Negotiation. But they would find a way. George's problem was that he just couldn't understand why his father didn't see the impracticalities of this new and, to him, unnecessary complication.

It was still bothering him the next morning at the MCU. Ottey picked up on it, but he wasn't one to discuss personal matters at work. He didn't think it was the right place for it. Over lunch in the canteen maybe. In the pub after work definitely, not that Cross ever went to the pub. For him, during work hours it bordered on the unprofessional. So when she asked what was bothering him, he was reluctant to discuss it at first. Finally, he told her that his father was being unreasonable. She didn't respond immediately, because her reaction was to want to give him a bloody good shake and tell him to grow up. But she knew that would be neither helpful nor useful.

'If it was my dad I'd be thrilled he was doing something, rather than just sitting around, festering his way into old age.'

'Isn't your father deceased?'

'Yes.'

'Then no wonder you'd be thrilled.'

She laughed, despite the fact that she was sure it hadn't been intended as a joke. 'Why don't you just go along and see him?'

'Because, as I've already said, that's the night we have dinner.'

'So change the night.'

'It's not that easy.'

'Surely it can't be that difficult.'

'I rather think you're straying into personal matters here.'

'And what's wrong with that?'

'We should talk about the case. It is, after all, what we're paid to do.'

'I can't understand why you're being so difficult.'

'Indeed you can't.'

She looked at him, not quite understanding what he was saying. He looked straight at her to clarify.

'Understand,' he repeated. An email pinged noisily into his desktop. He glanced over and then leant forward. 'It's from Clare.' He read it carefully, then again.

'What is it?' Ottey asked. But he was concentrating too hard. Then without warning, he suddenly leapt up from his chair and grabbed his cycling gear. 'George!' she protested, but to no avail. He was gone. She looked quickly at the email still open on his desktop. 'Okay...' she said, as if whatever she'd read was a bit of a game changer, and followed George out, intercepting him at the bike shelter.

'One word, George: "partners". We'll take the car.'

Having proclaimed this authoritatively and been followed by him to her car, she realised as soon as she turned the key in the ignition that she didn't actually know where they were going. The email had been from Clare, the pathologist. In it she'd said that the results had come back from the toxicology tests and they were a little surprising. Alex had tested for several what she had described as "performance-enhancing" drugs and abnormally high levels of testosterone. Most of the drugs, Cross discovered later, having spoken to Clare on the phone, were orally ingested. But some would have been injected. On closer examination she'd found injection sites in his leg. These weren't immediately apparent because of the state the body was in when it was discovered. He had been a regular user apparently, so the first thing Cross wanted to do was re-examine his flat.

They got the flat keys from Kostas and searched the place from top to bottom, with the aid of a couple of uniformed policemen. There was absolutely nothing there. Cross had another look at the bike. He examined the tyres and the bike generally.

'This has never been ridden. It's brand new,' he said.

'Perhaps he bought it for the L'Étape,' said Ottey.

Cross looked around the flat carefully. He wasn't looking for a stockpile of drugs. He was trying to build a picture of this young man, from the details of the apartment. It was clean and uncluttered, and had the feeling of not being really lived in. Not so much like a hotel, more like a set in the furnishing department of IKEA or Habitat. All perfectly co-ordinated. Like it had been ordered online and then unpacked and placed, exactly like it was in the brochure photograph. A large LED TV screen on the wall opposite the leather sofa. A Sky box. A Playstation. This was a bachelor pad. There were a few prints on the walls but, most striking of all, a racing bike was hung in pride of place above the sofa. Battle-scarred, it was obviously a relic from a past cycling victory.

In the bedroom Cross noticed all Alex's clothes hung up

neatly, freshly pressed. This young man cared about his appearance. This appealed to Cross' sense of organisation. He was particularly taken by the way Alex had organised his underwear and socks. Folded and stacked up neatly, side by side. It reminded him of the sock-display drawer in the menswear department at the old Maggs & Co store in Bristol. It was a wooden-framed glass drawer that slid out, with as much ease and perfectly formed manners as the salesman demonstrating his wares. The soundless mechanism was as subtle as the man's quiet patter. If Cross had been on his own he would have examined the way the socks, in particular, were folded. But even he knew that he would never be able to live down being caught going through a victim's underwear drawer.

The kitchen was the only area in the flat that felt used and properly lived in. No surprise there as Alex was a chef. It formed part of the open living room and was filled with knives, oils and well-seasoned pans. Cross liked that expression. A "seasoned" pan. He liked the implication of dedicated care and thoroughness.

After an hour they had found nothing.

'Are we sure he'd have a stash?' Ottey asked Cross.

'For the oral medicines I would have thought so. Clare said they would have been taken regularly. He has to have kept them somewhere.'

'He was a member of a gym,' she said.

'Do you think he might have had a personal trainer?' Cross asked.

'Worth checking?'

'I don't think he'd keep anything there, would he? People just use those lockers when they go, don't they? I was a member of a gym once.'

'Really?' she said, unable to disguise her surprise.

'Yes. Just the one month. So noisy, and presumably full of germs.'

They went out to the car and sat there for a few minutes, figuring out what to do next. Then Cross sighed. The kind of sigh people make when they think of something so obvious, they should've thought of it before, and now they feel stupid.

'The chemist. Patel,' said Cross.

'Yep,' agreed Ottey, and put the car into gear.

7

P atel was giving an elderly man an injection. The old man was sitting on a chair by the counter.

'There you go, Charlie.'

'Thank you, Mr Patel. You're getting much better with practice. I hardly felt a thing,' the old man said.

'I'll take that as a compliment,' said the chemist.

'Not a trypanophobic then, Mr Patel?' said Cross, inducing a turn of the head from Ottey, which annoyed her. She had decided to play it much cooler with his absurdly impressive vocabulary and ignore it.

'It's just a flu jab. I can cope. How can I help you, detective?' Patel knew he'd made a mistake as soon as he said the word "detective" – his customer, Charlie, was now rooted to the spot and wasn't going anywhere.

'Were you aware that Alex was taking performance-enhancing drugs?' Cross asked.

'I wasn't. No. Excuse me a second.' He turned back to the old man. 'Was there anything else, Charlie?'

'No,' said the old man.

'Good.' Patel then walked to the front door and opened it, inviting Charlie to leave. 'Give my best to Gloria.' The old man took another look at the two detectives. Cross stared right back. Ottey gave him a reassuring smile.

'He's a good man, Mr Patel,' Charlie said, with a hint of caution.

'I'm sure he is,' replied Ottey.

'Does a lot for the community round here. Brings your prescriptions if you're ill and can't make it in. Phones if he hasn't seen you around for a while. An absolute diamond,' he said.

'Thank you, Charlie. That's very kind,' said Patel.

The old man gave the police officers another disapproving look, then walked out of the shop. 'Goodbye Ajjay,' he said as he went through the door.

'Charlie,' said Patel, as he closed the door behind him and walked back to the other side of the counter. Cross noticed this with people in their offices; they often retreated behind their desks, workers behind their stations, when the police presented themselves. He wondered whether this was habit or defensiveness. With Patel, the way he stood up straight and put his hands on the counter, he was sure it was a way of imposing some sort of authority onto the situation.

'No, I wasn't aware of that,' Patel said in reply to Cross' question.

'His toxicology report came back positive for a few, including testosterone,' said Ottey. She handed him her phone so he could look at the results. He studied them briefly. His eyebrows arched, as if he was surprised but willing to accept what they were showing him as fact.

'Okay. Well there's no arguing with that.'

'You had no idea?' Ottey asked.

'None at all. But it doesn't surprise me.'

'And why is that?' she went on.

'He'd asked me about it in the past,' said Patel.

'What? To supply?'

'Yes. Of course I wasn't going to. I advised him not to on

both a health and sporting ethics basis. It's cheating and I told him it could have no place in our club.'

'What was his reaction?' Cross asked.

'Apologetic, actually.' Patel looked at Ottey's phone again and then handed it back. 'So this is disappointing, if unsurprising. Alex is, was, our best cyclist. Our star, if you like. He had no need to do this. He was so talented. But for some people that's just not enough.'

'Why unsurprising?' asked Cross.

'Because he was the kind of guy who always did things his way. He'd pretend to be interested in other people's opinions, but only if they agreed with his. If they didn't he just went his own way anyway. Recently he'd bulked up quite a bit. It didn't look natural. The speed of it certainly wasn't in any way natural. He had to be doing drugs. As for his performance – the spike in it was huge. He left everyone way behind.'

'So you didn't supply Alex Paphides with drugs of any sort?' said Cross.

'I did not,' he replied.

'Do you know where he might have got access to them?' Ottey asked.

'Have you got them with you?' Patel asked.

'We haven't actually found them yet.'

'I see. Well, he'll most likely have got them from the internet. If not, try his gym. I used to be a member there. It's why I left. Drug use, abuse, was prevalent there,' he said. 'I'm not telling you this but it might help you if you looked for a member called Danny.'

'Danny,' repeated Cross, making a note of it. 'What does he look like?'

'Oh, you can't miss him. You'll know him when you see him.'

8

'Drugs?' asked Kostas in disbelief, as he took them through to the staff room at the back of the restaurant. There was a row of metal lockers on one side, with a bench in the middle. Shelves were stacked neatly with laundry: table cloths, napkins and chefs' whites. Kostas opened one of the lockers. In it there were some clothes hanging, as neatly as they were back in Alex's flat. There were some shoes, trainers, clogs for the kitchen. Then at the bottom a small backpack. It was stuffed behind a large container of 'athletic supplements'.

'I knew about those. The supplements. He was always taking those and protein shakes,' said Kostas, almost hoping this was the extent of his late brother's appetite for performance aids. Ottey opened the backpack and started looking through it. Some tape, sun cream, a couple of pairs of Oakley sports sunglasses in their cases. Some protein bars and energy drink sachets – the kind riders opened with their teeth and drank during a race. Then a black, unbranded carrier bag. She opened it to reveal several plastic containers; some were supplements, but three of them were medical. There were also some unidentified capsule strips.

'We'll need to take these, Kostas,' she said.

'Of course.'

'Did you know about this? That your brother was taking drugs?' Cross asked.

'No. But it makes sense,' he said.

'In what way?' asked Cross.

'Like I said, he'd become obsessed with the Étape or whatever it was called. He said it was the only time in cycling where you could compare yourself to the pros – like the Marathon. Which is bullshit of course, but he didn't like hearing that.'

'Why "bullshit"?' asked Cross.

'Because the pros have already ridden about eight stages by the time they come to this one. The amateurs are all fresh,' he said.

'Fair point,' replied Cross.

'He'd bulked up a bit and he had these veins on his forearms. I mean he'd always had them before, obviously. But now, in the middle of a shift they'd be really bulging you know? Like Bruce Banner when he was changing into the Incredible Hulk,' he explained.

'And you thought this was as a result of the steroids, or whatever these are?' asked Ottey.

'No, like I said. I had no idea about the drugs.' Then he thought for a second. 'Do you think they had something to do with his death?' he asked.

'We don't know, but it's definitely something we will look into,' she said as Cross left the room. 'It looks like we're leaving.' She followed Cross out.

'You want to share?' she said as they got into the car.

'Patel, the head of the cycling club...'

'Is a pharmacist,' she said, and looked up and saw Debbie walking towards them. When Debbie spotted the two police officers she glanced at the restaurant entrance quickly, looked back at Ottey, then turned and walked back where she came from.

'So why's she running?' asked Ottey.

'She's not,' he replied. Ottey drove slowly behind Debbie. She went round a corner, out of sight of the restaurant, then stopped and turned to wait for the car. She tried the back door. It was locked. Ottey released the central locking.

'Hi Debbie. You okay?' she said as the young woman got into the back seat.

'Yeah. Do you mind if we drive somewhere else?' she said.

'Sure.'

Five minutes later they pulled up at the car park, just north of Bristol Zoo. Ottey switched the ignition off and turned towards Debbie.

'I thought it was just you. I didn't see him,' Debbie said to Ottey.

'DS Cross can leave if you'd rather,' Ottey replied, looking at Cross for affirmation.

'Yes. I can go for a short walk,' said Cross.

'No. It's fine. I guess,' Debbie said quietly.

'So how are you doing?' asked Ottey.

'Okay. I've been at college,' she replied.

'You go to college?' said Cross.

'Yes,' she replied.

Cross said nothing further, so Ottey filled in. 'What are you studying?' she asked.

'Hospitality.'

'Oh, interesting. Same field as Alex.'

'It was his idea. Said the hospitality industry was booming right now. I really enjoy it, actually,' she went on.

'You're back at college quickly. After all that's happened,' observed Ottey.

'I had to get away from Alex's mum. All the wailing and crying was driving me mad. She's lost her mind. And now Philippos is just obsessed with catering the funeral. He can't talk about anything else,' she said.

'Philippos?' Ottey asked.

'His dad. He's obsessed with doing his son proud. She's yelling at him for talking about the catering all the time, when their son is dead. They've closed the restaurant for a few days. But you know that. You've just been there.'

'We have.'

'Kostas didn't want to close but Helena said they had to do it out of respect. She's all in black now. Looks like one of those women you see on a postcard from Greece,' she said. It was like she needed to talk to someone who'd met them, and so knew who she was talking about, to get it off her chest.

'I can imagine even college is preferable to that,' said Ottey.

'Right?' said Debbie. There was a pause. She obviously had something to talk to them about. But both Cross and Ottey knew instinctively that the best tactic here was to give her time. It was a ploy gleaned from years of experience in such situations. So they said nothing and waited.

'Did you talk to my parents?' Debbie asked. Cross was about to answer then made the decision, as she'd hoped Ottey would have come alone, to hang back - as if he wasn't really there.

'We did,' Ottey answered.

'How were they?' she asked.

'Fine, I think,' Ottey said. She sensed Debbie needed a little prodding and so went on, 'Did you want to tell us something, Debbie?'

'It's just that... I don't want to get anyone into trouble...' she said. Was she, now that they were actually there, changing her mind about whatever it was she wanted to tell them?

'Of course you don't,' Ottey reassured her.

'Why were you back at the restaurant?' she asked.

'We were looking for something,' Ottey answered.

'Were you aware Alex was taking drugs?' Cross asked straight out, no sugar-coating.

'Yes. We had an argument about it,' she replied.

'Why?' he asked. She paused for a moment.

'Did you not approve?' asked Ottey. Cross sighed audibly. She gave him a sideways daggers look. It really annoyed her that he always thought he knew best and was "leading" these chats, when he was doing no such thing. Again Debbie said nothing, just sniffed the sleeve of her jumper, as if for comfort.

'Why didn't you approve?' Ottey persisted.

'It wasn't just me,' she replied.

'Kostas said he didn't know anything about it,' Ottey said. Cross was thinking, then looked up.

'How long have you known about the drug-taking?' he asked.

'Just a couple of months,' she replied.

'Do you know how long he'd been taking them?' There was another pause and she looked a little upset. Cross immediately came to the conclusion that this had something to do with why she was upset.

'Just over six months,' she said, quietly, sniffing her sleeve. Ottey offered her a tissue, thinking she might be wiping her nose.

'And he hadn't told you?' she asked.

'No.'

'And that upset you,' Cross said.

'Yes,' she almost whispered.

'Because you're pregnant,' he said. Ottey looked at him. Debbie looked up, a little surprised.

'How do you know?' she said.

'Good question,' Ottey muttered under her breath.

'Hyperemesis gravidarum,' he proclaimed to the mystified occupants of the car. 'Morning sickness,' he went on to explain. 'Quite badly, by the look of it. The slightest smell can make you feel nauseous. I noticed you sniffing the sleeve of your sweater to neutralise the smell. In this case it's probably DS Ottey's perfume which, I have to admit, she has been a little heavy-handed with this morning.' Ottey couldn't be bothered to object as she wanted to see Debbie's reaction.

'No-one knew except me and Alex.'

'Not even Alex's family?' Ottey asked.

'No.'

'How far gone are you?' Ottey asked.

'Sixteen weeks,' she said.

'Gosh, you hardly show,' Ottey said smiling.

'Is that bad?' she said quickly.

'No, no, not at all,' Ottey reassured her.

'He didn't know. Then you fell pregnant while he was ingesting a quantity of steroids and other noxious substances for his cycling,' Cross said. Debbie reached into her backpack and took out an asthma inhaler. She shook it and took a couple of puffs.

'What was his reaction?' Ottey asked.

'Surprised, then worried he'd hurt it,' she said.

'I can understand that,' said Ottey.

'He talked to his mate in the club,' she went on.

'A doctor?' asked Ottey.

'No, Ajjay. He's a chemist.'

Ottey looked at Cross, who pursed his lips. She'd noticed he often did this when told something that surprised him. She thought it was a technique he used to hide his reaction. So the chemist had known about the drugs. Why had he lied to them?

'And what was his advice?' Ottey asked.

'He didn't seem to think it would've made as much difference as if I'd been on them. But they had a huge fight,' she said.

'Really? Why?' Ottey asked.

'Ajjay said he was a cheat,' she said.

'Is there anything else you want to tell us?'

'No,' she said, opening the door and starting to get out.

'Tell me about London,' said Cross. She closed the door again.

'What about it?'

'When I asked you about it in the restaurant you were going

to say something. Then you looked at Kostas and changed your mind.

'Alex hadn't given up on the idea. He was going ahead with it,' she said.

'Was Kostas aware of this?' Cross asked.

'I don't know. They were real tight those two. Really close. They'd never tell people what they were talking about in the restaurant. They were like twins. But I don't know.'

'How far had things progressed?'

'We'd been up to London to look at a place. He said he'd worked out a way of doing it now so that Kostas wouldn't have to buy him out.'

'And how was that?' asked Cross.

'He was going to borrow,' she said.

'From the bank? Cross asked.

'No, he had another investor. He was dead serious. He'd hired a designer. He had a mood board and everything. Look.' She opened her photos on her phone and showed them pictures. It was very high-end, very unlike the Adelphi. It was everything the Adelphi was not. Very sleek with lots of steel and a giant charcoal pit in the middle of the room. 'He had a date and everything. I couldn't wait. The further I got away from my mum the better. He was going to train me up as a manager as well. That'll never happen now,' she said quietly.

'Do you know who the investor was?'

'No. It was someone abroad, Alex said. Another Greek bloke.'

'Are you sure Kostas knew nothing about this?' Cross asked.

'It was before... Look I don't want to get anyone into trouble but I think Kostas might have known. They had a huge row a few days before Alex died. They always argued, but there was something different about this one. Alex was off-his-head angry about something Kostas had done, it sounded like. I only heard bits, but I think it was about London,' she said.

'I'm sorry about all this, Debbie,' said Ottey.

'Yeah, it's a right fucking mess. You have no idea.' This time she opened the door and went. They watched her walk away, then Ottey looked at Cross. 'Poor thing, she's pregnant, which you kind of imagine may have been a bit of a surprise, and now the father of the baby is dead. But there's something else she's not telling us,' she said.

'There is,' he agreed. 'We need to get Alice to look through his laptop for a business trail. She's been concentrating on all the personal stuff. It's endless, apparently. I don't know how people find the time, and why on earth do they think their lives are of such interest to other people?'

9

They went back to the chemist at the end of the day. By doing this he couldn't use his work as an excuse not to talk to them. They also knew he had a training ride with the club shortly after work, which they wanted to follow him to.

'Recognise these?' said Ottey, holding part of Alex's drug supply up in front of a slightly startled Patel. He was wearing full lycra cycling gear. Cross noticed an expensive-looking racing bike propped up next to a door, which presumably led to a storeroom in the basement. The door had a coded lock.

'Should I?' Patel asked. She handed them to him. Patel put on a pair of glasses and examined the label.

'Human Chorionic Gonadotropin. HCG.'

'And what is that used for?' Cross asked. Patel sighed; he knew there was no way out of this.

'Mainly weight loss and the treatment of undescended testicles,' he replied.

'Now that I did not know,' said Ottey, slightly bemused.

'And...?' Cross pushed, well aware of the answer.

'And it's used by doping athletes to avoid the body crashing after steroid use,' said Patel reluctantly.

'Such as these?' said Ottey, holding up another box of pills. He took a look at them.

'Where did you get these?'

'We found them and a whole lot more at Alex's restaurant.' There was a pause. Patel looked grimly disappointed.

'I didn't know till just before Tenerife,' he said.

'You're a chemist and one of your team has a locker-full of performance-enhancing drugs. Objectively speaking, that seems quite a coincidence, wouldn't you say?' asked Cross.

'I genuinely had nothing to do with this.'

'Other than just supplying him?' said Ottey.

'I did no such thing. Why would I? I could lose my licence,' Patel protested.

'Because your team might win the L'Étape?' Cross volunteered.

'I couldn't give a shit about the L'Étape – I wasn't even going. That's for the diehards in the group. Look, you can get all this stuff on the internet. I told you that.'

'But only if you know what to look for and where to look,' Cross said.

'Anyone can find out. You don't need to be a chemist. Just Google "cheat".'

'Is he the only one in the group to do this? Any of the others?' asked Cross.

'Absolutely not. Matthew actually...' He was going to say something further, to prove his point presumably, but then changed his mind.

'Was it an issue within the group?' Ottey asked. Patel thought for a moment, then obviously decided to say nothing.

'Perhaps it's best if we ask them ourselves. Is Matthew training with you now?' asked Cross.

'He is,' he said.

'You don't mind if we tag along, do you?' asked Ottey.

They followed him as he cycled along Whiteladies Road and up onto the Downs. The group met under the old disused water tower, an imposing concrete structure whose sole purpose now seemed to be as a telecommunications mast. Cross had a morbid fascination with this tower as a child. To him it seemed huge and possessed of a looming, evil intent. For some reason he hated the very idea of this giant water container and had nightmares about being trapped in its dark, damp confines. He wasn't sure that it was much better now that it was empty. The cyclists had gathered at the café and were leaning against their bikes, talking and drinking water.

Ottey thought it best to wait until Patel introduced Matthew, which he duly did. But just as soon as he had, Cross wandered off to the group. Ottey sighed.

'This is Matthew,' Patel said.

'Hi Matthew, sorry for your loss. Can I ask you a few questions?' she said.

'Sure. It's terrible. I still can't quite believe it,' Matthew replied.

'How did you find out he wasn't going to join you on the Tenerife trip?' she asked.

'He texted me. Said he'd done his hamstring.'

'When was that?' Ottey asked.

'I don't know. I saw it when I got up that morning.'

'Can I see? Your phone?' she asked.

'Sure,' he said. He got it out of the pouch he was wearing round his waist and gave it to her.

Meanwhile Cross was examining one of the riders' bikes. 'Beautiful bike,' he said.

'Thanks,' said the rider.

'Pinarello Dogma F12, Dura-Ace Di2,' said Cross.

'Yes,' said the rider, who laughed slightly, impressed at his knowledge.

'I've not actually seen one before.'

'Do you ride?' asked the rider.

'Yes. Used to have a Trek, then a Boardman. But they kept

getting stolen,' Cross replied. One of the other riders laughed. 'What's so funny?' said Cross.

'Well, you're a policeman. It's a little ironic, don't you think?' he said.

'Yes, I suppose it is. Are these Fulcrum Racing Zero C17 wheels?'

'Yep.'

Ottey was still looking at Matthew's phone. 'Was this the last time he was in touch?' she asked him.

'Yes.'

'And you haven't heard from him since? Not when you were in Tenerife?'

'Nope,' he replied.

''Three thirty in the morning. Seems an odd time to find out you've pulled a hamstring, doesn't it?' she said.

'Not necessarily. Depends what you're up to,' he joked, and immediately regretted it. 'Sorry, that was stupid.' Ottey looked over at Cross, who was still with the others.

'Is it really light?' Cross asked. The rider pushed the bike over towards him.

'Pick it up. See for yourself.' Cross did so. He lifted it up with one hand.

'That's amazing.'

'Ten percent lighter than the last model.'

'Look, do you mind if we do this another time? The guys are all here and we need to get going. Some of them have families,' Matthew said to Ottey.

'Matthew, your friend has been murdered. This is a serious matter,' she said.

'Is that right?' he asked, looking over at Cross, who was now riding the bike he'd been examining round the water tower. Ottey couldn't believe it.

'Okay, point taken. Can I have your number? We'll get back

in touch if we need anything further.' She got his details, then walked back to the car. She sat there for a full five minutes while Cross talked to the riders, looking at some of the other bikes. She had a good mind to drive off and leave him there. The group finally got on their bikes and cycled off, in their matching lycra club tops. Cross stood there watching them as they rode away into the distance. He finally turned round, walked back to the car and got in.

Ottey drove off, not saying anything, as if to make her point. She then reminded herself that Cross had no compunction whatsoever about never speaking, and if she wanted to make a point, she'd have to vocalise it. So she finally said, 'Why did you just go off like that?'

'They had some very expensive bikes. It's not often you get a chance to see them like that.'

'This is a murder investigation, George.'

'I am well aware of that. You have no need to point it out. Did you look at the text?'

'I did.'

'And what did it say?'

'That he'd pulled his hamstring.'

'Was that it?' he asked.

'Yes. But it came at 3.30 in the morning,' she said. Cross thought for a moment. That was indeed an odd time to tell Matthew he was injured and couldn't make the trip. When and how did he do it? If indeed he'd done it at all. Which Cross was beginning to doubt.

'What exactly did it say?' he asked. She handed him her notebook. He looked at it and frowned. 'I can't read that. It's scribble.' She took it back from him, irritably, and read it out.

'Torn my hamstring. Won't make the trip. A.'

'It would've been better if you'd pulled over to read that,' he said.

'Are you serious?' she asked.

'Very much so. It's dangerous.'

'Well at least I was doing my job, George.'

'Indeed.'

'Don't you think that's an odd time to text Matthew about an injury?'

'Yes,' he replied. 'I do.'

10

There were often lulls in investigations while they waited for autopsy results or forensic findings to come back. And today felt like one such time. At the beginning of his career, Cross had found these moments quite troublesome. It was partly impatience but also the fact that a crime had been committed and, as long as it remained unsolved, he was acutely aware that there was an outstanding injustice. It was his responsibility to resolve the situation, was how he saw it. The fact that there might have been between another thirty or forty cops, in those days, working on it was of little comfort for him. But he gradually got used to the, at times, slow pace of these inquiries and understood how they functioned. He had worked out a system of priorities, which he adhered to assiduously. He knew that the endgame of these cases always lay in the presentation of the case to the jury. Not the arrest. Not the chase. A coherent narrative was the most important factor of all. So if it took time to find it, so be it.

Ottey was doing her best these days not to speak to Cross in a normal, everyday, colloquial way, as he often didn't understand interchanges in the vernacular. If she did, it would then require her to provide some kind of unnecessary explanation. Normally she might go into another detective's office at this stage of an investigation and ask them if they "fancied a chat". This would have thrown Cross. Because he didn't have "chats" and he was sure she must know that by now. A "chat" implied something personal. Nothing to do with work, and it was something he never indulged in.

'Shall we talk about what we know?' she asked.

'That would be useful,' he said. She had come to realise that constant repetition and conversation about what they knew in a case was a useful process for Cross. Nothing unusual in this. It was how many police officers worked. It was slightly different with Cross, though, in that he was capable of going over and over the same tiny details and information endlessly. He seemed to find it effective in a way that she didn't understand. But having seen what often came out of this navel-gazing, as she'd once described it, much to his consternation, she went along with it.

'Can we ask Alice to join us?' she said. He sighed. He preferred to have these conversations alone. Mackenzie still had a habit of interrupting at inappropriate moments. He knew this stemmed from her keenness to help, but he found it distracting. 'How else will she learn? I've told her just to sit and listen,' Ottey reasoned, realising this was the exact argument Carson had used with her, some months before. Which she had derided at the time.

'Very well,' said Cross reluctantly. Mackenzie was pleased. She found sitting around pretending to be busy absolutely draining. But what was the alternative? She had toyed with the idea that she could deliberately look as under-used as she was. But this had a couple of inherent dangers. Senior figures, namely Carson, might think she was lazy or, worse, redundant. She worried she could then lose her job. Her lack of useful employment didn't make sense to her, though. Everyone was constantly moaning about a lack of resources and yet here she was, in the midst of them all, a painfully underused resource, in her opinion. It was also a little humiliating going round the department like an over-eager puppy, volunteering to do anything anyone needed. So she'd stopped doing that as well.

What wasn't so welcome to Ottey was Carson appearing and asking, 'So where are we up to? Shall we go over what we have?' Even though it exactly echoed what she herself had said only moments before. How did he do this, she wondered? He always appeared when they were about to go through things. It was like he'd bugged Cross' office. Thinking about it, she wouldn't put it past him. But then thinking about it further, she realised that it would be pretty fruitless, as Cross sat there, for the most part, in complete silence.

'So, let's start with the text,' she began.

'The text is strange,' Cross said, thinking out loud.

'You mean the timing?' she asked.

'No, the actual wording. It's strange when you consider it in the context of the fight,' he replied.

'What fight?' she asked.

'Matthew and Alex had a fight. A physical fight.'

'What?' said Ottey, now slightly put out. 'How do you know that?'

'The other cyclists told me.'

'Go on,' said Carson.

'Wait a minute. Why didn't you share this with me in the car?' Ottey asked.

'You didn't ask,' Cross replied. With anyone else she would've thought he was trying to score points in front of Carson. Not so with Cross. But it was no less frustrating, all the same.

'But you didn't speak to Matthew,' she protested.

'The team found out Alex had been using drugs. Matthew was furious. He's virulently anti-drugs,' Cross continued, ignoring her. Carson wanted to ask, "What drugs?" but he

66

knew he'd look stupid and not up to speed, so in these situations he found it more sensible just to pretend he knew what was going on, and nod his head sagely, as if in agreement with everything that was being said.

'He still hates Lance Armstrong,' Cross continued, 'all these years later.'

'How did they find out?' said Ottey, still irritated that she was having to ask.

'Ajjay told them. They then confronted Alex, who tried to justify it. Ajjay told him the only way he could stay in the club was to pack in the drugs. He told him they had no room in the club for cheating. Told him he'd have to stop. Demanded the drugs were handed over so he could destroy them. Then he wanted Alex to do a drugs test every week. That's when Matthew stepped in. He said it was better if Alex just left there and then. They had no room for cheats. It soon got out of control. Punches were thrown. Then Alex left. But as he was going he reversed his car and rode over Matthew's bike. A high-end carbon fibre bike worth around ten thousand pounds. Next time Matthew heard from him was when he got the text.'

'So the wording *was* odd,' said Ottey, thinking it through.

'No mention of the fight, no apology. It was as if nothing had happened. Wouldn't you expect him to mention the fight at the very least? Say something about it? Apologise. Surely he wouldn't just text him about his hamstring as if nothing had happened. He couldn't have thought that he was still going on the trip. No mention of the drugs either. Wouldn't he say, "I've listened and stopped taking them"? Or even, "I know you don't agree with it, but can we sort it out after the trip?" But nothing? Doesn't that strike you as odd?'

'Actually, isn't it a little odd that they would still be expecting him to go?' said Carson.

'Good point,' Cross agreed.

But then again, it's not as if we actually know anything

about Alex. I mean about his personality. Maybe this was how he was,' said Ottey.

'He'd have to be some sort of sociopath to think everything was normal. Either that or on the spectrum,' said Cross. Ottey looked at him. No-one in the room could quite believe what they'd just heard.

'That was a joke,' said Cross. 'You said I should try and make more jokes to put people like Alice at ease.' This immediately made her feel uncomfortable.

'I did, I did,' agreed Ottey. 'Maybe we'll work on that. So what are you saying about the text?'

'I'm saying that in all likelihood, Alex didn't send it.'

'You think whoever killed him sent it?'

'I don't know, but whoever it was had no knowledge of the fight and the wrecked bike.'

'So that rules out everyone in the club, including the chemist,' said Carson.

'Looks that way,' said Ottey.

'But they knew about the Tenerife trip. Which implies it was someone known to him.'

'I don't agree,' said Mackenzie. There was a slight pause which, of course, she misread as them being taken aback with her interrupting. They were waiting for her to make her point, which she quickly realised. 'It could easily have been the chemist or Matthew.'

'Not Matthew,' interjected Cross. 'He has an alibi. Partner's dinner. Eight witnesses.'

'Okay, well the chemist then. He could still have sent the text, surely,' she went on. 'If he's killed Alex just before, he could've been in a blind panic. I mean, I'm assuming this is his first murder. Maybe he wasn't thinking straight.' Cross stared at her for a long, uncomfortable, time. Oh oh, I'm for it now, she thought.

'She has a point,' he said finally, 'but that scenario would point to it being an accidental death. Something which, as it were, took him by surprise, which he then had to cover up.'

'If it had been premeditated, he'd have thought it through more. He would've written the text in line with the narrative,' said Ottey. 'But you're saying Alex agreed to do what Ajjay had asked. So where's the beef? He wasn't even interested in the L'Étape.'

'So he told us,' said Cross.

'Oh, okay. Did you glean more from your cycling chums?' Ottey said, forgetting that sarcasm was wasted on him.

'Ajjay was going to step in. Take Alex's place.'

'Really?' she looked at Carson. 'That's not what the chemist told us.'

'Yes, he was desperate, apparently. Had been really upset not to make the cut,' said Cross.

'So he didn't feel awkward about it?' asked Carson.

'They said he was like the Duracell bunny, all over-excited; could talk about nothing else.'

'Get a warrant for the chemist's premises. Take a forensic team down there,' Carson said.

'What exactly are we looking for?' Cross asked.

'Drugs...' he said.

'Well there's a good chance of that, it being a chemist,' said Ottey, who just couldn't resist it.

'You know what I mean, Josie. There's one other thing. We don't have a scene of crime yet. He wasn't killed at the garages, we know that. So where was he killed? The pharmacy maybe?' With that he left. As if he'd just demonstrated a significant line of enquiry they should follow which hadn't occurred to them. Understandable, given that their policing skills were only a fraction as sophisticated as his.

'I hate it when he loves himself that much,' said Ottey. 'I'll get the warrant.' She left. Cross sat there thinking that a warrant was, in all likelihood, a waste of time. But it wasn't a waste of his, as yet. He then looked up and saw that Alice was still there. She had also been a little lost in thought. When they both realised that they were in the room alone, with no-one else there and nothing to say, they almost jumped in unison.

'I should go,' she said finally.

'Yes,' he replied, 'you should.'

11

Cross had just enough time to put his head round the door of the CCTV room before they exercised the warrant on Patel's business premises. He liked the way nothing ever changed in here. Sometimes there was a change in personnel, but he usually saw the same people as, being a creature of habit, he tended to visit at roughly the same time of day. He went up to Catherine's desk; she was still working on the CCTV, of the streets leading in and out of the garages.

'Any luck?' he asked, although he knew in truth that, if she had, he would've been told by now. She always managed to get important pieces of evidence or information through to him, wherever he was and whatever he was doing. She also had an innate sense of what could be important and what was irrelevant. This impressed him.

'Nothing clear; still on it.'

'We now have a time frame, which should narrow it down for you. He left the restaurant at around eight. On his bike. A bright yellow racing bike. Quite distinctive...' He stopped for a second as something occurred to him which he realised needed immediate clarification. '...except, of course, it won't be distinctive on CCTV images at all.' Happy to have cleared this up he carried on. 'But we don't know where he went. He texted his teammate at three – or someone did with his phone. We haven't found the phone yet. He then failed to show up at Bristol airport at seven. But I'm thinking he was dead by three,' Cross said.

'Okay, we'll start at the restaurant, see what we can find. We'll hold off on the garages.'

'You can't do both?' he asked hopefully.

'We're working five other cases but I'll see what we can do.'

In the car, on their way to the chemist with the warrant, Ottey thought it was maybe a good time to bring up Cross' situation with his dad. This was not only because they were, as always, enjoying a long silence, but because he couldn't get away. They were in a moving car. He was trapped – had nowhere to go.

'Have you ever missed a Thursday?' she asked.

'I don't understand,' he replied.

'With your dad?'

'A few times. When it was completely unavoidable, obviously,' he said.

'Because of work?' she asked.

'Yes.'

'And how was your dad about it?'

'He knew it had to be important for me to miss it. He understood.'

'Okay.' They drove on in silence for a while. 'So your dad's work at the Museum...'

'It's not work,' he quickly corrected her. 'It's a voluntary position.'

'You could still call it work, surely. Not being paid doesn't mean it's not "work".' He didn't reply. She went on. 'How important is this new job to your dad, do you think? Voluntary or not?'

'I have no idea.'

'Couldn't it be as important as yours to his way of thinking?'

'Of course not. We deal in murder.'

'That old chestnut. You can't denigrate everyone else's work just because they're not dealing with murder.'

'I don't. There are doctors, firemen, scientists, all of whose work I would call important,' he reasoned.

'And Bach?' she asked. 'Was his work important?'

'Well, obviously.'

'Not to someone who doesn't like classical music,' she countered. He didn't answer, which she found encouraging, so she continued, 'It's completely subjective, is my point. What is and what isn't important to people. So I'd argue your dad's new work, or whatever you want to call it, is important to him and will doubtless make a difference, however small, to all of those people who listen to him,' she said.

'That's not the point,' he replied.

'Then what is the point?'

'We have an arrangement. We always have dinner on a Thursday. They'll just have to find another time.'

'Why can't you find another time?' she asked.

'You don't understand,' he objected.

'So you keep saying,' she said.

Patel wasn't annoyed at the loss of business so much as the fact that several elderly and vulnerable people needed to pick up prescriptions and now wouldn't be able to. He made arrangements for one of his juniors to deliver them. Cross was interested in this. He thought this man's priorities were in the right order. They left forensics to it and went back to the unit. It was around two o'clock when the call came in. Forensics needed Cross and Ottey back on scene immediately. They had found blood. It had been cleaned up, but there was a trail leading to the door and outside to the edge of the pavement.

Also a major pooling by the counter inside. They had found a couple of actual traces near the base of the counter that had been missed and one on the door frame. Samples had been taken.

When they arrived back, Patel hadn't been informed of anything. The expression on the detectives' faces, however, told him all he needed to know. That things had just got serious. They took him down to the station.

'Am I under arrest?' he asked, when they walked into the Voluntary Assistance suite. Cross often wondered about this question, which was asked with irritating regularity. To him he thought it had to be clear whether they were or not because an arrest was always preceded by the words "Mr so-and-so, I am arresting you on suspicion etc..." and they were read their rights. Did they ask because they had an underlying fear of something illegal being discovered that wasn't necessarily anything to do with what they were being questioned about? Or was it a kind of inverted reminder to the detectives that they could leave whenever they wanted to? They never pushed this ability to leave, however, through fear of then being arrested and detained in a cell.

'You are not,' said Ottey.

'I told you I had nothing to do with his drug-taking,' Patel replied.

'You can see why that is a little difficult for us to accept at face value. You're in the same cycling club. You're a chemist. Bit of a coincidence, don't you think?' she went on. 'What *I* think is that he persuaded you. What harm would there be if no-one found out?'

'I am a respectable pharmacist and an amateur cyclist. End of. What would be the benefit to me of supplying him with gear?' he said.

'"Gear?"' Cross asked.

'Oh, come on. I can say "performance-enhancing drugs" if you want, but we all know that's what it's called.'

'Maybe you didn't actually supply him but just pointed him in the right direction,' Ottey said.

'Why would I do that?' asked Patel.

'Like we said. To win the L'Étape,' she said.

'I've already told you I have no interest in the L'Étape,' he protested.

'That's not entirely true though, is it?'

'I told you it's nothing to do with me.'

'Except that you're now in the team of eight. You were the reserve and have been bumped up. Why didn't you tell us about that?' she asked.

'Why d'you think? I knew you'd point the finger at me. Like you are actually doing now. Which is stupid. Let me make this very clear for you. Yes, I withheld the fact that I'm now on the team. Am I pleased about it? Yes, excited and also a little nervous. You see, I'm not the best cyclist in the club so I'm worried I'm not up to it. Did I kill Alex to get on the team? It even sounds stupid saying it out loud. No, I did not. Did I supply him with drugs? Which I have to admit does sound a little more plausible. No, I did not. Did I steer him in the right direction to get hold of them? No. Did he ask? Yes. Did I notice over the last six months that his behaviour had changed? Yes.'

'How did you find out that he was using drugs?'

'If you know what to look for it's fairly obvious. Anyway, I had the advantage of the fact that he'd already approached me. I kept an eye on him from then on.'

'So how did the group find out about Alex?'

'I told Matthew he'd approached me. Then with his stats and behaviour in the last few months I suspected he'd found another source.'

'Why did you tell him?' Ottey asked.

'Why do you think?' he asked, a little incredulously.

'Because drug-testing is a big thing on the L'Étape now,' said Cross. It was the first time he'd joined the conversation. 'They've trained for months, getting up early in the morning, cycling after work, sessions in the gym, in all weathers, making all sorts of sacrifices. Then, say they win. It's been all worthwhile until Alex fails his drugs test. They're disqualified. All of them. Then the entire team are branded as cheats.'

'And there you have it,' said Patel.

'Did you always want to be a chemist?' asked Cross, changing the line of questioning abruptly.

'What? Um, no, no, I'm one of those failed doctors, I'm afraid.'

'You studied medicine?'

'No, I messed up my A levels. Didn't get the grades.'

'That must've been disappointing,' said Cross.

'Not really. I think it was more my parents' dream than mine. They came over from Uganda during the Amin years. Very humble, hard-working and horribly ambitious for their child. Their only child. They worked hard because they were desperate for me to have a better start in life than them. A familiar immigrant story, I'm sure you're thinking, and of course it was. They wanted me to be a doctor. I think, maybe subconsciously, I fucked up my A levels deliberately. I'm very happy with the way things worked out, though. Mind you, since pharmacists have been allowed to give minor medical advice and flu jabs, people seem to confuse us with doctors – so I kind of ended up halfway there.'

'How so?' asked Cross.

'They treat us like the first port of call before they go to A&E. Or they go there, see the waiting time and come to us anyway. We often have a queue of people "waiting for treatment". So much so that we have a doctor's consulting room once a week.'

'Private?'

'No. I cover the cost myself,' said Patel.

'That's very generous of you,' said Ottey.

'It actually works out both ways. It solves the hassle of turning people away. Though it has caused a bit of an issue with people trying to treat it like their normal GP. It really is for emergencies or the "well-worrieds", as I call them, who can't get a GP appointment quickly enough. They're not treated, just examined and their minds put at rest. Unless there is a problem, in which case we either call their practice or send them to A&E.'

It was the word "emergencies" that got Cross thinking. He then got up and left the room. Ottey closed her eyes slowly.

'Am I free to go?'

'I'm afraid not.' She needed to wait for the results of forensics and the blood. Was it a match for Alex? 'Would you like something to drink?'

'A coffee would be great. Thanks.'

Ottey got Mackenzie to make the coffee, and Mackenzie was grateful, in truth. It gave her a chance to get away from looking into the ownership of the garages, which wasn't getting her very far. She'd decided to go down there later on that day and ask around. She felt sure she might get further that way.

Ottey marched into Cross' office without knocking. Not because she knew that would annoy him, which it did – he practically jumped out of his seat – but because she was annoyed. 'Why did you leave the interview like that?'

'It wasn't actually an interview.'

'Don't be pedantic. You know exactly what I mean,' she said.

'He didn't do it. Any of it. He's not stupid.'

'Like Alice said, it could've been an accident.'

'It could. But the likelihood is, I would suggest, tiny. I thought my time was better used elsewhere.'

'And what about mine?' she said.

'I couldn't possibly speak for yours,' he replied.

'And the blood?'

'He's a chemist. He said people treat chemists like A&E departments these days. They're encouraged to go into chemists for advice and flu jabs and it seems to have escalated to a minor trauma unit. It'll be something to do with that. Have you asked him?'

'Obviously not. I'm waiting for the results.'

'It might save you, and him, a lot of time if you just asked. He seems to be a very community-minded individual to my mind.'

Patel laughed when Ottey mentioned the cleaned-up blood.

'Perhaps you didn't hear what I said before? On some days, not that often, it's true, we're like an outpost of A&E. Just without all the facilities.' He then got out his phone and scrolled through. He showed her an article from the Bristol Evening Post from a few months ago. "Chemist delivers baby". It showed a picture of him in the pharmacy with a woman, sitting on a chair by the counter, holding a baby. She'd just given birth. 'That was a first!' said Patel proudly. 'They called the girl Angelica Justine.' Ottey looked at him blankly. 'Her initials are AJ, like my name Ajjay. It was a girl, so that was the closest they could get. They ended up calling her AJ for short. Isn't that sweet?'

'Sure. And the blood leading out of the pharmacy to the pavement?'

'It's actually coming into the pharmacy from a car. A stabbing. Young kid. They just dumped him. Stabbed in the leg. Some sort of gang punishment. But they'd nicked his femoral. We managed to stem the blood till the ambulance arrived. He could've died. Idiots.'

'He helped a woman give birth in the pharmacy and tended to a stabbing victim. But you already knew that,' Ottey said to Cross.

'I didn't actually *know* it but I'd come to the conclusion that in all probability it was something like that. Then Alice looked it up for me for confirmation,' he replied.

'And you didn't feel the need to share that?'

'No. I didn't want to interfere with your line of questioning.'

'You didn't tell me about any of the information you got at the water tower either. With the cyclists.'

'You didn't ask,' he said.

'I shouldn't have to ask. I'm your partner. You should share it.'

'I see.'

She could tell this didn't sit well with him. Deciding when to share anything was a difficult judgement for him to make. She had picked up on this. She was coming to understand that his awkwardness and reluctance to do certain things, things that were normal and everyday things for others, was not his being difficult. It was just the way he was made. He found it complicated.

'Maybe it would be easier if I asked you if you had things to share?' she volunteered.

'Yes. That's a good idea,' he said and started to pack his small backpack and put on his dayglo yellow cycling jacket.

12

That night, Cross went to church. Not because he was in any way religious. He was quite the opposite. These days he would describe himself as an atheist. For a while it had been agnostic, but then at thirteen he came to the absolute conclusion that there was no God and although he saw, both historically and around him, that it gave others comfort in life, he would just have to live with his lack of faith. In some respects he knew believing would've suited his personality; the regularity of a Sunday service, nightly prayer while kneeling beside his bed, even weekly bible-study meetings. Catholicism also, he concluded, would have been his faith of choice. Judaism ran it a close second. But with Catholicism it felt to him that there were very clear rules by which one had to abide. He liked the rigidity of its beliefs. He once thought that most religions would benefit from such clear guidance for their followers. But then fundamentalism sprang up in all its forms and all religions. So he had to redefine his opinion.

The reason for his visit that night was that he played the organ at this church. Not for services or anything. Just for himself. He thought playing during a service, a wedding or a

funeral would be an act of hypocrisy, as he would be partici-
pating in an act of worship. He couldn't reconcile this with his
lack of faith, and it had become a subject of much discussion
with the young priest, Stephen, who was engaged in an active
campaign to get George to agree to give a recital or two and
raise money for the church. But George was reluctant. Stephen
had even gone so far as to organise a committee to put a recital
together. He was met with obdurate resistance from Cross.

'Perhaps you could calculate how much a recital might earn,
and I could just make an equivalent contribution to the
church?' Cross had suggested.

'That's not the point. I think you should share your gift with
others,' Stephen replied.

He had once pushed this particular thesis too far and their
discussion had faltered almost terminally. Stephen made the
mistake of referring to it as a "gift from God". George's immediate response was that it wasn't a gift from anyone, particularly not from an imaginary God. It was actually the result of
hours upon hours of study and practice. Many priests might
have taken offence at the "imaginary" tag, but not Stephen, who
was obviously made of sterner stuff.

The deal they had brokered was that George could practise
in return for doing regular maintenance on the organ. Because
of course, George being George, it wasn't enough for him just to
learn how to play. He needed to know how the organ itself
worked. He was now something of an expert in not just playing, and the world history of organ playing, but also the fundamental mechanics of the instrument itself. So every Wednesday
night George would let himself into the church and play. He
often found it useful, not just as a break from the particular case
he might be working on, but actually in formulating fresh ideas
about it. He was in such a different state of mind when he was
playing. Not only did it relax him, but the sound of the organ,
the co-ordination between the different manuals and his feet

hovering over the pedals, instinctively playing the right ones, set his mind free. He found himself thinking about work in a different way, such was the mental release he found in playing. It was surprising how many times he'd solved a puzzle in a case, a conundrum that had befuddled them for weeks, while in church, playing the organ. Stephen doubtless thought there was some form of divine intervention going on. But he certainly wasn't going to say that to his musical detective.

But no fresh perspective for George this night. However, he felt that he'd cleared his head a little. The next logical step for the investigation was the gym. He finished playing and switched the organ off. But when he left, he was approached by a few women who had come into the church after he'd started practice. They immediately told him how wonderful his playing was. He was quite pleased by this: a little approval often went a long way with him, until he recognised one of them as being from the "recital committee" Stephen had introduced him to a few weeks before. That's how they knew when he practised. Stephen had told them. He was a cheeky, pushy bugger. But what was odd was that George found himself actually enjoying their comments and praise. It pleased him. Encouraged him. So rather than make his excuses and cycle home, he stood there for a good ten minutes basking quietly in their compliments. Until that is, one of them judged it the right time to say what a shame it was no-one else had the opportunity to hear him. Who knew that they had such talent in the congregation? This sentiment had a familiar ring to it. It could have come straight out of Stephen's mouth. Cross was quick to point out that he wasn't a member of their congregation. Nor was he a believer, which brought them neatly to the idea of a recital. It was at this point that he abruptly extricated himself from both the church and the conversation. He thought he'd done it with great tact and diplomacy. But they were left wondering why Stephen hadn't told them that the man he wanted them to encourage to play was so rude.

As Cross got on his bike, he looked up at the rectory and saw the priest at a window. Stephen waved and smiled. George just ignored him and cycled off, which left the priest with the distinct impression that his plan was working. It wouldn't be long now.

13

The next morning Cross and Ottey headed off to Alex's gym. As soon as they got into the car, Cross began talking to Ottey. This was really unusual for him. She had more than a sneaking suspicion that he was trying to head her off from reigniting the discussion about his Thursday-night dinners with his father.

The gym proved fruitless in their search for Alex's drugs. They had held out the hope that maybe there were members' lockers where they kept their kit. But there weren't. The lockers were used on a daily basis for members to put their belongings while they trained. The gym was on an industrial estate, occupying one of the medium-sized units there. It was the gym of a famous local boxer called Johnny Hazel, who was working his way through the amateur super flyweight category, nationally. The main room was dominated by a large boxing ring. There were boxing bags, racks of gloves and head guards littered all over the place. It was what you might describe as "hardcore". It was deliberately basic. No fancy machines and juice bars here. Old fashioned. If you looked closely you'd see that this was a very much curated appearance. Everything was deliberate. From the black and white pictures of old boxing fights on the walls, to the antique lockers and wooden benches in the changing room, and the clean towels on wire racks. If you came here, this place said you came to train, nothing else. This was serious, no-frills training. The smell of *Deep Heat* mixed with sweat, hung in the air.

At one end of the large room, the pictures on the walls changed from portraits of boxers and action shots from fights to bodybuilders competing. Standing in grotesque poses, flexing their absurdly large muscles, with more oil on them than a well-dressed salad. Weights were being pumped by some outrageously large, muscled individuals – men and women alike. It would surely not be too much of a stretch to imagine that you could tap a supply of steroids or whatever you had a taste for, thought Ottey. They met with Danny. As Patel had said, it was indeed quite hard to avoid him. An amateur body-builder, his biceps were twice the size of Cross' thighs. They were given use of the office to talk. Danny squeezed himself into one of the chairs opposite the two detectives.

'I heard Alex had passed. But murder? That doesn't make any sense,' he said.

'How well did you know him?' asked Ottey.

'Um, well, just inside of the gym really. I helped him with some muscle-toning in his legs. Not that he needed it.'

'What do you mean?' Cross asked.

'Well, he was a cyclist. Have you seen the thighs on some of them? Like tree trunks. Totally out of proportion to the rest of their bodies. But we worked on some stuff,' he said.

'That's quite the physique you have there,' Ottey remarked.

'Thanks. I'm coming up to a competition so I'm getting fully toned,' he said.

'I'm not in the least interested in the legality of how you obtained that impressive range of axial muscles, but I am curious as to whether you utilise some sort of additional chemical help to achieve it,' Cross said.

'No more than the usual supplements. Nothing illegal,' he replied.

'As I said, I have no interest in that. The reason we're here is that traces of various drugs were found in Alex's body. Performance-enhancing drugs,' Cross explained.

'Okay,' said Danny, giving nothing away.

'Would you know anything about that?' asked Ottey.

'About drugs or Alex using?' he asked.

'The latter,' she replied.

'No.'

'Do you expect us to believe that?' she asked.

'I don't give a shit what you believe, to be honest. I'm a member of the UKDFBA and I compete regularly,' he said.

'And that is?' she asked.

'The United Kingdom Drug Free Bodybuilding Association,' volunteered Cross.

'So you've heard of it?'

'No, it's just a fairly obvious acronym,' Cross replied.

'So I'm clean. Have to be,' he said.

'Did Alex ask you about getting hold of any drugs?' Ottey asked.

'Are you kidding?' he scoffed.

'She is quite obviously being serious,' said Cross. 'I think that must be quite apparent even to someone who doesn't know her.'

'We need to know who people go to, to score this stuff,' Ottey continued.

'Well that's easy. People here tend to go to the same guy. Best supply, best stuff apparently and easy to do business with,' he said.

'And that is...?' she asked, happy to play his game. People often did this when talking to the police, out of either a sense of drama or self-importance. Detectives had to indulge them and play along to get the information they needed. This was one such occasion.

'Alex Paphides.'

The detectives sat there for a moment, taking this in. It didn't surprise them so much as change the narrative, possibly. Cross, like so many other policemen, had come to the conclusion that nothing could surprise him in this line of work any more. He was intelligent enough to know he hadn't "seen it all" and he most likely wouldn't have when he retired.

'So, with him being dead, it wouldn't surprise me if it had something to do with that. Wherever he got the drugs from. Not nice people to deal with, and the other thought I had was – did he step on anyone's toes?'

At this point a heavily built man came to the office and knocked on the door.

'You good?' he asked Danny.

'Hey Tony, we don't have a session today.'

'I think you'll find we do,' Tony replied. Danny checked his phone and looked up.

'No, it's definitely tomorrow,' he said.

'I have it in for today,' came the response with the obvious implication that he hadn't made the mistake. Danny was about to say something further then changed his mind.

'You know what, it's fine. Let me finish up here and we'll do it.'

'I only have an hour,' Tony said, and left. Danny's attitude made Cross think that Tony wasn't someone you messed with. He also had a feeling he'd seen him somewhere before.

'Regular client?' Ottey asked.

'Yeah. Are we done here?' Danny replied.

'Sure.'

'I hope you find the guy, I really do. Anything else you need to know, I'll be here.'

They left and walked to the car, 'Did you recognise Danny's client?' Cross asked.

'Tony? No. But he looked like a piece of work. Danny certainly seemed a little nervous, didn't you think?' she said.

'I've definitely seen him before. Recently.'

Ottey started the ignition and then asked what had been bugging her all morning. 'Trypanophobia, spill.'

He looked at her, puzzled. 'What does it mean?' she explained reluctantly.

'Oh, I see. Fear of needles.'

'Ah.'

Back at the MCU, Cross summoned Alice to his office. It always felt like a summons to her, such was his tone. Not a request. An order. One she had learnt, over time, it was easier to follow at the earliest opportunity rather than prevaricate over. He gestured to a chair and she sat. He went through his notepad till he came to his action orders. Here he noted all the actions he had laid out to the team and the time and day in which they'd been ordered. They were ticked as soon as they had been fulfilled. It also had a time noted for him to follow up. This was what he was doing with Mackenzie now. He found her assigned task and looked up.

'Laptop,' he said.

'Yes. Nothing much, just usual social stuff. Loads and loads about cycling. How many pictures can you have of yourself and your mates on a bike, I ask myself?' He didn't furnish her with an answer. 'Pictures of bikes themselves, gears, brakes – it's all a bit anal.'

'Nothing about any business plans in London?' he asked.

'Nope,' she replied.

'No emails about it?'

'None.'

He thought for a minute. 'That seems unlikely,' he said.

'That's what I thought. I went through his trash. Everything. So it has to be elsewhere,' she said.

'My thoughts exactly,' he replied.

'So the question is, where? I wondered whether he might have another laptop, but you haven't found one, have you?' she asked.

'No I haven't, but then again I haven't specifically been looking for one,' he replied.

'By "you" I meant us.'

'That, in itself, is fairly confusing.'

'"Us" in the generic sense.'

'I see. Thank you for clarifying.'

'So I started doing random searches on the laptop we have around "restaurants", "London", "business plan"...'

'And did you find anything?' he interrupted impatiently.

'No, but I did find a couple of documents that couldn't be opened because they couldn't be found.'

'What does that mean?'

'It means they were saved elsewhere. On a drive, from what I could see. So we need to find that drive,' she said, quite pleased with herself, as she considered this to be right up there, legit, detective work. Cross sat silently for a few seconds then looked at his watch. It was just before ten. This was pertinent, because he knew it was when Ottey visited the ladies' room, prior to making her morning coffee. Like everyone, she was a creature of habit. As with everyone and everything, it was something that Cross had noted and would use as an opportunity to sneak out of the office when he needed to. Now was such a necessity and opportunity. He looked over to her desk and she was, indeed, not there. So he stood up, grabbed his bicycle gear and started to leave.

'Where are you going?' Mackenzie asked, immediately regretting the way it had come out.

'I beg your pardon?' said Cross.

'I was wondering where you were going, that's all,' she replied nervously.

'And why is that?'

She thought for a moment and remembered that being blunt and honest with Cross was often remarkably effective. 'DS Ottey asked me to. If she wasn't around to ask you herself. She finds it annoying when you leave without telling her where you're going.'

'Yes she does,' he said, and left. She found herself smiling. The better you got to know him, the more charming his manner became at times – unintentionally, of course.

As he attached his bicycle clips outside, Cross was thinking how refreshing their exchange had been. If only more people just told the truth instead of hiding behind badly concocted, feeble excuses. Everything would be so much more straightforward.

He left the office on occasions like this not because he didn't want Ottey to be with him. It was just that there were occasions where he didn't want to have to deal with social interactions and be on his best behaviour. Just a simple conversation in the car with Ottey was an effort for him to process and interact with appropriately. It took energy that at times he felt he just didn't have – or could've been used more effectively somewhere else.

On this occasion, as Ottey knew only too well when Mackenzie told her he'd left the office, it was definitely more to do with the fact that he didn't want to have to talk about his Thursday night conundrum with his dad. She thought this was because he was coming round to the view that she had a point and he didn't want to admit it. There was definitely an element of truth in this as Cross, cycling on his way to see Kostas, was secretly congratulating himself on avoiding exactly that.

14

'What are you looking for?' Kostas asked him as he handed Cross the keys to his brother's flat.

'I'm looking for an external hard drive for his computer,' Cross replied.

'He has one here in the office.'

'I think it's unlikely...' Cross stopped himself. 'Yes, that would be helpful.'

Cross was then installed in the back office with a coffee and left alone. The office was all you would expect from a family-run business but, Cross noted, it was very orderly. Receipts, invoices and paperwork were all clipped together and hanging off hooks in the wall. There was a whiteboard with weekly tasks and orders on one side. But the most affecting thing about it were the dozens and dozens of family photographs. Mostly taken in the restaurant with the two boys helping their mother and father. It struck Cross how much Alex resembled his father when his father was younger. There were pictures of the boys, aged no more than six or seven, Cross calculated, dressed as waiters in waistcoats and bow ties, serving tables. Their beaming smiles matched by the customers looking on fondly.

Alex had an amazing ability to carry four plates of food at one time when he was only five. There was a picture of Kostas with a huge circular tray above his head, dwarfing him, laden with meze. Alex standing on a chair to carve the doner, which was at least twice his size, as his father looked on proudly. The two boys, either side of their dad, cooking in the charcoal pit aged about eleven or twelve. Cross thought it was a little strange that there were no pictures of Helena, their mother. Then he realised the answer. It was so obvious – she was the one taking them.

There was nothing on the hard drive about London, which didn't surprise him. If Alex was keeping the dream of it alive, he wasn't going to let his brother find out on a shared computer. Cross had a chat with Kostas on the way out. He made a point of doing this with people involved in a case. If you had a legitimate reason for visiting them, in this case to get the key to the flat, you should never waste it. People acted very differently when you went to see them with specific questions or lines of enquiry than when you were there for a seemingly altogether different reason and you dropped the questions in tangentially. They were more relaxed at times like this, off their guard even. These occasions were often more productive than visits that were made specifically to question them. This was also in part because, if a detective made the visit specifically, it endowed the questions with way more importance than they probably warranted. So the answers became more considered and guarded.

'The bike in Alex's flat. It has to be worth around eleven thousand pounds,' said Cross.

'That doesn't surprise me. He'd been splashing the cash a lot recently,' Kostas replied. 'Mind you, how many bikes does a guy need?'

'Oh, I don't think it was for him. It's the exact make and specification as Matthew's. The one he destroyed. I think he was planning to replace it.'

'So, what? Do you think I have to give it to him?'

'I don't think anything. I'm just saying why I think he bought it.'

'Well, I don't need it.'

'Even so, it's brand new. I'm sure you could return it in the circumstances. It is worth a lot of money.'

'That's true. I'll think about it. I mean it feels like the right thing to do. If he'd not died he would've done it, so maybe...' Kostas' voice trailed off. It was a moment where the pain and reality of his loss hit home. Grief so often struck people out of the blue like this, unexpectedly.

'What did you mean by "he'd been splashing the cash a lot" recently?' Cross said. He noticed a minimal flinch in Kostas' cheek. He'd regretted saying anything, which was a cue for Cross to push. 'Had he changed his spending habits?'

'Yeah,' said Kostas quietly.

'Mr Paphides, we have nothing at the moment. Nothing to go on. We will have. But it takes time. Your brother has been murdered. That much we have determined, and we will do our very best to bring the perpetrator to justice. But at this stage in any investigation, it can be the smallest of things, things that seem innocuous to you, that could lead to significant leads and findings for us. Unless your brother had done anything illegal. In point of fact had he done something illegal, it's immaterial: he's dead. He can't get into trouble. Unless of course it was something you were also involved with.'

'No! No, I wasn't involved. What I mean is he wasn't doing anything illegal. I would've known, wouldn't I?' he said. Cross didn't answer. He wanted him to go on. 'Just recently, in the last year, he was definitely spending like it was going out of fashion. I thought he must've been maxing his credit cards, but I looked. I know all his passwords. He knew mine, and everything was fine,' said Kostas.

'Like the cars?'

'Yeah. He bought them both. On finance, obviously, but he arranged it and paid for it all himself – the deposits and repayments and that. I knew nothing about it until he showed up with them one morning. I couldn't believe it. But he wouldn't take no for an answer. Said it was good for the business, like I told you. Truth is we could have afforded it together, if we'd spoken about it, but it was the way he went off on his own and just did it.'

'What about London?' Cross asked.

'What about it?'

'Nothing,' Cross replied. But something about the speed of his answer made Cross think that possibly Kostas was aware of the fact that Alex hadn't given up on the idea of opening in London. He'd come back to it another time.

'You had an argument a few days before Alex was killed,' said Cross.

'Maybe. Like my dad said, we argued all the time,' he replied.

'But this one was particularly heated,' Cross went on.

'Maybe; I don't remember,' he said.

'Okay.'

His instinct that Kostas was hiding something was borne out by the fact that he seemed distinctly relieved when Cross announced he was leaving.

The first thing he did when he got to Alex's flat was get a glass, wash it, fill it from the tap and drink it. He took off his coat. He was looking for something hidden. So he checked all the normal places – the freezer, back of the wardrobe, under tables, drawers, air vents. He found nothing. He sat down, then his father rang.

'Cross,' he said.

'You know it's me. Why d'you answer the phone like that?' Raymond said.

'It's how I always answer the phone.'

'That's how you answer the phone at work.'

'I am at work,' Cross replied.

'Don't be deliberately obtuse. You know what I mean,' said Raymond, uncharacteristically terse. Cross knew that something had annoyed his father. He could tell from his tone. He assumed it was also why Raymond was calling him. He never called his son at work unless it was important.

'What is it?'

'This Thursday has been postponed for a week. We can have dinner as usual.'

'And the following week?' Cross asked.

'The following week I can't do. Nor any weeks after that for the foreseeable future,' said Raymond.

'Understood.'

'What does that mean?'

'It means we'll have to find another night to have dinner. I was thinking Wednesday might be the optimum solution,' Cross went on.

'I thought you had organ practice on Wednesday.'

'I do, but as it doesn't involve anyone else and as I've determined that the church is also free on Thursday evening it's just a matter of swapping the two,' he said, as if this was the obvious thing to do and he was surprised his father hadn't thought of it.

'Good. Well, I'm glad we sorted that out,' said Raymond.

'In point of fact I sorted it out, but there we are. I have to go.' He ended the call without a "goodbye" or giving his father a chance to say the same. Raymond was fine with that. He was just relieved that the Thursday night issue had been resolved. He knew from experience that these seemingly small things could become irretrievably catastrophic with his son.

For Cross this call had also been useful. Talking to his father had reminded him of things never being thrown out, and how he'd found Alex's old mobile phones in a drawer when he first came to the flat. He went into the bedroom and opened the drawer in the wardrobe. He lifted the phones out, and as he did so a small USB flash drive fell out of the tangle. He picked it up and put it in his pocket. He then pulled the drawer out and looked into the back of it. There was nothing else there except for a bunch of keys, a fitness heart rate belt and some sunglasses. He was about to put the phones back in the drawer when instinct told him to take them with him.

It didn't take long for him to find the documents he was looking for on the flash drive. There was an entire folder marked "Adelphi London". He was about to open it when Ottey walked in with that expression he now read as being extremely irritated. He thought he would head it off at the pass.

'I couldn't find you,' he said.

'Yeah, that tends to happen when you don't bother to look,' Ottey replied. 'Where have you been?'

'Back to the flat.'

'Why?'

'Because we've found no electronic footprint of the London project anywhere. It has to be somewhere. Debbie talked about an investor, a designer and a location. I think I've found it,' he said, looking at the screen. Ottey pulled up a chair next to him, sat down and leant over to look at the screen. Cross froze. Completely. His hands hovered over the keyboard as he stared fixedly at the screen.

'Well, go on,' she said. She hadn't noticed his sudden paralysis. When she did, she said, 'Sorry', got back up and put the chair back on the other side of the desk. 'I'll go and get my laptop.' She'd forgotten about Cross' personal space issues. She quietly chided herself for this as she crossed the open area to her desk. They had solved the problem of her wanting to look at the same screen as him and his not being able to deal with the proximity a few months earlier. A tech guy from IT had suggested that Cross shared his screen with her virtually – so he controlled the mouse and the desktop but she could see his desktop on her computer. This was normally used by computer technicians to solve people's computer problems, often on a completely different continent, but here it was just as effective across a desk.

In the folder they came across designs from a London-based architect, planning permission applications and licensing applications. Alex was a long way down the road with this. The one thing that wasn't in evidence was the line of credit. There was a business plan, which had obviously been sent out, and there was correspondence with a bank, which seemed to be offering finance. Initially it was a complete package, but Alex had said he couldn't afford it and would find finance elsewhere. In the end he had come up with a plan that was part bank finance and part investment. But as to who and where that investment was coming from, Cross couldn't find any information.

'So who is the investor?' said Ottey.

'That could well be a key question. We should dig a little bit deeper. Get Sean in tech to have a look at this drive and make sure there aren't any hidden caches or files.'

He told Ottey about his meeting with Kostas, who thought that his brother's spending habits had changed a lot of late. Cross was also fairly sure of another thing.

'What?' asked Ottey.

'I think Kostas knew about London. I think he knew it was still ongoing.'

'Do you think he was happy about that?'

'Alex bought them both the cars,' Cross said.

'Where did he get that kind of cash?' she asked.

'He got them on finance, but paid all the instalments as well as the deposits. What does that say about his mindset? He was optimistic. He thought this was just the beginning of something big for the two of them. There are plans here for rolling out to Manchester, Edinburgh, Leeds. These are big ambitions,' he added.

'Really?' said Ottey. She hadn't seen them, as he was such an irritatingly fast reader that he'd scrolled through the files at the speed of sound and she'd obviously missed it. 'Do you think Kostas was involved?' she asked.

'They were really close. They fought a lot but I believe that's the case with many siblings, particularly close ones. One city is missing from that list.'

'Bristol,' she said.

'Exactly. They weren't going to insult their father. They were just going to leave the Adelphi as it was.'

'Why fix it if it ain't broke?'

'Indeed.'

She noticed Cross' supermarket bag filled with mobile phones and charging cables. 'Are those his?'

'They are.' He got up and walked to the door. 'Alice, I have something for you.'

Ottey had observed over time that in the same way Cross didn't like being shouted at – it caused him real alarm and distress – he didn't inflict it on others. He would always place himself in a position where he could easily be heard. Mackenzie came into the room. He indicated the mobile phones on his desk.

'I need you to go through those and see if there's any recent activity,' he said.

'But those are his old phones. Wouldn't he have used his current one?'

'Quite possibly, but we don't actually have his phone. So there's no way we can check, and his phone records haven't, as yet, unearthed any unusual activity.'

Ottey stepped in. 'Look, we know he was supplying performance-enhancing drugs, but we have no evidence of how he did it. He had to communicate with his customers. He didn't use his personal phone as far as we can tell, for obvious reasons, but he had to have used a phone. We haven't found another, so it makes sense to look at these. Old phones with burner SIM cards. It's worth checking,' she said.

'Of course it is. I'm an idiot,' Mackenzie said.

'I wouldn't go that far,' said Cross, 'but you are still learning.'

Ottey looked at him after Alice left. 'She wasn't actually suggesting she was an idiot.'

'I know that,' Cross replied. 'I'm not an idiot either.'

15

A couple of quiet days followed. Mackenzie was dispatched to Alex's funeral. It was in a Greek Orthodox Church. She was surprised at how close to a Christian service it was. That was down to her own ignorance though, she thought, somewhat shamefaced. This was the second funeral she'd been to in her first six months with the unit. She didn't like funerals at the best of times, but this was a new experience for her. Witnessing a scene of such profound, personal grief that had nothing to do with her felt like an intrusion.

The police had nothing to gain, in terms of furthering the case, from attending, otherwise Ottey and Cross would have gone. She was told to go, as the family often got comfort from the presence of the police when cases were still open. She was about to ask Carson how they would glean any comfort from her, bearing in mind they'd never set eyes on her before, when she realised that the alternative was just to do more menial and meaningless tasks in the office. So she went.

It was a well-turned-out affair. Kostas spoke movingly about his brother. He said they might as well have been twins – they thought in such a similar way. That running a business together had been a blessing. Not that they had always agreed, and anyway, as anyone who knew them also knew, the real boss was their mother Helena. Going to work would now be a daily reminder of his loss. But he was trying to look on the positive side. That this grief would fade and, in the end, that daily reminder would become a blessing. Ajjay Patel also spoke on behalf of the cycling club, who were all there as a group. No mention of the drugs or the falling out. Just a tribute to how great a cyclist he was. How he made them all raise the bar and be better. She thought, perhaps uncharitably, how Patel managed to string together such a number of sporting clichés so seamlessly. But he was a chemist, not a public speaker, she reminded herself.

It was just as well she'd paid attention, because when she got back she was interrogated by Cross as to what she'd gleaned from being there. She described it in as much detail as she could. She couldn't answer as to whether Jean and Andy were there. She thought not. As the family stood by the church door thanking people as they left, receiving their sympathies and inviting them back to the restaurant, Debbie stood to one side. No-one deviated from the line afterwards to greet or comfort her. Except for Ajjay and the cyclists, no-one there seemed to know who she was, which Mackenzie thought was a bit strange. There was a big kerfuffle getting Alex's father, she assumed, out of his wheelchair and into the funeral car.

'Are you sure it was the father?' asked Cross.

'Yes,' she replied.

'How could you tell?'

'He was at the mother's side. It just made sense,' she said.

'But he doesn't use a wheelchair,' said Cross.

'Well all I can tell you is, he did today.'

That had interested Cross, which was why he was sat at a table in the Adelphi a couple of days after the funeral, having booked a table for dinner. For one. Kostas came over to the table with several small plates of meze as Cross was looking at the menu. Cross looked a little surprised.

'I didn't order those,' he said.

'I know. It's on the house,' replied Kostas.

'Oh, no. I can't do that. I have to pay for my meal,' Cross remonstrated.

'This is from my mother. It is a gift in return for your kindness,' said Kostas.

'Even so, I'm afraid I can't accept it,' Cross insisted.

'You want to argue with my mother? Because I know better,' said Kostas, putting some hot pitta breads covered with a bright red gingham cloth on the table, then looking in the direction of the back of the restaurant, where his mother sat in her usual place, knitting. Cross followed his look and the old woman nodded a stern acknowledgment at him.

'Perhaps you're right,' said Cross.

'Oh, I *know* I'm right,' replied Kostas.

'Very well, but I shall have to pay for the rest of the meal and I'll need a receipt,' said Cross.

'Of course,' said Kostas as he glided away and in one smooth movement greeted a couple of new customers and led them to their table. Meze was always a safe bet for Cross, funnily enough, as it was traditionally served on separate plates, which suited him perfectly. He had also spoken to Kostas on his arrival at the restaurant about his need for his food to be on separate plates and Kostas had taken it completely in his stride, as if it was the most normal thing in the world. Cross had anticipated that this would be Kostas' reaction. Had he thought otherwise he most certainly wouldn't have risked going there at all.

He surveyed the restaurant as he ate the meze. It was, as usual, completely full, with lots of families. One celebrating a birthday, for which Kostas paraded through the restaurant with a pudding adorned with a large lit sparkler and the plate decorated with a personalised greeting in chocolate sauce. The entire restaurant broke into a chorus of "Happy Birthday", as the delighted young woman feigned surprise. Cross thought she was pretending to be surprised, because as far as he could tell, from his limited visits to restaurants, it was de rigueur for such a cake to be delivered at the end of a birthday meal. And despite her pretence and protestations that her friends really shouldn't have, he suspected she might well have been disappointed if they hadn't. To round it off, Kostas provided each of them with a shot of ouzo. Ottey had told Cross that people often told restaurants that it was someone's birthday, when it wasn't, just to get the attention and maybe free shots.

There was also a group of fairly heavy-set men at one table. They were Mediterranean-looking, in all likelihood Greek, all muscled and toned. Cross recognised one of them as Danny's client from the gym, Tony.

The main course arrived. Cross surprised himself by how much of the meze he'd managed to get through. Kostas took away the plates with a look of proprietorial pride. As soon as Cross had booked, Kostas had told the staff that he alone would prepare his meal and serve the table. No-one else was to be involved. Cross' main course was on four plates: one with the lamb kebabs off the skewer and not touching, the rice on another and the salad on a separate one. Kostas had even gone as far as to put the lemon quarters on another plate. Cross was amazed at the tenderness of the meat. Kostas explained to him that it was his mother's marinade that did it. The meat was all organic, sourced from a local farm which they had visited, and was then marinated for twenty-four hours. The farmer was now a regular, when time allowed, and had attended Alex's funeral.

Tony and his group left. What interested Cross was the fact that no bill was asked for, produced or paid. They waved to the staff and left. Tony did up the button on his jacket as he walked, in that way that men do when they're trying to exude authority and control. Like he felt all eyes were on him. They weren't, except maybe for Kostas and his staff. And Cross.

Kostas joined Cross for some mint tea after he'd finished his meal. Again Cross protested that he hadn't ordered any tea. Kostas said Cross was doing him a favour by sharing a pot with him as it was his break and he was parched.

'How's the investigation going, detective?' the chef asked.

'We've reached a slight plateau at the moment. It often happens,' said Cross. Kostas was obviously disappointed.

'Do you think it will change any time soon?' he asked.

'I would've thought so. It doesn't strike me as particularly complex. Having said that, of course, the most simple-seeming cases are often the most complex,' he said.

'Do you think it had anything to do with the drugs?' Kostas asked.

'I'm not sure. I think he got most of those online. Well, except for one. I need to find the source of that one. But there weren't any third parties involved, we don't think.'

'Which one?' asked Kostas.

'Testosterone,' said Cross. He thought there was the smallest reaction at this from Kostas, which confirmed for him that he was on the right track.

'Is that a good or a bad thing?' Kostas asked.

'Neither,' said Cross. Kostas expected him to explain a little further, but he didn't. 'Where's your father this evening?'

'Upstairs.'

'Does he not work in the evenings?'

'Silly bugger's broken his ankle. Fell in the shower and couldn't stop himself with his busted arm,' Kostas explained.

'He is in the wars,' said Cross.

'We had to take him in a wheelchair to the funeral. My mother was very angry,' said Kostas.

'Yes, I heard. I'd like to see all of your father's medicines.'

'What? Why?'

'I need to see them. Will you ask your mother, as I assume it will depend on her?' Cross said.

Kostas didn't argue any further, but walked back to his mother to explain Cross' request. It didn't appear to go down too well in the first instance. There was much shouting and remonstrating in Greek. Finally she got up and stomped off upstairs, giving Cross an irritated look on her way. Kostas came over.

'Please. Follow me,' he said.

'Thank you,' said Cross, who got up from the table and went upstairs with Kostas. The apartment was absolutely spotless. The furniture was dark mahogany with a fair amount of kitsch Greek ornaments and pictures. There was a sofa with a plastic cover over the top of it and plastic covers on the adjacent matching chairs. The old man was in his vest and shorts and was being shouted at by his wife, who was trying to get him into a dressing gown. He looked up as soon as Kostas and Cross walked in and yelled something in Greek.

'Could we go to the bathroom, please, or wherever he keeps his medicines?' Cross asked.

Kostas spoke to his mother in Greek. She replied and he turned back to Cross. 'This way.'

They went into the bathroom. Kostas opened a mirrored cabinet over the sink. In it were various mouthwashes, tooth-pastes, spare soaps and on the top shelf a lot of bottles and packets. Cross examined them, finally settling on one. He looked at the label. 'Mr Patel's pharmacy,' he remarked.

'Alex's mate from the cycling. Good man. Always brings my parents' prescriptions with him when he comes to eat. Saves them going to him,' said Kostas. Cross walked out with the pills back into the living room. He held them up in front of Kostas' father.

'For your osteoporosis,' he said.

'Yes,' replied the father.

'Kostas, you said your father was suffering breaks in his bones more and more often recently.'

'He is.'

'Can you remember when it started?'

'Last year some time,' Kostas replied.

'And how long have you been suffering from it, Mr Paphides?' Cross asked.

'Five, six years,' he replied.

'And no real problems until these last few months?'

'No,' said Paphides.

'When Alex persuaded you to let him start taking them instead of you,' said Cross.

'What?' said Kostas. Helena, the mother, looked like she was trying to take this in. The father didn't answer immediately.

'It was my idea, not his,' said the father finally. 'He was working, training so hard for this race. I thought it would help.'

Suddenly his wife launched into him, slapping his face and shouting in English.

'You stupid, stupid man! What did you do that for? What good can come out of something like that?' she screamed. Kostas grabbed hold of her and stopped her.

'No, Mama, no! You'll hurt him! Leave him alone!' She started sobbing into her son's chest. The father slumped back into his chair. Kostas turned to Cross.

'This hasn't got anything to do with...' he said

'No, it's just another line of enquiry we can eliminate,' Cross replied.

'Did Ajjay know?' asked Kostas.

'Only after we told him. I think if he knew about the increased frequency of your father's fractures he'd have put two and two together. But he wasn't responsible. That lies very much with your father and Alex.'

The mother had left the room. Kostas turned to his father. 'Why? What were you thinking?'

'I was just trying to help,' said his father.

'What? Why? Why would you do that?'

'Because he was so desperate. He wanted to win this race very much and why shouldn't he?'

'Did he ask you or did you offer?' Kostas asked. Philippos hesitated, as if he was calculating which answer would cause less controversy.

'I offered,' he said.

'I don't believe you.'

'I did.'

'How would you know anything about drugs for cycling? I'm not stupid. He asked you and look what's happened. You're in a fucking wheelchair!'

'Don't swear at me,' he said.

'Seriously, you're going to say that after what you've done. You're a fucking idiot. The both of you are a pair of fucking idiots. I'm going downstairs,' Kostas said and left. Cross followed him.

As Cross was leaving the restaurant, following a protracted argument about his paying for the bill, Kostas said,

'I can't believe Alex would do that. I mean, where was his head? It's just a bike race. It's just a hobby. Did Debbie know about the drugs?'

'Only recently,' said Cross.

'But Alex knew Dad was getting more fragile. This is the third break in seven months. How could he think that was okay? I mean we discussed it. Talked about going private, getting another opinion, and all the time he knew it was because he was taking my father's medication,' he said, confused.

'Tell me about Tony,' Cross said.

'Tony? What Tony?'

'He was here tonight? Big individual with three male companions,' explained Cross, even though he knew full well that Kostas knew who he was talking about.

'Oh yes, good customer.'

'Such a good customer that he doesn't even have to pay? Does he have an account, maybe?'

'No, no, he was a friend of Alex.'

'Where did they know each other from?' Cross asked.

'I'm not sure – the gym, I think.'

Cross said nothing; he just looked at Kostas in his uncompromising way. The way that implied he'd asked Kostas a question and was still waiting for the real answer. Kostas looked uncomfortable then said, 'Alex owed him money. He borrowed it. That's one of the things Tony does, lends money.'

'And the interest is extortionate?'

'Yes, he ended up owing him more money than he'd borrowed. But now Tony, well he wrote off the debt when Alex was killed. He was very upset.'

'How much was it at the time of Alex's death?'

'It was down to only a few thousand.'

'So in return for writing it off he gets free meals?' said Cross.

'No, not so much. This was the first time he'd been in since Alex died. I offered it. He didn't ask.'

'He frightens you,' Cross suggested.

'No! He's our vegetable supplier. He runs a wholesale business but also organises all the other suppliers. They help each other out when they need to. But he has lots of other businesses,' Kostas said. Cross nodded as he took this in then turned on his heel and left.

A few days later the CCTV crew, well, that is to say Catherine, had been making some progress. She called Cross and Ottey into her office. What she showed them was some blurred footage of a van going down a side street that led into the garages. Cross asked her to repeat it time and time again.

'It could be something or... nothing,' she said.

'I'm tempted to go with something,' Cross replied.

'Particularly as we have absolutely nothing else to go on right now,' added Ottey.

'Someone had to get the body there somehow,' said Cross.

'A plate or some idea of the logo would be helpful,' said Ottey.

'Alisha's trying to enhance it as we speak,' said Catherine. Ottey looked over at a girl glued to another computer screen and gave her a smile of encouragement.

'Anything on Alex?' Cross asked.

'Still working on it. We've got him leaving the restaurant at just after five thirty. He's heading sort of south-east,' Catherine replied. Cross turned and left.

'Thanks Catherine,' said Ottey.

'It's not much. I'm sorry – we'll keep plugging away.'

'It's a start,' said Ottey, and left.

16

In many ways, Mackenzie's impatience with cases was similar to Cross' when he first joined the force. She wasn't experienced enough to appreciate the fact that investigations were, for the most part, a series of tiny steps. Small pieces of seemingly innocuous information, whether it be names, locations or dates, often had an incremental effect when placed together or in a certain, not immediately obvious, order. She thought going through Alex's old phones was pointless. She comforted herself, though, by thinking that she was actually handling pieces of evidence. This cheered her up a bit. She wondered whether she should be wearing gloves to handle them. She wasn't at all sure, and it delayed her for a good ten minutes as she weighed up the options of just finding a box of latex gloves, putting a pair on and risking widespread laughter if she was wrong. But if she asked someone, they might well tell her she should, knowing full well she didn't need to, just for a laugh and to set her up for widespread ridicule anyway. So she decided to go ahead without them, and if she was wrong risk admonition from Cross – which on balance she thought would be a lot less humiliating than a widespread piss-take.

She decided, in order to make her task more interesting, to

google the models of all the phones then go through them in order of manufacture. There were about ten of them. Alex liked tech and new stuff. She thought he must've been one of those people that had to have the latest version of the phone they happened to use. She could never understand the annual news item that appeared on TV, without fail, about people queuing for days, some even with tents and Primus stoves, to get the latest version of the iPhone. Why such urgency? Why did they have to have it right now? Right this minute? How could the phone in their pocket, which they had queued for with the exact same desperation and anticipation only twelve months before, be so old fashioned in such a short amount of time? Have gone from the indispensable "must have as soon as possible, if not before" to the absolutely dispensable, replace as soon as possible?

She knew that Cross would appreciate her manufacture timeline approach, as pointless as it was. These things appealed to him. There wasn't much to look at in the old flip phones. Basic texts and the directory, but things got more interesting as technology moved on. She was quite shocked at how much the old iPhone had weighed when it first came out. But as she went through the later phones, when technology advanced to the point that they were now cameras, she found her attitude to the whole case changed. Here were hundreds of pictures of their victim with his brother. They were obviously close. They were a tight family. So many pictures were taken in and around the restaurant with their parents. Bad haircuts featured, along with many questionable sartorial choices that she couldn't believe were ever fashionable.

What was happening, of course, was that a picture of Alex was forming in her mind. He went from victim to real person with a life and people around him. She found this surprisingly affecting. She actually got to know this young man. His character, his attitudes, his sense of humour. She didn't know it, but this was a major lesson for her in her police work. Getting to know the victim was so much easier these days, even after their death, because of phones and social media. Before the advent of this technology, police officers' knowledge of their victim was pretty sketchy, to say the least. Cross knew all of this, and his giving her the phones was actually deliberate. Not just to do the donkey work of going through all the information. He knew from experience that if she was any good, which he was beginning to suspect she might be, this would be an invaluable lesson.

She actually found some interesting activity on one of the older phones. Not a smartphone. All of the phones had activity on them – calls and old texts – but they related to the time that the phones were in use. However, Alex had suddenly started to use one phone again which he hadn't used for many years, about twelve months previously. There were several calls made from it in the last year. Also texts about meets and drops. She was tempted to analyse it all and present Cross with a dossier of dates, times, numbers and all sorts of amazing correlations. But he had instructed her that as soon as she found anything on them she was to let him see.

He took the phone and asked her to close the door as she left. Ottey looked up. 'Whatever you found has impressed him,' she said, looking at Cross in his office, now poring over the phone Alice had just given him. 'Well done. What was it?'

'Seven-year-old phone that he suddenly started using again about a year ago,' she replied.

'Excellent. Let's wait and see what he gets out of it.'

Mackenzie was pleased but disappointed at the same time. Cross got to do the juicy bit now. She was annoyed he hadn't been out of the office, which would have given her the opportunity to go through it and present him with her findings. Another time. There would definitely be another time. Maybe next time, instead of being carried away with her excitement of finding something relevant and rushing into Cross as soon as she'd found it, she would bide her time and delve a little bit deeper. Do some investigating of her own. Might even impress him. Unless it was time-sensitive of course. Then she would take whatever it was straight into him.

It was clear from Alex's bank statements that his spending seemed to have peaked at the beginning of the year and that by the time he died he was in a fairly precarious financial situation. Another conversation with Kostas had confirmed this. Alex had tried to borrow from him. This wasn't unusual, Kostas had said. It'd been like that since they were young. Alex would spend any pocket money he got from his parents almost immediately. The same with the bits of cash they got in their early teens when they helped in the restaurant. Initially it had been on sweets and football magazines. Then Playstation games. He was the first in their family, including his parents, Cross was amazed to discover, who had a mobile phone. His father thought they were unnecessary. He said he was always in the restaurant, where he had a phone with which he could make all his work calls. Why would he need a mobile and spend all that money? He was of the "why text when you can phone" generation, whereas with the new generation it was "why phone when you can text", and now it had gone even further with WhatsApp and Messenger. Cross often wondered whether technology, having irrevocably damaged the literacy and willingness of the general public to write, would now discourage them to even bother to speak. Virtual life – life on a smartphone – seemed so much more important than actual life these days. Why was it, when talking to people, that if their phone buzzed with whatever it was, text message, whatever, it required their immediate attention and interrupted whatever was actually going on in "real life"?

It took a few days for all the information from the USB drive and the phone to be collated. In the meantime, Cross had had the last of his Thursday dinners with his father. They had more to talk about than usual, and instead of watching a recorded episode of *Mastermind*, Raymond brought up his talk that he was giving at the air museum the following week about Concorde. He'd written the first draft and was quite pleased with it, he told George. He was then completely surprised by his son's offer to look through it. Or, if he preferred, to hear it. This was so unlike George, he wondered whether this was to do with Josie's influence. He suspected it was. Unbeknownst to Cross, he and Josie had been in regular contact since George and he had gone round for Sunday lunch. It was in fact a real pleasure, a relief even, for Raymond to have someone to discuss his son with. He'd actually never had this throughout George's grown-up life. And he was right. Cross was trying to change the way he interacted with people at Ottey's instigation. He'd concluded that there was no reason his father should be left out of this experiment, as he saw it.

Cross made several changes and edits to the talk. This wasn't so much a collaborative effort, as he just took Raymond's pad away from him and concentrated on the text. He didn't ask his father whether it was all right for him to cross great big swathes of the talk out and rewrite several paragraphs. He just did it. Raymond put aside his pride and let his son get on with it, as he was actually thrilled that they were doing something together. Well, all right, not entirely together, but as together as George was able to do anything together. It was a hopeful step forward. Cross asked his father to read the piece out to him again. If Raymond was expecting any praise or encouragement, which of course he wasn't, none was forthcoming. No sooner had he finished the last sentence than George was clearing up their Chinese takeaway and was out of the door.

Cross was reading all the information from the phones and USB at Tony's cafe early the next morning. He had got Alice to print everything up, which obviously for someone of her generation was completely puzzling, but he liked hard copy.

Although he worked on a computer most of the time, he liked annotating facts on paper. He would put the sheets into a ring folder in different sections so he could access them easily. He then collated all of this with his actions list and calendar, all of which was printed out. He had done this since his A levels, and as that had been incredibly successful he had seen no reason to stop.

He was preparing everything for Ottey to present to Carson, who had called a meeting. The reason he was doing it in the cafe was that here he was left in peace. At the office, with the impending meeting, people would've been constantly sticking their head into his office, despite the fact that he'd closed the door, to check on various things before the meeting. He wrote all the pertinent points down in a bullet list in capitals for Ottey. The latest question that needed answering, to his mind, was who and what was "Hellenic"? She was up to speed with everything, of course, but he liked it to be presented in a certain order. He had to do this, as he found himself incapable of conducting the staff meetings himself, being much more comfortable listening and commenting if needed.

Cross liked to listen. He liked to hear the team's progress. Where they were going next. Which actions had been completed. New ones assigned. All listed out loud. He found it really useful to hear it all laid out in this way so he could picture the overall operation in his mind.

'We're opening another line of enquiry into our victim's finances. He definitely over-stretched himself about twelve months ago. We don't really know why...' Ottey started.

'Optimism. Unfounded. But optimism,' said Cross, inter-rupting.

'What George is referring to is Alex's plan to open in London and then roll out nationwide. He was quite far down the road with it. But it was contingent on his brother buying him out of the Adelphi, which Kostas wasn't willing to do. It would've stretched them too far. Alex was unhappy about this, particularly as his father, unexpectedly, supported him and tried to persuade Kostas to change his mind. Even though this meant possibly jeopardising everything he'd built up, he was insistent. This caused a certain amount of friction in the family with Alex and his father on one side, Kostas and his mother on the other. It was all resolved at the beginning of the year when Alex had a change of heart. This is a strong family, but he could see how he was tearing it apart. So the project was off. But Alex was now in a hole financially. Kostas helped him out as much as he could, but Alex never revealed to his brother the true extent of his financial woes. This is when he found a new source of income and a new investor – Hellenic, who we're looking into. He started supplying drugs to other amateur athletes in the area for short-term cash flow, presumably. Getting his supply from the internet. He made quite a fist of it. Maybe people were willing to pay him for the convenience, I guess. But it could have something to do with his death. Johnny?' she said to a detective sitting at the front of the room.

Cross sat up at this point. DI Johnny Campbell was very much not part of his brief. He tried to get Ottey's eye, but she was studiously looking elsewhere.

'The performance-enhancing market is one of the fastest growing in the whole of the UK. Don't ask me why, but people seem to be taking their sport a lot more seriously these days for some reason – if you can call it that. Now, there is money to be made, obviously, and when that happens it's no surprise that the dealers who deal in cocaine, heroin and crystal meth all want in on the action. So it is possible our victim found himself in hot water with one of these guys,' said Campbell.

'Pure conjecture, complete theorising, based on what? Nothing,' Cross blurted out. 'Can we please save some time and get back to what we know? However little that may be.'

'George, this is a credible theory,' Campbell said.

'Credible theorising is, in the main, based on some sort of factual foundation. This is nothing more than water cooler gossip,' Cross replied.

'You're such a fucking wanker when you want to be,' spat Campbell. Cross flinched as if he was about to be hit. He sometimes did this when under attack. Years before, this would have been the end of the meeting for him. He would've reacted by leaving through the door, which he always sat next to. But he now consoled himself with the fact that such a virulent reaction was because he'd said something near the knuckle.

'Okay, Johnny, I think you can go,' said Carson.

'Seriously? This is a joke. Why do you always let him get away with this?'

'Probably because when this kind of thing happens I generally happen to be in the right,' said Cross, which made Mackenzie laugh out loud. Ottey glared at her. She apologised and looked back at the floor. Ottey was, however, laughing inside. She didn't like Campbell and, truth be told, when he'd insisted on presenting his theory, she let him because part of her knew this might happen and it was better it was dealt with now.

Campbell left the room.

'While there is no evidence that the drug dealing community were involved as yet, I think you'll agree, George, that while not pursuing it, we should be open to the possibility if evidence leads us that way,' said Carson. Ottey was thinking that this was an especially long-winded piece of man-management speak from her boss.

'So we know that Alex started dealing,' Ottey continued, 'but everything seemed to change about eight months ago. An investor became involved in the London project. What's interesting is that Alex was very secretive about it, even on his USB. He didn't tell Kostas, so had he changed his mind about telling him? Like I said before, we've managed to get a name, well part of a name. We think it'll be something like Hellenic Trusts, or

Holdings, Financials. So the next line of enquiry is to look into this.'

'Why?' asked Carson. A perfectly reasonable question, Cross thought, in the circumstances. Ottey hadn't furnished him with much detail, which might have been a mistake.

'Because Alex had a meeting with someone at this Hellenic corporation, or whatever it is, the night of his murder,' said Cross.

'Hellenic?' said Carson. 'Wasn't there some kind of Hellenic shipping line back in the day? I'm talking the Onassis era.'

'I believe there was,' Cross affirmed.

'Right then. Let's do this!' said Carson, as he strode out of the office with some purpose. What purpose that might be, however, was anyone's guess, and what exactly it was he wanted them to do he hadn't made clear.

Cross, Ottey and Mackenzie had gone through all the numbers on the "drug" phone and called several numbers of Alex's clients, they presumed. Almost all of them went to voicemail. Those who answered claimed to know nothing when they realised it was the police. Some others were unobtainable. Because Alex felt this phone would never be discovered, he had helpfully entered names against some of the more regular numbers. Danny didn't appear in the list but Tony did. Several times. Much more often than the other regulars and with increased frequency leading up to his death. Ottey called him and arranged to meet.

17

Franopoulos Fruit and Vegetable wholesalers was located in a large unit on an industrial estate in Easton. As they drove there, Ottey said to Cross, not a little mischievously, 'I'm so glad you had a good evening with Raymond and sorted out your dinner night.'

Cross was slightly distracted, thinking through his line of questioning with Tony. 'Yes,' was all he offered.

'How was his talk?' she asked.

'Wait a minute. How do you know all this?' Cross asked.

'I spoke with him this morning,' she replied.

'You called my father? Why?'

'He called me, as it happens,' she replied.

'And you spoke to him?' he asked, somewhat absurdly.

'That's what I tend to do when people I know call me. It seems rude not to unless I'm busy,' she said. He made no reply, which made her immediately regret her flippancy. 'Look, he was really happy that you managed to accommodate the change in date, and he said you were incredibly useful with his talk. He was really pleased. You did a good thing. All is great.' He still made no reply, so she decided to let it be until she figured out exactly why it seemed to upset him. Then she might, only might, discuss it with him.

The unit was modern, basically a delivery bay for a few lorries, and a warehouse. A lorry was delivering pallets of Spanish oranges, all packed in slatted boxes with straw. The scent was amazing. Like someone had lit a dozen scented candles to get rid of the underlying smell of rot. The place was clean. Indeed, a man in a Franopoulos sweatshirt was brushing up all the debris from the floor as they arrived. Inevitably, a small percentage of the products perished in transit, Tony went to great lengths explaining to them as they sat in his small office, looking down on the bay. There were several monitors showing CCTV cameras covering all angles of the interior and exterior. They recycled as much as they could, he said, and almost on cue a pickup truck with a trailer attached pulled up. A young, tattooed man with long hair, plaited beard and combat fatigues strolled in.

'That's Billy come to get swill for his pigs. He's one of those organic, rare-breed pig types.' He picked up Ottey's slightly disdainful expression and laughed. 'Don't be fooled by his appearance; that boy is loaded. Organic, free-range – his pigs are just the best. He supplies to all the top restaurants, Michelin-starred and everything. He even supplies two three-starred restaurants in London. He used to go as far as Scotland, but then he told the chefs they should be using local produce and stopped supplying them. Same with London; that's why he only supplies two. He's got a blog, has about thirty thousand followers or something. Does butchery courses, everything. The man's an undercover entrepreneur!'

'It's great you recycle in that way,' said Ottey.

'Put it this way – I'll never be out of pork. Just as well I'm not Jewish.' He said this, Ottey thought, as if he hoped it might cause a little offence. 'What did you eat the other night?' he asked Cross, who was completely at a loss as to what he was talking about. 'At the Adelphi; I saw you there – recognised you from the gym.'

'I had the lamb kebabs, with rice and salad,' Cross replied.

'The lamb comes from Billy's father, their pork from Billy and the chickens from his uncle. All top quality.'

'You seem to be very knowledgeable about where they source their produce,' Cross observed.

'I saw a gap in the market years ago, before organic really took off. These guys didn't have a clue about distribution, so I stepped in and helped. I'm like a meat agent, if you like. But they don't really need me any more – with the internet everything's changed. Still, I have a great address book.'

They sat down. He offered them fruit from a bowl on his desk, which they declined. He was a very confident man, but they'd met his like before. Beneath their veneer of charm and openness lurked an often quite malevolent threat. All would be well until you crossed them, then all bets were off. He was balding but took no pains to disguise this. The top of his head shone with a well-maintained tan. His hair was greased back at the sides, curly but not long, and jet black. He'd had work done on his teeth, Cross noticed. He was wearing an expensive pinstripe suit, the type that said "I'm a businessman", and a crisp white shirt, open at the collar to reveal a delicate gold chain round his neck. He wore cufflinks. This man paid a lot of attention to his look. His suit was tailored in such a way that it tapered in an exaggerated fashion at the waist, emphasising his broad shoulders and well-packed torso.

'So you said on the phone you wanted to talk about Alex,' he said.

'Yes, that's correct,' Ottey replied.

'It's tragic. Definitely murder?' he asked.

'Without question,' replied Ottey, who knew that her partner had now gone into silent observation mode. Something she'd hated when they first worked together. She felt she was doing all the heavy lifting in situations like this. But then he'd come out with something so fundamental to whatever case they were working on, that she realised it was part of his process. Which she'd then come to think of as "their" process. It made it a lot easier for her. Working with him was obviously not easy. He never indulged in what she called "banter-interviewing", where the police would act as some sort of double act. Not so much good cop, bad cop, but just two cops thinking out loud about the absurd story that had just been trotted out for their benefit and pulling it apart ironically. She'd had a great rapport with her last partner and absolutely none with Cross. Cross had no understanding of rapport and so couldn't indulge. It drove her nuts at times. The worst thing was that he didn't know he was doing it. It was also a skill that she prided herself on, and now it was something she never had the opportunity to utilise. She had an inkling that Alice might be quite good at it, and she had resolved to put it to the test at some point.

'Such a nice family. I feel for them, I really do,' said Tony, looking at the floor.

'Have you been their supplier for a long time?' she went on.

'No, not at all. About two years. Philippos never really took to me. Thought I was too dear. Didn't buy into organic. Quite old fashioned. Not to be too critical but he was never as interested in quality as the boys. Even he'd admit, though, that their business has done really well since our partnership,' he said.

'Partnership?' Ottey remarked.

'Wrong choice of word. What I meant was working together.'

'So how did you meet Alex?'

'I have to say it doesn't reflect that well on me. I met him at the gym. Stalked him if you like. I knew immediately who he was, but he only appeared there about three years ago. I'm afraid I'm all out when it comes to business. Nothing annoys me more than when someone turns me down. Like his father.

So it was unfinished business, kind of. It's a good concern, that restaurant, especially since they extended.'

'When was that?' Cross asked.

'About a year after the boys took over from their dad. They wanted to realise the full potential of the place, but I think they may have moved a little too quickly. They ran into a bit of trouble financially. They were quite stretched at the bank,' he said.

'You seem remarkably well-informed about their business.'

'I make everyone's business my business. A bad habit, my wife tells me,' he said. 'So I got to know Alex; we started to train together and gradually talk about business. I was a guest at his restaurant a couple of times, for his birthday, a cousin's wedding. The food was good but it could have been so much better with better ingredients.'

'And you were the perfect supplier?'

'Of course. Kostas was like his father at first: cautious, "stuck in the mud". Thought the prices were a rip-off. I persuaded them to try it for a few months, but Kostas was worried about losing the suppliers they had by leaving them for someone else, even for a short time. So nothing happened – we trained. But Alex, he was very competitive. He didn't like it that the restaurant was, in his words, second best. But really Alex didn't like being told he couldn't have something. He always wanted to try something new. Be the best. So he eventually persuaded his brother. With us supplying, their business was up by five percent after six months. The extra cost of the supplies cost fifteen percent more than before, but supplies only accounted for, I don't know, maybe forty percent of their outgoings. Do the math. The extra cost was more than covered by the additional profit even then. Now the business is up ten percent from then. Even Philippos gives me a smile now.'

'That's impressive,' said Ottey.

'Yes, but like I said, the friendship was made initially under false pretences. Do you think friendship ever gets beyond that?

I don't know. Do I feel guilty? Come to think of it, no. It was a win-win. And now he's gone,' he said sadly.

'Why did he call you from his drug dealing phone?' Cross asked.

'I beg your pardon?' he asked.

'I heard him okay,' said Ottey, who had started feeling a little nauseous from the cloud of aftershave that wafted off Franopoulos, together with his overpowering charm.

'He only called you from a phone he used for his drug dealing. You know about the drug dealing?' Cross said.

'I did,' he said.

'Is that how he got to know you? You were a customer?'

'No. Absolutely not.'

'I don't believe you,' said Ottey.

'I don't use drugs. I never have. I've worked hard to be in the shape I'm in,' he said. The two detectives said nothing, but looked sceptical. 'Really? You don't believe me? Okay, no problem. Easily sorted.' He got up and grabbed a paper cup from the water dispenser in the corner of the room and disappeared. Ottey looked at Cross.

'You don't think...' she said, without finishing the sentence. Five minutes later Franopoulos reappeared with the paper cup, which had been covered with cling film, and put it on the table.

'There. You can test it to your hearts' content,' he said triumphantly. It was a cup of fresh urine. They said nothing. Then Cross looked up.

'That doesn't prove a thing. You could've got someone else to urinate in that,' he said.

'Fine,' said Tony, getting up and going over to the water dispenser.

'Really, there's no need. Mr Franopoulos, please,' said Ottey.

'You sure?'

'Totally.'

He sat back down.

'There are several calls on Alex's second phone to you up until his death. If it wasn't drugs, then what was that about?'

'Just business calls.'

'Then why didn't he use his regular phone?'

'He did and I called him on it.' He got his smartphone out and scrolled through it. There were calls from Alex, and when Cross looked closely he could see that both of Alex's phones were listed.

'But you don't appear in his call records for the other phone?' said Cross.

'You're looking for the wrong name. Try Fanny,' he said. Ottey looked at him quizzically. 'People call me Franny. One day Alex misspelled it when he put it in his phone. Thought it was hysterical and it stayed that way.' He then pointed to his desk, where another two phones lay. 'I have three phones and I'm not a drug dealer. One for business and one for the family.'

'And the third?' Cross asked.

'That's personal,' he replied. Now Ottey liked him even less.

'What do you know about Hellenic?' she asked. This annoyed Cross, firstly because, in his opinion, it was far too soon in this interview and, secondly, because they didn't even know its full title yet.

'I don't know. What is it?' he said.

'Well, we're not entirely sure, but Alex seemed to be having dealings with them... or it,' she said, thus proving Cross' point, he thought. It made them look like they weren't leading the investigation – it was leading them.

'Why didn't you pay for your meal the other night?' Cross asked.

'That's a private matter,' Tony replied, smiling.

'This is a murder investigation; such niceties neither count for anything nor do they interest us,' said Cross. Tony breathed in and held his breath as if deciding whether to go on.

'Alex owed me some money. Like I said, we'd become quite

close. In the circumstances I let it go. It was just a few thousand,' he said.

'That would've been very generous of you, were it not for the exorbitant rate of interest you charged him. The truth is, you'd been paid back the original amount plus interest, months ago. It's hardly as if you were genuinely writing off a debt,' said Cross, a little distastefully. Tony didn't answer.

'I think we're done here,' said Ottey. She normally left it up to Cross to end these meetings, but her instinct said he'd had enough as well. They got up and walked towards the door.

'Haven't you forgotten something?' said Tony. Ottey turned to see him holding out the cup of piss towards her. Cross, anticipating what was coming, hadn't bothered to stop.

As they walked to the car, a Luton and a transit van pulled in. They were light blue, decked out in Franopoulos livery, which consisted of a large picture of the Acropolis against a beautiful clear sky with various crates of produce in the foreground. They got into the car, and as they drove off Cross noticed Tony appearing in the bay and watching them leave. In his experience, when people did this it was often because they felt they hadn't seen the last of the police and were working out their next plan of action.

'Nasty piece of work,' Ottey observed. 'He could easily be wrapped up in all of this.'

'And just as easily not,' Cross replied.

18

C arson saw them walk back into the unit from his office and came into the open area.

'Something's come up in the door-to-door. Alice will tell you,' he said as he walked over to her desk. She looked up.

'Yes?' she said, as she hadn't heard him. She had headphones on. Cross had been meaning to tell Ottey to ask her to stop wearing them at work. Ottey had miraculously sensed this one day and pre-empted him by telling him that Alice was actually listening to a suspect interview on another case, which Carson thought was educational for her.

'You spoke with uniform,' Carson explained.

'Oh yes, sorry, a couple of residents saw a van matching the one on CCTV at the far end of the garages – possibly at the one where the body was discovered – at around two twenty one morning two weeks ago.'

'Date?' Ottey asked.

'Ninth,' Mackenzie replied.

'The morning of the trip to Tenerife,' said Ottey.

'Why are we only hearing this now?' asked Cross.

'There's more,' Carson said.

'One of the witnesses was just returning home, so just saw the van parked. The other was having a smoke and watched for a while,' Mackenzie said.

'Number sixty-two?' Cross asked. Mackenzie checked her notes.

'Yes. How did you know?' she asked.

'Her girlfriend works lates. She waits up for her. Their curtains are closed till late afternoon – her girlfriend is a non-smoker,' Cross said. 'Continue.'

'She said the van was driven erratically. The man...' she went on.

'Is she sure it was a man?' Cross interrupted.

'She thinks so. But he was too far away for her to be able to identify him. He opened the garage door and reversed the van right back in.'

'He doesn't want to be seen,' said Cross, thinking out loud.

'Yes, but more interestingly, he scraped the van on the side of the garage entrance. She thinks it must've done some damage because it was a heck of a noise,' she said. 'One more thing...'

'He sounds rushed, maybe in a state of high anxiety. It was the ninth, so the murder has only just been committed,' Cross said, interrupting again.

'There was writing on the side of the van – some sort of trade logo,' Mackenzie said.

'CCTV are having a look at it now,' Carson added.

'We should check local body shops, particularly our dodgy friends, and see if anyone's brought in a van for repair in the last couple of weeks,' said Ottey. Oh not body shops again, thought Mackenzie, who had had her fill of them on their last case.

'Tommy, can you handle that?' said Ottey to a uniform at the back of the office. He nodded and made a note. Mackenzie was relieved.

'Alice could help him,' said Cross. 'She knows quite a lot

about them from the Carpenter murder.' She was both flattered and irritated by this. If she never saw a dodgy car body shop again, it would be too soon.

'We should go back to the dump site,' Cross said to Ottey. 'Forensics concentrated on the digger. The place was covered in paint, oil, graffiti, cement. Paint residue on the door frame wouldn't have been unusual, so they might've ignored it.' He left the room. He was privately really annoyed with himself for not asking the witness if she had seen anything the night of the murder when he spoke with her. It was crassly inept of him. He was always hard on himself when he made mistakes like this.

'You not going with your partner, Josie?' Carson asked mischievously.

By the time Ottey had gathered herself together and got outside, Cross was already leaving the car park on his bicycle. When she passed Cross in her car, she gave him a hoot of annoyance for leaving without her. It gave him such a start that he lost his balance and fell off his bike. She felt terrible and slowed down to make sure he was all right, looking in her rear view mirror. He was, so she accelerated away before he realised it was her.

Cross had insisted that work should not continue with the demolition, much to the chagrin of Morgan, the contractor. He had, of course, been proved right to do so, as they now found themselves going back to look for traces of automotive paint. All of this would've vanished had work continued. Car paint had been an important factor in one of their recent cases, Ottey reflected as she parked up. Cross arrived not long after her. She asked him if he was all right. She immediately regretted it, thinking it might give her away as the honking driver. He replied in the affirmative and made his way down to the remains of the pertinent garage. It didn't take long for him to find what he was looking for, as the wooden frame that went round the door was still pretty much in a couple of large pieces. He found some paint on one part of it.

'Paint. Metallic, I think. We need to get forensics down here,' he said.

Twenty minutes later, after she'd told him that no forensic teams were available, Ottey watched as Cross strode over to the pile of garage debris and started pulling away at the wooden frame.

'George, it's still technically a crime scene,' she said.

'There's no point in preserving the scene if we don't have a forensic team to come down and analyse the evidence,' he replied. But the wretched thing wouldn't come away, however hard he tried. He looked at it indignantly then tried again. But it wouldn't budge. She sighed and went over to help.

They drove back to the station. Just as well she had an estate car, as the boot now contained not only Cross' bike but also a large part of the door frame. It had only just fitted in the car. One end of it stretched the entire length of the car, lying through the gap between their seats, stopping inches from the windscreen. She hoped that she wouldn't have to stop suddenly before they got to the MCU. She was pretty sure she had windscreen insurance included for free in her car insurance. Why did they do that, she wondered? Give it away like that? It can't have been out of the goodness of their hearts. It had to be a business decision. Maybe people didn't smash that many windscreens. So it looked like a generous offer when it was nothing of the kind.

Cross was annoyed, as he had a bloody great big splinter in his finger. He'd got most of it out but the end had snapped off. He would get it out later with a sterilised needle as efficiently as a fully qualified doctor in A&E.

Carson looked up from his desk then back to his computer. Wait a minute, was that...? He looked up again and yes it was – an enormous door jamb being marched towards him by an irate Cross. He had it over his shoulder as one end trailed on the floor. Carson didn't want to say what had occurred to him as his political sensitivity kicked in promptly, but Cross looked like he was on his way to his own crucifixion. Carson walked into the open area where Cross had stopped.

'George. I had no idea you collected driftwood,' he said, laughing. Others joined in quietly.

'What?' Cross asked, puzzled, 'I don't. Why would I collect driftwood?' Then he understood what his boss was referring to. 'This is from the crime scene. It's the door frame.'

'Then what is it doing here? This breaks every tenet of Chain of Evidence,' Carson stated. He looked at Ottey as if she might venture some explanation. But from the look on her face he realised that this wasn't going to be forthcoming. She was pissed off enough as it was.

'So what else was I supposed to do? There's no-one available from forensics, apparently. How are we supposed to solve a case when we don't have the resources to do it?' asked Cross.

Carson didn't have an answer to this. He felt, from experience, that trying to have this discussion with Cross in public again would only end up with him losing and looking a little foolish.

'I'm bringing pertinent forensic evidence to the station, because apparently no-one from forensics is available today,' Cross went on.

'That's true,' Carson agreed.

'Is it indeed? Are you actually sure of that?'

'It's what I, like you, have been told,' said Carson.

'Because I happen to know that one Eric Walsh is sitting at home doing nothing. Paint, plastics and synthetic materials were his specialisms, that we could now have made use of had he not been let go last month thanks to departmental cuts,' said Cross. Carson made no attempt to refute this. 'So, if it's not too much trouble, I would like someone to take this down to the lab and ask Eric to come back in and identify these paint scrapings.'

'I'm afraid that's not possible. But you already know that

because you know as well as everyone else that I've had to find cuts. Something I dislike as much as you,' Carson said.

'I appreciate that, which is why, in the circumstances, I thought it would be helpful to bring the evidence in. The question is what I'm supposed to do with it now,' Cross said.

'Leave it with me and I'll deal with it,' said Carson, trying to ameliorate him.

'Thank you. I'll be in my office,' Cross replied, and turned to walk away.

'You're welcome. It'll take a couple of days.'

'What?' said Cross, stopping in his tracks.

'We just have to send it out now, that's all. It's no different,' Carson explained.

'It's completely different,' Cross retorted.

'I agree with George,' said Ottey unhelpfully. 'We'll be sending crime scene photos to Boots next.'

'No we won't,' said Cross irritably. 'They're all digital. No need.' A couple of the other detectives in the room sniggered.

'I was trying to make a point, George. To back you up,' Ottey protested.

'You can't back anything up with inaccurate information,' he retorted. She gave up. He could fight this one on his own, she decided. She went over to her desk.

'You said it'll take two days. That makes it different for a start,' Cross said, his attention now firmly back on Carson.

'Hopefully. I'll order a courier now,' he said.

'A courier?' Cross spluttered in disbelief. Carson left quickly before he said anything else that might cause further unrest.

Cross was sitting in his office. He was taking a break from the case and had gone back to preparing papers for court in the Carpenters' murder case. A husband and wife, murdered fifteen years apart. It had been complex and quite surprising in the end. He, as usual, wanted to make his narrative for the case as clear as possible for court. The jury could have no doubt, the prosecution find no chink, no technicalities to prevent them from finding the accused guilty. Everything had been done by the book, as it always was with Cross.

Ottey appeared. 'I need coffee and fresh air. Would you like to join me?'

Cross looked at his watch. 'I don't have coffee for another half hour. No.'

She knew better than to argue, but she actually wanted him to go with her. She wanted to run through the case with him again without anyone else. So she waited. Thirty minutes later they were driving into Bristol, at Cross' insistence, to a café run by a couple of New Zealanders, who according to him made the best flat white in the South West. New Zealanders, he went on to tell her, had become world leaders in making coffee. Indeed, they claimed to have invented the flat white, although that had become the subject of fierce debate down under where an Australian from Sydney now laid claim to the fact that he had invented it way back in 1989.

When she got back to the car (he had determined, through the car window, that the café was too full to enable him to concentrate and have a proper conversation with her) and tasted the coffee, she was forced to agree that it had been well worth the trip. Cross then insisted on going through the few facts they had, out loud. She had found this fantastically tedious and laborious when she had first been forced to partner with him. But she had to admit that some of his best thoughts and ideas about investigations had come out of these repetitive sessions.

'So what are your thoughts about the fruit and veg man?' Cross asked.

'He's involved somehow,' she replied. Cross looked at her, slightly surprised. 'Sorry, I don't mean in the murder, necessarily, although I wouldn't rule it out. But he was definitely mixed up with Alex in some way.'

'And Hellenic?'

They had come up with a blank on Hellenic. It was a Greek company, based out of Athens as far as they could tell. Its presence in London comprised solely of a brass plaque on a Georgian building in Mayfair and a PO Box address. No phone, no details at Companies House. Hellenic had, indeed, been a major shipping company back in the day, which had been sold off by the son of the founder, a Euro-Trash playboy as far as Ottey could tell. Several wives, even more girlfriends and dozens of children, legitimate or otherwise. Even with his prodigious appetite for excess he wasn't able to make his way through his inherited billions before he fell off his boat somewhere in the Cyclades. His body was never found. His beneficiaries were many, but even with that number, his vast wealth meant they could all count themselves as well off. One of his daughters ran a charitable foundation in her grandfather's name. Some of the other children were in various businesses, including real estate and the media. One of them was even an artist. But currently they couldn't figure out why the name should've cropped up in Alex's affairs.

'It could be all manner of things,' said Cross.

'True,' she said. 'There's a Hellenic travel company in Leeds.'

'So what else do we have?'

'The pharmacy was clean. That we know,' said Ottey.

'Which only means that it wasn't the murder scene. It doesn't rule the chemist out. It could've happened somewhere else,' Cross pointed out.

'True.'

'We need to concentrate on the text.'

'Why?'

'Because it doesn't make any sense. His making no reference to their fight. Behaving as if nothing was wrong. As if nothing had happened. Something's missing.'

'So, as we've said, in all probability he didn't send the text,' she said.

'Exactly. But then there's the packing. He'd packed and was clearly still going, which is also important. It means something definitely happened we don't know about, between the fight and the text. But the key is who sent the text.'

They sipped their coffee. Then Cross had a thought.

'His hamstring. We could have Clare check whether there's any damage.'

'Can she do that in post mortem? I mean, you actually see a pulled hamstring in the flesh?'

'I'm not sure. But when sportsmen have an injury they have an MRI... You should call Clare and ask for a post mortem MRI.'

'Why me?' she asked.

'You know very well why, and I think you are teasing me now,' he said. They both knew that Clare had a love/hate relationship/respect for Cross and could never be sure at any given moment of time whether she was on the up or down-swing of her feelings towards him.

19

Cross sat in his office, door closed and blind down, for a few days. In at the start of the day, earlier than anyone else, and out last. No-one saw anything of him during this time. Ottey had joked with him once that he could just take a few days off with his office closed up like this and no-one would be any the wiser. He was completely baffled as to why he would want to do such a thing in the middle of a murder case. His actions indicated that he didn't want to be disturbed. People had become used to respecting this, because when he appeared he would, more often than not, have discovered something of significance for the case they were working on. It wouldn't be some great insight worthy of Sherlock Holmes, who would eloquently spout forth a confected and well-configured theory of what had happened. In Cross' case it was normally a tiny speck of information that no-one had noticed, and therefore passed blindly over, which then had a fundamental knock-on effect on the case.

He also only ever retreated in this way when he felt they didn't really have a lot to go on and were chasing half leads, trying to piece together a narrative with few facts. Which was of course what police work was often about. He just knew that if he concentrated he might come up with something. Sometimes it only took a few hours. Other times it could be days at a stretch. He was poring over Alex's emails in an account Alice had found via the USB. There was a lot of correspondence with a man called Angelo Sokratis at Hellenic Holdings in Athens. But it was the name of the person who'd introduced them in the first place, Franny, that stood out to Cross. So Tony had been involved. Most interesting of all, however, was a meeting Alex had in his diary for the evening he died. It was in the Hampton by Hilton hotel at the airport. Cross checked the flight plans for private aircraft that day and discovered that a flight had arrived from Athens at five thirty that afternoon and left just after one in the morning. He hadn't realised that Bristol was an airport that operated twenty-four hours a day. There were two passengers and a stewardess. The passengers were Angelo Sokratis and his business manager, Theo. It seemed that, over time, Angelo had gone from wanting to be a co-investor to sole investor. This was around the time that Alex had told the bank that he wouldn't need their loan.

There had been a to-ing and fro-ing over terms as Theo was trying to strong-arm Alex, who, it had to be said, stood his ground. He finally informed the Athenians that he didn't need this deal. He would just go back to the bank, bide his time and find another investor. He was confident that his proposal had become more and more attractive to potential investors, the more work he did on it. The more he crunched numbers, the more potential profit he was able to find. One of the big decisions he had made was moving the location from the new King's Cross development to Camden, saving a huge amount in overheads. He thought that King's Cross was way over-priced and that, even though he said it himself, he had been seduced by going into what was fast becoming one of the trendiest, and so most costly, retail areas in London. Better to set up shop somewhere less expensive, make a name for themselves and then, maybe, move to KX when they had a firm customer base.

But something had gone sour in the last few weeks. What that was, Cross couldn't determine from what was in front of him. But it was important enough for Angelo to fly over and meet with Alex in person. The third thing, possibly the most important of all, which could easily have been missed in the hundreds of emails between Alex and Theo was a "cc" in one of them. It was the name which surprised Cross, because this person was supposedly ignorant of the continued London project.

Kostas turned up at the unit one afternoon asking for Cross and Ottey. When they settled in a VA (voluntary assistance) suite, Kostas emptied the contents of a black refuse sack he had brought onto the table where the coffee machine resided. There were several boxes and bottles, all containing pills of some kind.

'I found these hidden in the back of our food storage room,' he said. Ottey examined some of the packets. The names meant nothing to her. They were mostly pharmaceutical as far as she could tell. Cross, on the other hand, seemed to have no interest in the drugs, but was watching Kostas closely.

'Were you looking for them?' asked Cross.

'No,' said Kostas.

'But if they were hidden, how did you come across them?' he went on. 'Were you looking for them?' There was a nanosecond as Kostas obviously made a decision as to how to answer this.

'No, we were doing our usual provision stock check,' he said. 'Perishables,' he added, as if this might give it more veracity, Cross thought.

'All right, well as you're here, maybe we could have a talk?' Cross said. Kostas looked uncertain. Maybe he was just expecting to be thanked and sent on his way.

'Sure, I can't be too long, though. I have the evening service to prepare for,' he said.

'Of course. Would you excuse me?' said Cross, leaving the room. Kostas looked at Ottey, a little confused.

'Coffee?' she asked. 'The only thing I can guarantee about it is that it won't be anywhere near as good as yours.'

'Thanks, I will,' he replied.

Cross returned, pushing the door open with his back. He was carrying a small table, the size of a card table. He placed it in the middle of the room then disappeared again. Kostas looked at Ottey.

'Most times he's okay without the table, but today, it seems, is one of those days he needs it,' she said. Cross re-entered without a word, placed a chair behind the table, then set about organising his papers. He looked up at Kostas.

'So, Kostas,' he began, 'I think it's about time you started telling the truth and not deciding for yourself what you will divulge and what you won't.'

'I don't understand,' Kostas protested.

'Your brother is dead, murdered. A nice young man, who I think may have got himself into a bit of trouble. Now you, yourself, are not in trouble, but how long that lasts will depend entirely on how honest you are with us. Because you've been truthful, to an extent, but you've also been sparing with what you've told us. Which is inconvenient. You see, it costs us time to find out what you haven't told us. Pointless, really, when based on the knowledge you could've given us, we could've spent those hours trying to get a clearer picture of what happened to your brother. When people don't tell everything it's normally because they have something to hide. They've done something which they need to cover up because they're implicated in some way in what the police are looking into. You, I'm convinced, are not involved in your brother's death, nor, I suspect, in his drug dealings.'

'His what?' said Kostas.

'Your brother was not only taking performance-enhancing drugs but had been dealing in them for the past eighteen months. You didn't think those,' he said, indicating the pile on the other table, 'were for his own consumption, did you?' Cross went on.

'The fucking idiot,' said Kostas. 'So that's where all the money came from?'

'It would seem so. We thought from the regularity of his trade that he had a stockpile somewhere, and you've found it.'

'I don't believe this. Is this why someone killed him?'

'We're not sure, is the truth. Now you're saying you knew nothing about this?' Cross said.

'Absolutely nothing,' Kostas said.

'And that's where you now find yourself at a distinct disadvantage, Kostas,' said Cross.

'How d'you mean?'

'Well, in normal circumstances we would believe you. By normal, I mean if you hadn't been less than truthful on both previous occasions when we came to see you. You didn't tell us about Debbie, you didn't tell us about his drug-taking...'

'That's because I didn't know. Honest.'

'I'm not sure I believe you. You two were, according to both you and Debbie, extremely close, like twins. You talked about everything,' said Cross.

'Not this, I swear.'

'What about London?' Cross asked.

'What about it?' Kostas replied. This was an interesting reaction. Defensive, a little argumentative – a new attitude from him.

'You say that you knew about it at the beginning?'

'Yes, he wanted us to go into partnership but I wasn't interested.'

'And why was that?'

'We were doing just fine, but he always wanted more. To be the best, like I told you,' he said.

'No more than that?'

'I didn't want to upset my parents. They'd built the business up from nothing. They're proud people.'

'And that was part of his problem,' suggested Cross. 'It was their business, not his or yours.'

'But it is now,' said Kostas.

'That's the point. It wasn't of his making. You were both given it on a plate, if you'll forgive the pun, and that rankled with him. Did it rankle with you?'

'No. Like I said, I thought we were doing fine. There was no need for it.'

'Is that really true?' Cross asked.

'I don't know what you mean.'

'He's always been the competitive one. He was a leader, you were a follower. Isn't that true?'

'When we were younger maybe, but not so much now.'

'So you're a little more competitive now. A little more ambitious, perhaps?'

'Were…' Kostas corrected him. 'Maybe; it's not a crime.' Again, defensive, thought Cross.

'But not to the extent that you'd join him in his extension plans.'

'Like I said, I told him no and that was an end of it,' said Kostas. Ottey noted how the tone of the conversation had changed ever so slightly. She had no idea where Cross was going with this, as they hadn't had a chance to talk after he'd emerged from his office.

'It wasn't an end for him though, was it?' said Cross.

'What's going on here?' Kostas asked.

'We're just talking about your brother's business ambitions. His plans.'

'Are you thinking I had something to do with this?' Kostas asked.

'DS Cross made it quite clear that he doesn't think you've done anything wrong. That you weren't involved in his drug dealing nor his murder. He's told you he thinks no such thing,' said Ottey.

'It doesn't feel like it,' he said, looking at Cross. If he was expecting an apology he was going to be disappointed.

'It wasn't an end for him though, was it?' repeated Cross, as if he hadn't just asked the same question.

'No, he wanted me to buy him out, like I told you. But when we did the numbers he saw it couldn't work. So he backed off and dropped it,' he said.

'So you keep saying. But did he? In truth, drop it?' Cross asked.

'He did try the bank again, to go on his own. But he already had a mortgage on his flat, and with all the costs of setting up in London he didn't think it made sense.'

'So he dropped it,' repeated Cross.

'Yes,' repeated Kostas.

'You're sure about that?'

'Yes.'

'You're completely committed to the Adelphi, aren't you? I mean, it's a time-consuming job. You're not married. Do you have a girlfriend?' Cross asked.

'Not at the moment, no. I don't have time; I'm always working.'

'Would it be fair to say that you did more than your share of the work? I mean you and Alex own the restaurant jointly, but it seems to me you carry the heavy load.'

'Maybe.'

'All the orders and invoices in your office were signed by you. The staff rota was in your handwriting. The reservations book is the same. And you double up as chef, Maître D'.'

'People like to see the owner. They like to build up a relationship.'

'Which is fine as long as the owner is there, or should I say, owners. Alex was spending less and less time at the restaurant, what with his cycling and his other extra-curricular activities.

Was he not? The training for the race was always in the evenings, after everyone else had finished work. But for you and Alex that was one of the busiest periods of the day.'

'He'd make up for it at lunch service,' said Kostas.

'But going back to my original point: it wasn't exactly a fifty-fifty partnership, was it?'

'Less so recently, yeah. But I didn't have a problem with it. I enjoy what I do. Maybe a little more than Alex. I enjoy cooking and serving food for people.'

'Was it why he bought you the cars? To make up for it.'

'A bit, yeah, but now it looks like he paid for them, well, the deposits and the payments, with his dodgy money,' he said. 'Ironic really. You know what I just found out? The debt on the cars doesn't disappear with his death – it carries on.'

'It becomes the responsibility of the estate and the executor,' Cross affirmed.

'That's the problem, isn't it? What if there is no estate? I'm now lumbered with paying off two cars I never wanted in the first place.'

'Talk to the lender or car financier. They may well take Alex's car back off you as they're relatively new, but I think you may be stuck with yours. Still, not a bad car to be "lumbered" with.'

There was a lengthy pause.

'Would you like to go through the drugs you brought in and keep any that might be legitimate? By that, I mean not actually illegal?' asked Cross.

'No, just get rid of them, thanks. We done here?'

'We are.' Kostas got up and offered his hand to Cross. Ottey stepped in and offered her hand.

'Thanks for coming in, Kostas; we'll be in touch,' she said. Cross had gone back to his notepad and was diligently making notes. Kostas walked to the door and opened it. Cross looked up.

'Oh, one other thing. What do you know about Hellenic?'

'Hellenic? Hellenic what?'

'It's a holding company operates out of Athens.'

'Never heard of it. Should I?' he said.

'Not necessarily,' Cross replied, and went back to his pad. Kostas looked at Ottey, presumably wanting to know if it was still okay for him to go. She smiled, which he took as an indication that he could, and left. She sat back down and looked at Cross. He never wrote things on his pad to give the impression that he was finished with someone, that their meeting was over. It was because he laid great store by contemporaneous notes. He wanted to get his thoughts on paper so he could refer to his initial reactions later, when they were less fresh and instinctive. She waited for him to finish, but when he did he closed his file, picked up the table and left.

'For fuck's sake,' she said, and followed him.

'As a rule, when you are writing something in your notes and I stay in the room, it's because I'm expecting there to be a conversation about what has just happened,' she said as she walked into his office.

'Then you should say so. How am I supposed to intuit that you want to speak?' he said.

'It's not just me; it's what people do. They have just done something together and if one of them is occupied at the end of it and the other waits, the implication is that they expect to discuss whatever has just happened,' she said,

'Right, I shall bear that in mind.'

'If you could, I'd be very grateful.'

'Well, as I just said, I will know next time,' he said.

'Which is what you said last time,' she replied. He looked at her, not really knowing what to say, so she went on. 'I get it. These things don't occur to you naturally like they do with other people, and it's an effort for you to think about it. But I would appreciate the effort.'

'Of course, and I shall attempt to make such an effort,' he said.

'Thank you. So Kostas – nothing really there?'

'On the contrary...' He stopped abruptly, aware that this kind of contradiction annoyed other people, and bearing in mind what had just transpired, he knew to tread carefully.

'So, what's your thinking?' she asked.

'Like everyone else in this case, he's holding something back. I'm curious as to why he felt the need to bring Alex's drugs in. Why not just destroy them? Why the need to even tell us?'

'Because he thought it was the right thing to do?' she suggested.

'Or because he's trying to steer us away from something else. To keep us thinking Alex's death was something to do with the drugs?'

'Why would he do that?'

'As yet, I don't know.'

'Why did you ask him about Hellenic?'

'Because I discovered something when I was looking through Alex's emails. Kostas claims to know nothing about them and yet he was copied in on an email Alex sent to their lawyer Theo Doukas.'

'When was this?'

'Two months ago.'

'Which is, what, four months after Alex turned down the bank and said London was off?' she thought out loud.

'Exactly. So Alex was going ahead, with sole financing from Hellenic and, it would appear, the support of his brother.'

'You think Kostas was involved in the London expansion?'

'I know he was. We just need to piece the narrative together. Why is he lying about it?'

She wanted to know why he hadn't asked the chef about this in the meeting, but she wasn't in the mood to worship at the altar of Cross' investigative process that morning. The fact was that Cross often wanted to know why he was being lied to, before he alerted the person in question to the fact that he was aware of their mendacity. The more he allowed them to maintain their false front, or story, the more it inculcated a sense of security on their part, which he would later rip away mercilessly. He always wanted to know why, because he wanted them to realise, when they discovered he was aware of it, that he also knew why. This, in turn, made them alarmed at the prospect of how much more he might know. Did he know the full story? Would it be better to come out with it now? It implied that he was in possession of more facts than, at times, he actually was. With Kostas, he knew he wasn't involved in his brother's demise, but he felt that whatever Kostas was shy about sharing might well be pertinent to the case.

20

Cross had asked a Greek-speaking detective to get hold of the police in Athens and see if he could glean any information about Hellenic Holdings and Angelo Sokratis. He'd also got in touch with a contact in GCHQ and asked whether Hellenic was on their radar. Toby Fletcher's wife had been murdered a few years before in their home just outside Bristol. Cross had been the lead detective on the case. Toby had been initially sceptical about this West Country detective's abilities, and thought the secret service, that is to say people he knew in MI5, would be able to solve the appalling tragedy more quickly than Cross. There had been a lot of territorial posturing by those above Cross, including Carson, while he just quietly got on and investigated. Ottey thought that Carson couldn't believe his luck in having actual dealings with MI5. But in his usual, methodical way, Cross solved the case with some speed.

Fletcher was both impressed and grateful, and told Cross that if he could ever help with anything, he would be delighted to. There was also a female operative from MI5, Michelle, a university friend of Fletcher's, who had been intrigued by Cross' instincts and doggedness. She told him on one occasion that he would've made a great spy. Anyone else might have been really pleased by what was, essentially, the highest praise from someone inside MI5. He had responded that he didn't have a sufficient capacity for deceit or indeed a skewed enough moral compass to have been a great spy. This unintended insult endeared him to her even more, to the extent that she had been in touch no fewer than three times in relation to terrorist threats in the South West for his advice and help. No-one knew this in the department, as he hadn't shared it. But it explained how he sometimes had access to precious information that other detectives simply had no idea, even where to start to mine such gold.

A dossier on Angelo came back from Athens. He seemed to have started off as a legitimate businessman in Greece with interests in property and tourism. Once the most eligible bachelor in Greece, he had caused consternation a couple of years before by coming out. He and his partner had since been great advocates for same-sex marriage. Then, when they realised it was an impossibility in Greece at the time, they had spent their time campaigning for the equivalent of civil partnerships for couples of the same sex in their native country. However, they were still encountering fairly widespread opposition. Angelo had made a foray into construction a decade ago and suffered for it with the downturn and crisis in the Greek economy. Then he turned his attention outside of Greece. Again without much success.

But, according to the police, this man had money to lose – to an extent. When things got truly difficult he turned his attention to turning a profit from various illegal ventures. This interested Cross, because this man presumably had enough money, like his siblings, to live a life of luxury and not even have to work. But that wasn't for him. His major success, for which he was currently under investigation in Greece, was a large, pan-European, money-laundering business. A bit of an Anglophile, he made several trips over here seeking investments. But with laundering money came the associated problems. He was now linked to several murders in Greece, as well as a major drug-trafficking network. But there was also a strange philanthropic side to this man. He'd donated thousands of Euros to help the refugee crisis in Lesbos. It was an ethical nightmare for Greek politicians, as he lobbied for various causes and tried to make political donations. His reputation was now such that his donations were rebuffed. Politicians didn't want their reputations tarnished. But according to the police, Sokratis found a way round this, and the politicians were happy to take his money then, as long as no-one knew about it. It was fairly safe to assume, therefore, that this man had some influence in Greek political circles.

Hellenic was also on Toby and Michelle's radar. Angelo had been making several attempts, without success, to establish his laundering operation in the UK. He'd toyed with the idea of buying a country pile somewhere in the South West – even going as far as to look at a couple. The word was that he wanted to settle here so that he could marry his long-time partner. But he discovered that there was as much interest from the police in his business here as there had been back home. He had a reputation for stealthy corruption on a huge level, to oil the wheels of his operation in Greece. Cross wondered whether he'd come to the conclusion that there was maybe less use for that skill set in the UK – not that Cross believed that was necessarily the case. Also, if he lived in the UK he would attract the interest of the authorities here and therefore have two police forces monitoring his every move. Twice as much chance of getting caught, maybe.

Mackenzie had taken it upon herself to look into Tony Franopoulos and his business. As well as his wholesale supplier, he had a small but respectable property portfolio and several investments in other local companies. He was a big noise in the Bristol and Bath Greek community. He was on the board of trustees of some Greek charities and was a regular churchgoer. But his reputation was fairly evenly divided between sainthood and the devil, because he'd got into the loan business a few years before. It had started accidentally, but demand was such that he found himself able to charge extortionate interest rates and get away with them. But such a business inevitably flirted with the illegal in one obvious way. Enforcement. After all, what could you do if someone didn't pay up? Initially he'd taken businesses, or parts of businesses, as collateral. But with several of them it wasn't too long before he discovered why the owners had needed to borrow from him in the first place, and as a result they went belly-up, despite his efforts.

He got hold of a couple of good ones, though, where the money had been needed to settle gambling debts. Then the money borrowed had itself been gambled, in the belief that the next one was a "sure thing" and would solve all their problems. He had acquired a car dealership and taxi company in this way. The latter had done particularly well for him. He'd come up with a not completely original idea, admittedly, of it being a female-drivers-only cab company. It was for this very reason that he'd managed to fight off the threat of Uber – although he had lost business to them, of course. He'd acquired a computer programming company, which he then tasked to come up with an app to hire his women-only cabs way before the arrival of Uber, so his clientele were already used to ordering their cabs through an app. This was another reason his company stood up to Uber so well.

But it was the family business he'd inherited, the fruit and veg wholesale business, that was his main love. He embraced organic a long time before his competitors, and a few years earlier had realised there was a whole market he was neglecting – home delivery. Up until then the business had been entirely business to business – he only supplied restaurants, hospitals and large corporations. He was ignoring the single customer. The customer at home. So he set up an online delivery business. He did so well that he ended up buying a couple of farms in Somerset that were struggling. He told them what he wanted them to grow, including much that had been imported before. He installed polytunnels and was able to sell not only organic veg, but also veg which had no air miles – well hardly any miles at all – on them. Less transportation costs meant that he was able to sell competitively. He was suddenly at the forefront of a new breed of ecologically minded food entrepreneurs. Mackenzie even found a clip of him on YouTube talking on local news about his farms with a carefully orchestrated air of secrecy. He was growing Mediterranean fruit that no-one else in the country was, and he wanted his location kept secret.

But it was a photograph of him at a local charity event for a Greek hospice that caught her eye. It wasn't the size of the cheque he was holding (both in a monetary and physical sense), it was the man standing next to him. She cross-referenced the photograph with a couple of others and then got up to tell Cross. This was a breakthrough. She was sure of it and, what was more, no-one had asked her to do it. She could practically taste the gratitude and surprise. She knocked on Cross' door. He asked her in. He was sitting with Ottey. They had been discussing the case and Ottey was looking decidedly pissed off.

'I've found something,' Mackenzie said eagerly. Cross said nothing.

'Go on,' said Ottey.

'Tony Franopoulos was, or rather is, known to Angelo Sokratis,' she proclaimed, maybe a tiny bit theatrically. The two detectives said nothing, then looked at each other, weighing up the import, the precise implications this bombshell was going to have on the investigation.

'DS Cross has just told me that Franopoulos introduced Sokratis to Alex Paphides,' said Ottey. What? Shit! thought Mackenzie. This was the second time in as many cases – well, she'd only been there for two cases, admittedly –

where she'd discovered something and informed him, only to be told that he already knew, taking all the wind completely out of her sails. Ottey then turned to Cross. 'George?'

'Yes? Oh yes. Alice, were you tasked by me to look into Tony Franopoulos?' he asked.

'I was not,' she sighed.

'I take it from that exhalation that you are fully aware of what I'm about to say. Had you kept to what I'd tasked you with, rather than "going freelance", I believe is the expression, then you might not have wasted your valuable time ascertaining something you couldn't know that I was already aware of. Was there anything else?'

'No,' she said, turning towards the door. She stopped and turned back to him. 'One slight problem with what you just said. You haven't actually tasked me with anything.'

Cross thought about this for a moment, 'That, Alice, is an excellent point.'

'Thanks,' she said, amazed that she'd come out of this with anything positive, however small.

'And something I shall rectify immediately. I shall come over to your desk with an assignment,' he replied. Cross looked over at Ottey and raised his eyebrows as if to say, 'You see? I am learning.' She shook her head and left the office.

Catherine had been asked to look at the CCTV footage at the hotel the evening of Alex's death. She came to the office later with her results. Ottey saw her from her desk and got up to follow, as did Carson, who saw her crossing the department. The last time they had all gathered like this, the previous day, Cross had been appalled to be told that Catherine had "sent away" the footage of the indistinct logo on the side of the suspect van for enhancement.

'What do you mean, "sent away"?' he asked.

'Well, what do you think it means, George?' said Carson.

'Why is it we seem no longer capable of doing things that

only a few months ago were routine and deemed essential for the proper facilitation of police work?'

'Improved efficiencies, as you well know,' Carson said.

'I know nothing of the sort. You can't tell me that her having to do this is either more efficient or cost-effective in her effort or time,' Cross continued. 'So the purpose of these cuts, namely "improved efficiency", is clearly not working.'

'George, it's not as if she actually had to go out to the post office, put it in a jiffy-bag and buy a stamp.'

'Well, obviously not,' said Cross, thinking this through. 'It's an electronic image, which would have made that impossible. Unless of course she printed it out first. Then she could have sent it in an envelope, as you suggest, but that would surely have defeated the whole purpose. The pixels are what need enhancement, so it would have to be sent electronically.'

Carson had immediately regretted making his little quip, and made a note that in future, to save time if nothing else, he would refrain from making such jokes. Catherine showed them some clips she'd edited from the airport hotel footage. First of all, two men arrived. This was Angelo and his business partner Theo. They were dressed incredibly well, in suits that said they were there to do business. They had booked a meeting room, according to the hotel. The next footage showed Alex arriving and being greeted by Theo in the reception of the hotel. It was quite a formal, stiff greeting, Cross thought, as if what was about to happen held no attraction for either of them. It was probably going to be an awkward meeting. Alex left an hour later. Then shortly after, Tony Franopoulos was seen walking through the hotel to the meeting room. The timecode said this meeting lasted just under forty-five minutes.

'They're not in the least bit bothered about being seen on security cameras. They spend time in the reception area. They visit the rest rooms. They even go for a drink in the bar. Why haven't they left yet? What are they waiting for? They have nothing to hide, whatever it is,' he said. Catherine smiled. She really liked Cross. She liked the way it was all business with him. What they had in front of them – nothing else. But what she really liked was the way, on every occasion, he seemed to be one step ahead of everyone else. As he was here.

'They were indeed waiting for someone,' she said, and then moved the tape on. At ten pm, which was around the time they thought Alex had been killed, in walked his brother. This time it was Angelo who met him. It was a warm embrace, then Angelo led him by the arm into the meeting room. They all left two hours later. Big hugs between Angelo and Kostas. Warm handshakes with Theo. Then they left. The two Greek men flew straight back to Athens. It was a really quick turnaround.

They all sat there and took this new information in.

'So they didn't kill him,' said Carson.

'No-one had suggested they had,' said Cross.

'No, I was just thinking out loud, as it were. So what does this mean, George?'

'I think I'd like to pay Tony Franopoulos another visit before making any comment,' he said.

'Do you think he's involved?' asked Carson.

'He's certainly more involved than he has previously let on. He meets with Hellenic at the hotel and leaves shortly after Alex,' he said.

'So you think he might have killed him,' Carson stated.

'I don't think anything of the sort, but I would certainly like to know where he went after their meeting. His company vans are also the same shade of light blue as the paint left on the garage frame, which might be interesting,' he went on.

'You're kidding,' said Carson.

'Why would I joke...' started Cross.

'George...' said Ottey, indicating that he'd got the wrong end of the "literal" meaning stick again.

'No. It's true. I'd also like to see Kostas again, just for my own curiosity.'

'Do you think we have time for that?'

'If we can send pieces of forensic evidence out for examination as well as digital imaging, I think I have time to look into Angelo Sokratis' dealings with Kostas Paphides. Because if that man is suddenly going to have business dealings and concerns in Bristol, I think it would be wise to know exactly what they are. I don't, for a minute, think we've seen the last of Sokratis, and from what Athens and MI5 are telling us, he's a nasty character we'd do well to keep our eyes on.'

'MI5?' said Carson, but Cross got up and grabbed his coat and bike gear. When he got to the door he stopped as if he'd remembered something, and turned to Ottey.

'DS Ottey, will you be joining me?' he asked.

'I will, George,' she said, smiling. He put his bike things back on the table and they left. Carson was trying to figure out what was going on and, not for the first time, who the hell Cross knew in MI5. He saw Catherine looking at him, so he did what he always thought to do in such a situation. He issued an instruction designed to give anyone within earshot the impression that he was very much in charge.

'Let me know when you hear back on the van logo.'

21

Tony wasn't at his work. His secretary told the two detectives that he was at the gym. 'He's there more often than here, these days,' she said. As they went back to the car, Cross and Ottey took a closer look at the fleet of light blue vans then turned to each other.

'They're wrapped,' Cross observed.

'So that rules them out,' she agreed.

'It would certainly seem so.'

Danny was stretching Tony when they got to the gym. From Tony's drenched T-shirt, Danny had certainly put him through his paces. He asked them if they could wait while he showered but also made a point of asking them what they needed, as he felt he'd told them all he knew last time.

'We'd like to talk about Hellenic,' Ottey said. Tony thought for a moment. Was he working out whether to deny any knowledge again? If he was, he obviously decided that, with them asking again, they had to know more than they did before so it would be pointless.

'Sure. There's a café on the main road. Take a left, about a hundred yards. There in fifteen minutes?' He walked off to the showers.

'How are you getting on?' asked Danny.

'We're making progress, thanks,' said Ottey.

'Do you think it had anything to do with him supplying the drugs?'

'We're not sure. Why? Have you thought of anything since we were last here?'

'No. But it would make sense, wouldn't it? I mean a lot of these guys aren't just selling performance-enhancers, you know; they do rec stuff as well. Maybe he trod on someone's toes,' he went on.

'Someone came to the gym, didn't they? More than once,' Cross suggested.

'How'd you find that out?' asked Danny.

'You just told us,' said Ottey. He frowned a second as he tried to figure this out. 'Name?' she asked.

'I don't know. I'd tell you if I did.'

'Would you be willing to come down to the station and look at a few mug shots with one of the detectives who deals with that?' she asked.

'Unfortunate choice of word,' he said, 'but sure, if it'll help. I can come down tomorrow.'

Tony arrived in the café about ten minutes later, hair still wet from the shower. He bought himself a bottle of water and offered both of them a drink, which they declined.

'Why did you tell us you hadn't heard of Hellenic?' Cross asked.

'Did I? I don't remember. I don't know why I would've done that. Maybe I didn't hear you properly.'

'What do you do for them?' asked Cross.

'I don't know what you mean. I don't do anything for them,' he said.

'I'm not at all sure why you're being so evasive, Mr Franopoulos,' said Cross. Tony didn't answer. 'What's your relationship with Angelo Sokratis?'

'I don't have one. I've never even met the man.'

'Do you meet a lot of people in your line of business?'

'No more than anyone else.'

'Sokratis is a big name in Greece, is he not?' Cross asked.

'Yes.'

'Important enough to remember whether you'd met him or not, presumably,' said Cross. Franopoulos didn't answer. Ottey opened a picture on her phone and showed him a photograph of himself with his arms around Sokratis.

'Taken at one of your Greek fund-raising nights here in Bristol. Sokratis made a contribution of five hundred thousand pounds that night. Half a million. Do you get so many of those that they just slip your mind?' she asked.

'Okay, fine; why don't you just cut to the chase and ask whatever it is you want?' said Tony.

'Well, because it would be pointless if you are either not going to answer the questions or not tell us the truth. We're happy to "cut to the chase" as you call it, if you're willing to do the same.'

'I guess the closest thing to describe it would be that I act as a consultant for them,' he said.

'Could you elaborate?'

'They want to expand their business out of Greece. I mean, who wouldn't with the state of that economy?'

'You didn't answer my question,' said Cross.

'I keep my ears to the ground. Look out for any business or markets they might be interested in.'

'Like the restaurant business?' Ottey asked.

'Well, you might say that is an area of expertise for me. I have a lot of contacts nationwide in the food business. But they're interested in anything underperforming which could do better, or even businesses that are doing well, where they see room for improvement.'

'Which is how you brought Alex to their attention.'

'Yes.'

'What was the plan?' asked Ottey.

'Simple. Alex wanted to expand, as you probably know, and Angelo was interested in investing. Perfect for both sides.'

'Something went wrong, though,' Cross suggested.

'Alex began to have cold feet.'

'Why?'

'I don't know. You'd have to ask him,' Tony replied, ice coldly. Cross looked at him, trying to work out whether this was just a product of irritation or a menacing challenge – implying that he had something to do with the murder and they couldn't touch him. Cross came to the conclusion that this man had nothing to hide but was getting annoyed by the questioning all the same. So he sat there in silence, and Ottey took her cue from him and said nothing. After a while it was Franopoulos who was the first to cave.

'Look, Angelo is a major player in Greece and maybe he will be here. But the one thing he values more than anything is discretion. He could be very good for me; I don't know yet. But he's certainly someone who can open doors for me here and at home. That's why I'm being cagey with you. I don't want to piss him off. It's as simple as that.'

'Maybe you could tell me what you were meeting him about the evening of the eighth of this month?' Cross asked.

'I don't remember.'

'How often do you meet with him, would you say?'

'Every couple of months, sometimes every month.'

'Where?'

'If it's London, at his hotel. He takes a suite at The Connaught.'

'And Bristol?'

'He's normally in and out on the jet, so mostly in a hotel near the airport. The Hamptons by Hilton, I think it's called.'

'Where were you on the eighth of this month?'

'You know where.'

'Well obviously we know where you were in the early

evening. You were meeting Angelo and his lawyer Theo at that hotel. What was that meeting about?'

'That would be confidential.'

'Well, we know that it was about Alex, as he left shortly before you arrived. This is the last image of Alex alive.' Ottey showed him the CCTV footage on her phone.

'I'm not going to say any more about the meeting. Sorry, it's private and I can assure you it won't help you with poor Alex's murder,' Tony said. Cross turned to Ottey with an expression that she knew meant he wanted her to wrap it up and for them to get out of there.

'Mr Franopoulos, where did you go after your meeting with Hellenic?'

'Well, that's easy. I had dinner with my wife.'

'Where?'

'At Paco Tapas.'

'Very nice.'

'Michelin Star.'

'I know. How did you manage to get a table?'

'How d'you think? I supply their fruit and veg.'

'Of course you do. How can you remember it so well? No looking at your diary, no checking your phone'

'Wedding anniversary.'

'You won't mind if we check?'

'Of course not. The booking was in my wife's name and we said hello to the chef after.'

Cross looked at his phone, which had buzzed with a text, then got up abruptly and left.

'Where's he going?' Franopoulos asked.

'You should be encouraged; that generally means you're no longer of any interest to him, which is a good thing for you, I assure you,' she said, getting up and following her partner out of the café.

She opened the central locking and they both got into her car.

'Something happen? Or you just had enough?'

'Both. I don't think Franopoulos was involved. I don't think Hellenic was involved. I think this is a dead end and the sooner we move on the more time we'll save,' he said.

'Move on where, exactly?' she asked. He thought for a moment.

'I have no idea,' he replied.

'Great. I can't wait to see Carson's face,' she said.

'I don't think he'll be very happy.'

'Exactly.'

'Oh I see. I would've thought in the circumstances you might have more important considerations, bearing in mind we currently have nothing to go on in this murder case,' he said. She ignored him. Months ago she would have thought this kind of comment, which admittedly he used to make with more frequency, condescending and rude. She now knew it was his way of saying what he was thinking. Literally. There was no side or slight intended. It was just his way. So she let it go.

'So what happened?' she asked.

'Alison...'

'The family liaison officer?'

'Yes. Texted. Debbie's in hospital. The BRI. Miscarriage.'

'Oh... shit. We should go down.'

'Indeed.'

When they arrived at the hospital, Debbie was about to go into theatre for a D&C. Cross held back and let Ottey go in and talk to Debbie. Cross was not in any way familiar with pregnancy, and the causes of lost pregnancies. But he thought it wouldn't be too far-fetched to think that maybe the murder of her boyfriend and all the related stress and anxiety of Alex's murder had played a prominent part in this. They were there to comfort and support Debbie, Ottey said. They both felt that she was best placed to do this on her own. Mainly because she was a woman and a mother, but also because Cross didn't perform well in these situations. People felt, on occasion, that he was

161

cold and detached. Cross waited patiently outside the room until some theatre porters arrived with a trolley to take Debbie to theatre.

Ottey was quite surprised by how calm and accepting Debbie was. She wondered, with the situation Debbie was in – estranged parents, living with her late boyfriend's family – whether maybe losing the baby might have in some way been a relief for her. She then told herself off for such an unkind thought. She sat on the edge of the bed and held Debbie's hand. Helena, Alex's mother, was also there. She had been crying. She actually looked more upset than the patient. But this would have been her first grandchild, Ottey thought, and all that she had left of her dead son. It was an awful double blow.

After Debbie had been wheeled away by the theatre staff in their scrubs and shower caps, Ottey emerged with Helena. Cross stood up.

'Mrs Paphides would like to speak with us,' said Ottey. Interesting, thought Cross, mainly because he'd made a wrong assumption that she wasn't much of an English speaker, although he'd witnessed her shouting at Philippos the night she'd discovered he'd been giving Alex his testosterone. Cross admonished himself for making such a judgment based on her appearance. He was pretty sure it was racist of him. He had made the assumption, with her being dressed all in black with a scarf around her head, peeling vegetables in the restaurant, that she didn't speak English. How wrong he'd been. They went to the hospital café and sat and listened.

She was not only fully aware of Alex's plans for London and his nationwide expansion, she was supportive.

'Who'd you think did his mood boards he took to the designers?' she asked. 'Alex discussed everything with me. I love my two boys equally. What mother doesn't? But they were very different. Alex was much more ambitious. He discussed everything with me because he couldn't with his father or brother. They are very alike, those two. Alex was much more like me. I started this restaurant. Everyone thinks it was Phil, but he was just the chef. A bloody good chef, but I was the brains. You probably think it was Phil who encouraged Alexander but you're wrong. It was me. When Alexander couldn't make the numbers work and Kostas wanted nothing more to do with it, Alex started looking elsewhere. That's when Tony F introduced him to Hellenic and Angelo. I wasn't happy. He has a bad reputation back home. Very bad. He mixes his good businesses with others not so good. Alexander persuaded me that Angelo wanted to have a legitimate business in England. He was really grateful, and the deal, I have to say, was good. Reasonable targets. Proper organised roll-out once they'd worked out if the concept was working.'

Ottey was completely taken aback by the way this woman spoke. It was absolutely not what she was expecting. A bit like Cross, she castigated herself inwardly for judging her before she spoke to her.

'So everything was going well?' said Ottey.

'Did Kostas know about Alexander still going ahead?' asked Cross.

'Of course. They talk about everything, those two. No secrets. The only one who didn't know was Phil. Because it would have broken his heart. He's a sentimental old fool. He pretended to support Alexander when it all started. But secretly he was so happy when it fell through and he thought Alexander had given up on the idea. But would the boys be happy just running our restaurant, was always the question I asked myself? That was our life's work, not theirs. I had great respect for them having ambition. Much better than just taking what they'd been handed down. What kind of a life is that? Where's the self-respect? But Kostas was going to stay in Bristol. It suited him better. Alexander, though, told him the door was always open. That was kind.' She lost control of her emotions for a second as she thought about her late son affectionately. 'But recently something happened with Angelo, and Alexander didn't want to go ahead any more.'

'What was that?' Ottey asked, partly to give this woman a chance to take a breath.

'Alexander found out that Angelo wasn't being entirely honest. Now there's a surprise. One of the biggest criminals in Athens turns out not to be a man of his word. He's a criminal, detectives. All this nonsense about legitimate business in the UK was all lies. He's a gangster. He wanted to clean money. Launder money using the new restaurants. When Alexander found this out Angelo actually offered him a deal – a small percentage of the money he'd washed. Alexander said no. That's where he was the night he died. Calling it all off. Angelo wanted to have one more attempt at persuading him. But Alexander said no.'

'Are you sure?' Cross asked.

'Yes. He told me and Tony.'

'What was his reaction?'

'Tony? The truth is I think he was scared. He's frightened of Angelo. He'd introduced them and now Alex was pulling out. This wasn't going to look so good for Tony. He may be a big man in the gym all the time but he's all mouth. He should stick to fruit and veg if you ask me.' Ottey smiled; she liked this woman.

'And that's what I think,' Helena finished.

'What is? You haven't actually told us what you think.'

'Hellenic had him killed. Angelo killed him.'

'No. They didn't,' said Cross firmly. Helena sat there for a moment and thought about this. It was a shock. It was what she believed. What made sense to her, and she'd probably thought the police would be grateful for the tip.

'Yes, they did,' she repeated. Cross and Ottey made no answer. The silence seemed to carry a weight of inevitability and certainty for her. She looked down at the floor, a little confused maybe. After all, she had been so sure. She'd worked it all out.

'They left almost immediately after their meeting and flew straight back to Athens. There would really have been no reason for them to kill your son. It was just a deal that they couldn't make. There wasn't that much at stake for them. They could just leave it,' said Ottey.

'But it was the person who came to see them after Alex's meeting which confirmed it for us,' said Cross. The woman thought for a moment and then looked up.

'Kostas,' she said quietly.

'Did you know?' asked Cross.

'No, but it makes perfect sense. Kostas has always felt he lived in the shadow of his older brother. It would be just like him to do this. Show us all that he could be the smart one. Silly boy. I'll talk to him.'

'There won't be any need,' said Cross. 'As soon as Alex was killed, Hellenic's interest cooled. It would've drawn too much attention to them. Not an auspicious start to a business venture when one of the principals is murdered.' She nodded slightly. Ottey gave him a look, so he turned back to Helena. 'I meant no disrespect,' he said. The grieving woman smiled at him as if she understood him a little, Ottey thought. Helena was obviously a good reader of people.

22

C ross decided to indulge in a little organ practice that night. Sometimes he would come to the church just for its tranquillity. Tonight was such an occasion. He wanted to clear his mind of what he was now sure were certain irrelevancies in the case. Make a fresh start. He wanted to expunge Hellenic, Tony Franopoulos and Alex's side-business in sports drugs. On occasions like this, he would come and sit in the pews for ten minutes or so, relishing the peace and quiet. The church was also always cool, sometimes freezing in winter, as they couldn't afford the heating to be on when the church wasn't being used. To his embarrassment, the priest had started putting on the heating every Wednesday night, when he came to do his weekly practice. He remonstrated with Stephen, who replied that he couldn't have George practising with cold fingers as he could hear him in the rectory next door. It was, therefore, a selfish and completely self-interested gesture on his part. It was an argument George had no chance of winning. Then, one evening, when he was having tea and cake with Stephen, he came up with a solution. The priest was a good baker and had to rebuff his congregation's annual attempts to enter him in *The Great British Bake Off*. One year, a group of his congregants went even further and applied for him.

He should've noticed, when they came round for tea, that they were suddenly taking pictures of his cakes and scones on their phones. He had thought it flattering, though puzzling, at the time. It was when he got a phone call from a researcher on the programme that he realised what they'd been up to. He, of course, declined. This was then followed up by one of the producers trying to persuade him. That having a vicar – 'I'm a priest, actually' – would be wonderful not only for the programme, but surely for the Church across the country. He replied, politely, that it wasn't that straightforward; he would have to approach the local bishop to get permission which, with the present incumbent, he felt would be virtually impossible. The producer then replied that she knew for a fact that the Archbishop of Canterbury was a huge fan of the show, and that maybe the programme could get in touch with him. Stephen had replied again that he was a priest, a Catholic priest, so that wouldn't do them any good – unless of course the Archbishop of Westminster, Vincent Nichols, was also a fan, he joked. She thought for a moment and then said she wasn't sure, but she could check. He reiterated that he wasn't interested.

He thought this was the end of the matter until he received an email from the executive producer of the show, asking him whether he would be interested in taking part in a one-off charity special. Competing against an Imam, a Rabbi, a Sikh Granthi and a Buddhist Monk. It would be fantastic for a greater understanding of multiculturalism in the country, as well as inter-faith relations. But when Stephen asked who the other contestants were, they confessed that he was the only "preacher-baker" they had found, and that was the end of that.

He always made individual cupcakes for Cross, as he knew this was preferable to him. On occasion, Cross helped Stephen with the church accounts. He was just as proficient as the church's regular accountant, Stephen had discovered. Quicker and, of course, he didn't charge. On this particular evening, a couple of days after Cross had discovered the "heating for his practice" issue, he asked Stephen if he could just catch up with the bills.

'But you only checked the accounts two weeks ago, George.'

'I'd just like to keep ahead.'

So they were provided and Cross quickly found what he was looking for: the gas and electricity providers for the church and the particular tariffs it was on – there were so many these days, to entice customers, it was bewildering. Cross felt there was something fundamentally wrong in some people paying higher prices for the same gas and electricity than others who had taken advantage of some new offer. How could you justify neighbours, living next to each other, having a differential of hundreds of pounds a year when they were using the same quantities of power? Of course, it was the elderly and vulnerable, who had no understanding of the plethora of different companies, different tariffs, fixed or not fixed, who suffered the most. Anyway, that evening Cross got two power bills, looked at the tariff costs, analysed the kilowatts and cubic metres and the total amounts of charges. When he got home that night, he calculated what the extra charge for heating the church during his practice came to and, from then on, made a donation in the collection box for the exact amount, every time he practised. Stephen knew what was going on – it wasn't difficult, as suddenly the collection box had money in it every Wednesday night, regularly – but his protests fell on deaf ears.

Cross hated thinking about cases when he had nothing in front of him. Nothing solid evidentially, that is. Clare had performed the MRI and confirmed what they already suspected. Alex wasn't suffering from a hamstring injury. As Cross played the organ that night he realised he was now speculating. This was something he hated others doing, because he felt they sometimes did it way too often and that it was much easier than doing real police work. But because they were "discussing" the case, they fooled themselves that they were indeed working. But he was allowing himself to do that this once. To run through the possibilities. He had come down to two. That Alex had been killed by a stranger, which he dismissed out of hand, as how would the stranger have known about the Tenerife trip and then texted Matthew to cover his tracks? Or delay the discovery that Alex was missing?

He was sure it had nothing to do with the cycling club. The name Danny had given them, when he came into the station, turned out to be a dealer known to the drug squad. He had been to the gym to score some performance-enhancers for his brother, who was an amateur bodybuilder, not to have a beef with Alex. This really only left one option to examine, in Cross' mind, and at the moment it didn't really make any sense – and that was to look at the two families themselves. Alex's and Debbie's. But Kostas had an alibi. He'd told them right at the beginning, understanding the importance of their need to exclude him from the investigation as soon as possible and thereby not waste any valuable time looking into him, that he'd been to a meeting in the early evening then returned to the restaurant. He had dozens of witnesses and the hotel CCTV bore witness to his story. Cross was curious as to what that was about though, even so.

At the end of his practice on this occasion, he had come to the conclusion that Debbie's parents warranted further investigation. As he left the church, he found the priest sitting in the stalls, having listened, as he often did.

'I can't say I recognised that, George,' he said, getting up from his pew.

'Johann Kuhnau's Biblical Stories. A late seventeenth, early eighteenth-century German composer. He was appointed organist of the Thomaskirche in Leipzig at the age of twenty-four. So young,' Cross mused.

'Gosh. Speaking of which, I hear you haven't taken up the offer to play the St Mary's Redcliffe organ yet.'

'No,' he replied.

'Well, I enjoyed that very much. A pleasant surprise, as it's not your usual evening.'

'No, it was a spontaneous decision. But from now on I can't have dinner with my father on a Thursday night. Something we've done for over twenty years. So I need to change my night.'

'Is everything all right with Raymond?' the priest asked, concerned.

'Yes. He's going to start volunteering at Aerospace Bristol. Thursday is the only evening they can manage, apparently.'

'Well, that's marvellous.'

'Yes, but not very convenient. I will now be coming on Thursday night, instead of Wednesday nights. I assume that will be all right, as the church never seems to be in use,' Cross said, with an unintentional lack of tact.

'Yes, of course. That's bridge night, but we play in the hall, so it's not a problem. Do you play, George?'

'I don't.'

'That's a shame. One of our regular players has died. It's her funeral next week. She's played her final hand, you could say.'

'If you feel it necessary to employ a cliché, then you certainly could, yes,' replied Cross, and went to gather up his bike. Stephen smiled, not just because he found Cross' eccentricities quite touching but because it made him think Thursdays might come in quite useful for his 'George Cross organ recital' campaign.

Cross cycled back to his flat, his mind now clear and refreshed, ready to start the investigation anew in the morning. It was another of his innate skills, that he was able to compartmentalise bits of any investigation. Those that became irrelevant found their way quickly and irrevocably into his mental trash.

A meeting at the MCU was convened, this time by Ottey. She wanted to get everyone up to speed with the change of direction they were going to make, after the events of yesterday and viewing the hotel CCTV footage. Cross was obsessed with everyone being up to speed, and that no-one wasted any more time chasing old leads that had now been dismissed. Carson was less impressed. While he appreciated Cross' instincts – actually that was completely the wrong word; it was Cross' evaluation of the facts, at any given point in time in a case, and his analysis of what was pertinent and relevant that he admired – he found Cross' willingness to throw out days, sometimes weeks of work wholesale, difficult. As did many of the others who had done this work. But what he knew was that Cross wasn't working on instinct. He was working on facts that he determined to be conclusive. Carson's issue was trying to justify these, often ninety-degree, turns in a murder investigation to the higher-ups. Particularly when only a few days previously, he'd used his salesman-spin to tell them how well the investigation was progressing in the direction they'd decided to pursue. This man never learnt from his mistakes. He was always too happy to tell them how efficiently the department was working – under his expert command, being the implication – and how much extraordinary progress they were making in a case, so he could bask in the short-term praise and approbation. Then he would have to go back, only days later, and inform them that the amazing progress he had sold them at the beginning of the week was now being completely thrown out, as it transpired it was completely wrong. One name always seemed to crop up as being the party responsible in these conversations with the brass – DS George Cross. It certainly didn't enhance his reputation with middle-management.

Ottey was, like Carson, slightly apprehensive about the sea change in this investigation. When they had discovered Alex trading in drugs, albeit performance-enhancing ones, and then his connections with Hellenic and Angelo Sokratis, it seemed to make sense that the answer would lie somewhere therein. But that was, she realised, a rookie-mistake. Things so often weren't what they seemed. But she felt Cross owed her some reassurance, at the very least. At the end of the meeting, Ottey and Cross went to visit Jean and Andy.

'George...' she started. He knew instinctively what she was going to ask. This wasn't the first time this had happened.

'Yes I am,' he said.

'What?' she asked.

'Certain we should be moving on. You need to put everything we had before to one side. I don't believe any of it is relevant. It would be easier if you discarded it. Completely.'

'But don't you find it a bit strange that we've been pursuing leads, convinced we were onto something, and then dump them just like that?'

'No.'

'Why not?'

'Because I was never convinced.'

'Oh yeah, I forgot you're perfect.' He didn't reply for a moment, during which he decided that she wasn't being serious. It was irony, so he felt no need to point out that he was no such thing.

'It's always a mistake to be "convinced" early in an investigation, as it narrows your focus, which means you are inevitably going to miss something.'

'But you follow early leads with conviction.'

'Indeed, but there is a distinct difference – semantic to an extent, granted. But being convinced of something in a case is not the same as pursuing something with conviction. Which you should always do to fulfil the pursuit of it adequately. Being convinced of something before you have sufficient proof – proof which your conviction will either give you or not – can be essentially misleading,' he finished. She thought he had a point. She just wasn't sure, as she parked the car outside Debbie's parents' house, that she knew exactly what it was.

Their first visit to Debbie's parents had been to inform them of Alex's death and have an initial look at them. Now things had changed. For Cross, Jean and Andy had become persons of interest. This wasn't just because they had nowhere else to look; they had looked elsewhere and come up short. But, as Cross had explained to Mackenzie, it was as important to exclude things in an investigation as to include them. Statistically, as everyone knows, most murders in the United Kingdom happen within the family. Had Alex's slightly colourful – certainly more colourful than they had anticipated – business "interests" not diverted them for a while, they would have been here in Eastville maybe a week earlier.

'Do you think they know about Debbie's miscarriage?' Ottey asked, before they got out of the car.

'I doubt it, somehow,' Cross replied.

'Should we tell them?' she asked.

'It doesn't really feel our business to. But then again, if you think it might be revealing, then perhaps yes.'

'So, you'd like me to do it.'

'I think that's best, yes.'

Andy let them in. He made them a coffee as they all waited for Jean to appear. She eventually came down, hair a mess and obviously unwashed. She wasn't happy they were there. A cloud of stale alcohol wafted over them as she went into the kitchen and got her cigarettes.

'We were just wondering if anything had occurred to you since we were last here? Sometimes things just pop back into people's heads,' Ottey began.

'No. Sorry,' Andy replied.

'No problem; we were in the area anyway,' said Ottey.

'Yeah right,' Jean muttered as she took a long drag.

'Jean....' Andy cautioned her.

'Have you seen Debbie since our last meeting?' said Ottey, ignoring Jean.

'No.'

At this point, Cross noticed that the jigsaw on the table hadn't been finished.

'You don't seem to have got very far,' he commented.

'No,' said Andy. 'Like you said, the sky's a bugger.'

Cross thought for a moment. 'Do you mind if I have a go?' he said.

'Um, no,' said Andy, a little taken aback. 'Help yourself.' Ottey ignored her partner as he went over to the table, took off his coat, sat down and looked intently at the puzzle.

'First things first, Andy,' said Cross.

'Yes?' Andy replied, thinking it was something to do with the case.

'You need to organise your pieces properly and segregate them. First by content, then obviously any sides; but organise them in sections that roughly correspond to the picture,' said Cross.

'Do you need the lid? To see the picture?' Andy asked politely, not quite believing he was having this conversation.

'No, not necessary,' Cross replied swiftly, moving the spare pieces into groups on the table. Andy looked back at Ottey, obviously a bit thrown by Cross' behaviour. She continued as if this was completely normal – which, of course, to her it now was.

'Not been in touch? Debbie?' she continued.

'What's it to you?' said Jean, still pissed off at this intrusion.

'Jean, they're only trying to help,' said Andy.

'No they're not. I told you this would happen,' she replied.

'Told him what would happen?' asked Ottey.

'That you lot would be poking your noses around,' she said.

'It's kind of our job, when someone's been murdered, Jean,' said Ottey. Jean didn't reply. She took a sip of her coffee, but it was way too hot.

'Fuck! Did you put any cold water in it?' she said to Andy.

'Why hasn't she been in touch?' Ottey asked.

'I don't know. I don't know anything about the way that child's mind works,' said Jean.

'Her boyfriend's just been murdered. That's a lot for anyone to take on board, let alone a sixteen-year-old girl. I would have expected her to be in touch with her mother,' Ottey continued.

'Well that just goes to show how much you know her. Or rather don't. Doesn't it?'

Ottey looked over at Cross, wondering whether he was going to take any part in this, but he was engrossed in the jigsaw.

'So things must be pretty bad between you then?' Ottey continued.

'You got that right. That's why she fucked off.'

'Okay,' said Ottey. She asked them more questions about their relationship with Debbie. It seemed to her that the relationship with the mother had broken down irretrievably. But there was something in Andy's demeanour that had an element of regret about it. That he was sad it'd come to this. Ottey did a little mental maths. She thought Jean actually looked pretty young for a mother of a sixteen-year-old. A bit ropey; she didn't look after herself. But she was still quite young.

'How old were you when you had Debbie?' she asked.

'What's that got to do with anything?' Jean spat.

'It's just a question,' said Andy.

'Well it's none of her business. I think it's time you left. I need a piss.' She got up and left the room.

'Sorry. She's been putting it away since you told us about Alex. Actually she's been putting it away ever since Debbie left. She's always a bit rough in the mornings. Might be best if you come in the afternoon next time,' he said helpfully, then added, 'That is, if you need to come back at all.'

'George. We're leaving,' said Ottey.

'Just a minute,' he said. They noticed that he'd made huge progress with the jigsaw. With a final flurry, he finished it and was about to put the final piece in, when he stopped himself and got up. He put his coat back on and looked at the jigsaw with great satisfaction.

'That's amazing. Aren't you going to finish it?' Andy said.

'Oh no, I'll let you do that,' Cross replied.

'But there's only one piece left.'

'That's true, but it's very bad form to finish someone else's jigsaw,' said Cross. He looked over at Ottey in an attempt to show her that he could be well-mannered.

'But you might as well,' Andy laughed.

Cross looked at Ottey. She gave nothing away, which he took to be an admonitory silence.

'I couldn't possibly,' said Cross.

'I insist,' said Andy.

'Oh, very well,' said Cross, far too quickly, putting the piece in place. He looked childishly pleased with himself. He looked back at Ottey, as if expecting to be congratulated, but her expression hadn't changed.

'He did insist,' he said, in his own defence.

'It's true, I did. Anyway I was about to pack it in. I'd had enough,' said Andy. They left and as they walked away from the house he called after them.

'Sixteen. She was sixteen when she had Debbie. Jean.'

They walked down the road towards Ottey's car. After they got in, Cross turned to her.

'They have a shed in the back garden.'

'What about it?' she asked.

'It's an old shed. Been there a good ten years but it has a brand new padlock. Very large, brand-new padlock.'

'And...?' she asked.

'We've seen one just like it before,' he replied. 'Why didn't you bring up the miscarriage?'

'She'd buggered off upstairs before I had a chance and it didn't feel right, telling the stepfather before the mother. Like you said, it's really for Debbie to tell them, anyway.'

23

The next two developments came in rapid succession. The first was an alert from a uniformed unit which had been called to a disturbance at the Adelphi Palace. Cross and Ottey were notified by uniform because they knew one of the owners was the victim in a murder investigation. When Cross and Ottey arrived they found a police car and a custody van outside the restaurant. The exterior back door of the van was open. Jean could be seen inside behind the bars of the interior gate. She looked in a terrible state, red-faced, hair unwashed. The two detectives ignored her, not wanting to get drawn into an unnecessary altercation. The front window of the restaurant was smashed. Inside, two uniforms were talking to Kostas and his father. Debbie was crying in the back of the restaurant, being comforted by Helena.

Jean had arrived during lunch service, apparently, to see her daughter, who was upstairs in the family flat. They were obviously busy, so Kostas persuaded her to come back a little later. She came back at around four that afternoon, the worse for wear, having waited in a pub around the corner. Debbie didn't want to see her mother, which Jean had refused to believe. She quickly became abusive and Kostas asked her to leave, eventually forcing her out of the door.

'I wasn't aggressive, I swear. It wasn't that difficult to get her out. She's well pissed,' he said.

'What's she so angry about?' Ottey asked.

'That Debbie won't see her. But why would she all of a sudden? She didn't even bother to get in touch after Alex died.'

'So why now?' Ottey asked.

'Because of the miscarriage. Little bit late to start behaving like a mother, if you ask me. I know Debs told you that she left because things were bad at home, but it's not true. Jean threw her out.'

'I didn't know that, no. We thought she'd just left.'

'Well, she didn't. She's not fit to be a mother, that woman.'

'How did she know about the miscarriage?' Cross asked.

'Debbie told her stepfather,' Kostas said, 'and she's been kicking off about that as well. That a daughter should call her mother not her stepfather. I've called him.'

'Who?' asked Ottey.

'Andy. He's on his way.'

'Well, he's not going to be happy about that,' Cross said, indicating Jean in the police van.

'We're not pressing charges,' said Kostas.

'Why not?' asked Ottey.

'It's my mum. She won't let us. My dad and I wanted to, but she said no. Thinks that woman's got enough to deal with. A stretch in prison might do her some good though, don't you think? At least it'd dry her out.'

Ottey went to talk with Helena and Debbie at the back of the restaurant. One of the constables wanted Kostas to finish his statement, even though they weren't taking any action. Cross was pleased to see this young constable going through the proper process. He made a mental note of his name. He then sat down, and waited for Ottey to finish with Debbie. Philippos brought him a coffee.

'Thank you. You make very good coffee. The best Greek coffee I've had in Bristol,' he said.

'You're welcome,' said Philippos.

'Mind you, I think it's the only Greek coffee I've had in Bristol, to be honest. But that doesn't in any way take away from the quality.' The old chef didn't quite know how to react to this, and so backed away deferentially.

Andy arrived fifteen minutes later, looking stressed and none too pleased. He had the briefest of words with Jean through the grill at the back of the van, but walked away as soon as she started yelling abuse at him, telling him to do something and get her out of there. He walked into the restaurant and said hello to Cross, very politely. As soon as Debbie saw him, she ran across the restaurant to him and hugged him, bursting into tears. He held her for a few minutes, stroking her hair and kissing the top of her head. Whatever problems she had with her mother, she didn't have them with her stepfather, it would seem. He was extremely solicitous to both Helena and Philippos, and was apologetic. He told Kostas that he had already called a glazing mate, who would come and measure up later that evening and replace the window. Andy would, of course, pay for the cost. The family seemed to be completely disarmed by his attitude. When Kostas suggested that he might want to get Jean out of the van and take her home, his response was that she could wait. Debbie made her stepfather a cup of tea, which he gratefully accepted. Cross and Ottey observed what was, to all intents and purposes, a family discussing how to move forward in the immediate future with Debbie and her loss. Well, double loss.

When Andy decided to leave, Ottey said they would be calling him to arrange another visit. It would be better if he was there. They watched as he warned Jean that if she made a fuss, he'd just leave her where she was and she could sleep it off in a cell. After her initial abusive reaction to this, she tearfully acceded and she was released. Andy took her to his van, a black transit, Cross noted. They said goodbye to the family. Cross made a point of talking to Debbie. He told her that she should get in touch with them if she had anything else to tell them. He thought she looked a little frightened, and wondered what it was like to be that frightened of your own mother. It also confirmed for him that she was still holding something back. He decided to pursue it.

'Debbie, you're not telling us something,' he said.

'No I'm not,' she replied. It took him a second to work out whether this meant she was agreeing with him, or denying it.

'You are. It would be best to tell us now and save a lot of time. We'll find out in the end,' he said.

'It's inevitable,' said Ottey, joining in.

'What is it?' Cross pressed.

'Nothing,' Debbie insisted. Cross just kept looking at her, trying to make an assessment of what it could be. There could only be one option, with the way things were going.

'You know where Alex was going that night. Is that it?' he said.

'He was going to a meeting at the airport. You already know that,' she said.

'But you know where he was going afterwards,' he went on.

'No I don't.'

'But you have a pretty good idea,' Cross said. She didn't reply. She looked at Helena and Kostas, who both seemed to be waiting expectantly. She looked down and started fiddling with her nails. Helena looked up.

'Maybe she'll tell us and we can call you,' she said, trying to be helpful.

'We don't really have time for that, Mrs Paphides. Need I remind you, we are looking for your son's killer, and if Debbie knows something, or even if it's just that she thinks she knows something...'

'I think he was going to my mother's. I know he was,' Debbie said quickly.

180

'Why would you think that?'

'Because he said so. We had an argument about it,' she said, bursting into tears. 'The last time we talked, we were having an argument and now I can't even say "sorry".' Helena comforted her and looked up at Cross as if to imply that he'd got what he came for and now should really leave.

'One more question, Debbie. Why? Why was he going?' Cross asked.

'To tell her about the baby,' she said. The very mention of the lost baby upset her even more. Cross turned on his heels and left.

'Thanks, Debbie. That could be really important,' Ottey said and looked at Helena. 'Call us if there's anything else, or if we can help in any way.' Helena nodded silently and Ottey walked out of the restaurant.

'Just as I suspected,' Cross said, as he and Ottey got back into the car. 'It answers the one outstanding question. Who told Jean and Andy about the pregnancy. Alex. He was there that night.'

The second development happened the next day, when Catherine from CCTV knocked on his office door, carrying her iPad.

'So we've had a bit of success with the van's logo.'

'At last,' said Ottey, before correcting herself. 'I'm sorry, that wasn't meant as a criticism, more an expression of relief, Cat.'

'No worries. Anyway, it's part of a fleet belonging to South West Plumbers. This is their website.'

She showed them her iPad. On it the plumbing firm's website, with the boss standing in front of a vanguard of vans, arms out. He looked like one of those American car salesmen who adorn huge billboards down the sides of American highways. He was dressed a little smarter than them, though. His smile had more to do with smug self-satisfaction, Cross felt, than a warm, friendly welcome.

'The vans are the same shade of blue as the paint on the garage, aren't they?' she asked Cross.

'It looks like it,' he said quietly, almost to himself.

Later that afternoon, they drove to Andy and Jean's house, as arranged. It was a miserable afternoon. What Cross referred to as "wet" rain poured down. It felt as though it was only falling out of the sky because each drop was too heavy to actually stay up there. They got horribly wet as they ran from the car to the house. They knocked on the door. Jean appeared at the window to see who it was. They could almost hear her sigh through the glass, despite the thundering rain. She didn't appear and open the door for a while, by which time the two detectives were well and truly soaked through. Ottey thought this was a deliberate ploy on Jean's part, after yesterday's time in the police van. Cross thought it was because she was downing a glass of wine, before hiding the glass in the kitchen.

'Seriously?' she said, as she opened the door.

'Oh yes,' replied the drenched Cross. Andy appeared from behind her.

'You said you were getting the door, Jean!' he exclaimed.

'I did. I was,' she muttered.

'Look at the state of them; come in, come in,' he said, ushering them into the house, not before directing a "for fuck's sake" at his wife. They sat down, as Jean reluctantly made them some tea, and Andy went to get them a couple of towels. Cross smelled his towel, appreciatively, before drying himself. He always did this, smelled things. His sense of smell was important to him. Smell interested him. One of his obsessions as a teenager was being able to identify both men's and women's perfumes, until a woman complained at his sniffing too close to her when he was seventeen. He never did it again, but Ottey had, on occasion heard him mutter to himself "Penhaligon's Blenheim" or "Opium". He went through a phase in his early teens of collecting tiny free samples at the perfume counter at Maggs & Co in Clifton. He was quite a familiar figure there after a while, and the women took to him. They would occasionally ask him to show off his talent for identifying perfumes, blind, to their customers.

Cross patted down his head, then neatly folded the towel up and placed it on his lap. He looked at Ottey. She was going to start the conversation, as they wanted it to be relaxed. To make both Andy and Jean feel confident and unworried. This was her skill set.

'First, thanks for seeing us again. I'm sorry about Debbie – that must be very upsetting for you.'

'It wouldn't've happened if she'd been here,' answered Jean.

'And how d'you work that one out?' Andy asked. Cross noticed a distinct change of attitude in Andy with his wife. He seemed irritated, angry. Maybe he was still annoyed by the previous day's scene at the restaurant. He was no longer the protective presence for her that he had been in their first meeting. Well, it couldn't be easy living with a drunk, thought Cross. Particularly one who started so early in the day. He imagined she must be in quite a state, every night, when Andy returned home from work.

'Well, she wouldn't have got pregnant for a start.'

'You can't know that. Don't be stupid,' he replied.

'*Don't* call me stupid,' she spat, as if it was a reiteration of something she'd already said several times before.

'Was it easy for you to get time off work?' Ottey continued.

'Yeah, my boss understood. He knows the situation,' he said, instinctively looking at Jean.

'And what's that supposed to mean?' she said.

'What d'you think? The miscarriage, obviously.' He turned back to Ottey. 'I'll work a few nights to make up for it. We're twenty-four hours, seven days a week.'

'You sound like a bloody advert. Why don't you give her your card while you're at it?' said Jean.

'Oh shut up, Jean. If you've got nothing better to say, why don't you just go and wash?'

'We'd rather she stayed,' said Cross.

'What do you do for work, Andy?' Ottey asked.

'I'm a plumber,' he replied.

'You work for yourself?'

'Used to. Thinking of going back to it, as it happens,' he said.

'So, who do you work for now?' Ottey went on.

'South West Plumbing.' There was an indiscernible pause as the two detectives took this in.

'Oh, I know them; they're all over the place,' Ottey said.

'Yeah, it's a big fleet.'

'Light blue, with the owner plastered all over them. He must be quite a character, face all over town,' she went on.

'Yeah, he does love himself a bit,' Andy laughed.

'I didn't see a van outside. Do you leave it at work?'

'No, no; we bring them home. It's the black transit,' he said.

'Why a black one?' she asked.

'My regular one's having a service.'

'Just a service?' she asked.

'Yep.'

'No repairs at all?'

'Well, they'll fix anything they need to,' Andy said.

'Anything need fixing?' she asked.

Andy thought for a moment then, when nothing came to mind, he pursed his lips and shook his head, quickly followed by, 'Oh, what am I talking about? The back door. It got broken into.'

'Recently?' she asked.

'Yeah, last week.'

'Last week and you forgot?'

'No, just slipped my mind. That's all,' he said.

'Okay. Andy, where were you the night of the eighth?' Ottey asked.

'The eighth? When was that?' he asked.

'Two weeks ago Tuesday,' she replied.

Andy got out his phone and checked his diary.

'Normal work day, then I was back here with Jean. Back at eighteen thirty, according to this. I do everything on the twenty four hour clock. We need to keep the hours for our time sheets.'

'Isn't that all computerised these days?' she asked.

'Exactly, which is why we keep a note. The computer isn't always right; the wifi drops out all the time and it never accounts for travel properly. It's like one of those sat navs. It records a journey in your work log by how long it thinks we should take, sometimes the way the bloody crow flies, by the look of it. Has no idea of real traffic and delays. So we have to cross-check,' he said. Cross had a feeling this man was trying to be as helpful as possible. Or at least come across that way. Ottey looked at Jean.

'Can you confirm that, Jean?'

'Yes,' she said.

'What did you do that night?'

'Can't really remember. We had dinner, probably watched a DVD,' she said.

'There's nothing worth watching on the TV these days,' said Andy.

'Funny, that's exactly what DS Ottey says, isn't it?' said Cross, joining the conversation for the first time since they arrived.

'Yep,' she concurred.

'I don't watch television myself so I wouldn't know.' Cross went on. 'I listen to the radio, though. Well, when I say "radio" it's really only Radio 4, although I do like Jazz FM for, well, jazz obviously. And there's no beating Radio 3 for classical – they play symphonies in their entirety. I can't really be doing with these stations that play Bach's best bits or Mozart's greatest hits. Did you see Alex that night?' Neither of them answered. 'Mrs Swinton?' he asked.

'What? No, like I told you, we haven't seen him in months,' she replied.

'Okay...' he said, then took an inordinate time to write something down in his notebook. He looked up at the two of them as if he expected them to have something further to say. They said nothing, looked at each other, then back at him. Yes, he was still staring. Then, after what seemed like an eternity, he asked, 'Mrs Swinton, how did you feel about Debbie being pregnant?'

'What? Well...' she said, trying to search for a response.

'Only sixteen,' he went on.

'What are you trying to say?' she asked.

'Nothing. I'm merely asking you how you felt,' he replied.

'We were disappointed, if I'm honest,' said Andy. Jean didn't bother to contradict him.

'Were you angry? When she told you?'

'No,' replied Andy.

'More... sad,' Jean added.

'When did she tell you?'

'A few weeks ago.'

'When you last saw her?' Cross asked.

'No, I think she phoned,' said Jean.

'Really? Not the sort of news you'd expect to hear over the phone,' he said.

'Why not?' said Jean.

'Well as you know, things have been a little tense recently,' said Andy, jumping in. He looked at Ottey, who smiled reassuringly. She often did this to fill in for Cross.

'Of course. Well, that's all pretty straightforward,' said Cross. 'I think we've got all we need. You were here. Together. Didn't see Alex.' If you didn't know him, you'd think Cross was a little plodding, dense even.

'No,' Andy affirmed.

'Thanks again for your time,' said Ottey.

As they walked towards the front door Cross stopped and looked out of the back window into the garden.

'What do you keep in your shed?'

This seemed to take Andy by surprise, as if it'd come out of the blue. 'Um, lawn mower, garden stuff and, well, a load of crap to be honest. You know how it builds up.'

'Big lock for a "load of crap", said Cross, 'and quite new by the look of it.'

'I keep my tools in there overnight. Not safe in the van. Like I told you. It was broken into last week,' he said.

'But you can't decant the entire contents of the van into the shed every night, surely?'

'No, no, I'd be at it all night,' he laughed. 'Just the power tools, things people like to nick. I mean, it's pretty secure. Like last week – they couldn't get into the van, but they make a right mess of it trying.'

'They'd be safer in the house, wouldn't they? Having said that, looking at that shed, they'd probably be safer in the van,' Cross said.

'Jean doesn't like them in the house.'

'Of course,' said Cross, as if this was a very valid point he hadn't thought of. 'And that's a pretty mighty lock.'

'Yep.'

'Did you change it recently?'

'I did, as it happens. We had a break-in a few months ago. Chased the bloke off, but the lock was screwed. We've got a motion detector light on the back of the house now. Floods the garden if anything moves, and sends a text to my phone,' he said.

'No!' said Cross, seemingly impressed by such technology. He turned to Ottey. 'Did you know there were lights that could send texts to people?' he asked her.

'I did not,' she replied.

'That's amazing. Could you show me how it works?' he asked.

'George, I really don't think we have time for a demonstration,' she said. They made a move to leave, then Cross stopped again, and said to Andy apologetically, as if he knew that what he was about to ask was probably out of the question.

'Is it all right if I have a quick look?' he asked.

'What?'

'In the shed,' said Cross.

'No,' replied Andy.

'No?' said Cross, sounding genuinely surprised that such an innocent enquiry should've elicited this response.

'I think we've told you all you need to know,' Andy said.

'Really? I don't think that's possible in all reality, is it? I mean, how can you know how much we need to know when you don't actually know how much we already know? What might be useful to us, in the course of our investigation?' Andy offered no response so Cross insisted, 'I'd like to look in the shed.'

'Don't you need a warrant for that?' asked Jean.

'A warrant?' Cross asked, as if he couldn't work out why she would say that. 'Why would you want us to go to all that trouble?'

'Because we know our rights,' said Andy. The tone of the conversation had now shifted significantly. He was no longer the man happy to help, kind enough to get them towels when they got soaked. He was now defensive and they had quickly become unwelcome.

'Of course you do. But why would you bring them up all of a sudden?' asked Cross, puzzled. They offered no response. 'I'd be grateful for an answer, lest I'm under the wrong impression. You see, I'm thinking it's because you're trying to prevent me from going into your shed. But why would you want to do that if all you keep in there is a "load of old crap"? There has to be another reason, wouldn't you say? If you were me? Another reason for your not wanting me to look in the shed?' He stared at Andy, inquiringly. Andy didn't flinch.

'We'll see ourselves out. Oh, and commiserations.'

'I'm sorry?' Andy replied, confused.

'For Debbie's miscarriage.' He looked at Ottey uncertainly. 'Isn't that what you're supposed to say?'

Andy and Jean watched them run back to the car in the rain.

'That man's a bloody idiot,' said Jean as she went back to the kitchen to pour herself a glass of wine. Andy watched the two officers talking in the car, before it eventually pulled out. He wasn't so sure.

24

The investigation was at a point now where the difference between Cross' approach and that of his colleagues became apparent. Carson and pretty much everyone else wanted to get a warrant for the Swintons' house and shed. But not Cross. It was this difference in approach that went some way to explaining his staggering conviction rate in court. It was a success rate that no other detective in the area (possibly in the country, Carson once thought, but hadn't bothered to check) came anywhere close to. It was the fact that Cross wanted everything in the case presented in the most convincing, vice-like grip of certainty. He wanted it laid out on a plate for the jury. He didn't want them to have any choices if he could possibly help it. He wanted them, in a case where he knew the evidence pointed with no uncertainty to the guilt of the accused, to have no alternative but to find them guilty. So in this situation Carson was having a little trouble understanding why his best detective was resisting his offer of a warrant to search the shed in the Swintons' garden. This was compounded by two events. The first was Cross, at the beginning of the meeting, producing a photograph of the wreckage of the garage in which Alex's polythene-wrapped body was found. He pointed to a large, new-looking padlock still attached to part of the door.

'It's the same make of padlock on Swinton's garden shed,' said Cross.

'And now you're going to tell me that it's quite a common make of lock,' said Carson, who knew that this was a habit of Cross' – he would produce something which seemed incontrovertible proof in a case, only to shoot it down himself, immediately afterwards.

'Exactly,' said Cross. 'So we need to find a receipt, because my thinking is, as they were both used in the covering up of the same crime, Swinton will be in possession of a recent receipt for both locks.'

'Fine, I'll make sure the warrant covers the house as well as the shed,' said Carson, reaching over for his desk phone. He started to punch in a number, then Cross jumped forward, in a way that surprised himself as much as it surprised Carson, and cut the call off.

'No!'

'George,' said Carson, startled and implying that Cross was way out of order here.

'I don't think we should do that,' said Cross, as near to apologetically as he could. 'Not yet.'

'What more do you need?' he asked when, as if on cue, Mackenzie came in with what Carson thought had to be sufficient justification for even Cross to be happy to go back to the house with a warrant.

'As you know, the black transit van used by Swinton was a temporary replacement for his regular one. I've just spoken to the head of the company, the bloke on the vans. I didn't know people still had Bristol accents that thick...' she said.

'Alice...' said Ottey, encouraging her just to get on with it.

'Oh yes, I'm sorry. Anyway, it was in for repairs, but not for the back door as he claimed. It had extensive damage down one side. The bloke said it was like a huge gash.'

'Right, ducks in order George? I'll get the warrant.'

'No!' replied Cross for the second time.

'George, for fuck's sake, what else do you need?'

But Cross was already leaving the office. Carson turned to Ottey. 'Will you do something about him, please?'

'Sure,' she said. 'What do you suggest exactly?

Cross wanted to keep an eye on the Swintons' house overnight, but Ottey couldn't help. 'I have a parents' evening tonight; what about tomorrow?' said Ottey.

'Tomorrow will be too late,' Cross replied.

'Then let's just get the warrant.'

'No. This way is conclusive.'

'Maybe we could ask Carson for some help,' she said.

'I can't do it. I have a PTA tonight,' said Ottey.

'Seriously? This is a murder case,' protested Carson.

'They always are, boss. But I'm not missing this one. Not after the arse-ripping I got from the head teacher last time.'

'Okay, fair enough, but I don't have any spare bodies,' he said.

'What? At the risk of repeating you – this is a murder case,' said Cross.

'We've just had another come in. I've had to take some people off Paphides, just to do the preliminaries on that. Tomorrow will be different.'

'Tomorrow will be too late,' said Cross.

'Which is why I'm going to get a warrant and you can get the search done this afternoon, and have the man in custody in time for Josie to get to school,' said Carson.

'I don't want a warrant.'

'Why ever not? You have a pair of matching padlocks, a receipt which you are certain you'll find in the house, and a van with damage caused by contact with the side of the garage. Paint traces which will confirm that it was driven by the man whose house I would like to issue the search warrant for,' said Carson, rapidly reaching the end of his tether.

'You may be persuaded, but a jury may not. My way is conclusive,' said Cross, standing his ground.

'As would a search be. I don't have the people, so I'm afraid you lose this one. I'll get the warrant,' he said with all the authority he could muster, before looking up and seeing that Cross had, again, already left the office. He was calling for Mackenzie, who was about to protest that she actually had plans for that evening, but he'd gone.

A couple of hours later Cross and Mackenzie found themselves sitting in the road Debbie's parents lived in. They had stopped off, on the way, at Greggs. Cross bought them both a sandwich. When Mackenzie asked how long he thought they were going to be, doing whatever it was they were about to do – he still hadn't actually told her – he said probably till the early hours. He then watched with interest as she loaded up a basket of treats: sausage rolls, crisps, fizzy water, diet coke, nuts and some fruit. When they got to the counter, she turned as she was told the total cost, and looked at him expectantly. It took him a full ten seconds before he reached for his wallet and paid.

'Can I ask you a question?' she said, as they tucked into the contents of the carrier bag that was propped up between them in her car.

'Yes,' he replied.

'Why are we here? I mean, I know it's a stake-out and everything, but what exactly are we staking out?' she asked. He was about to tell her but then remembered that it was his responsibility to teach her. To make her think, rather than spoon-feed her.

'What haven't we found, as yet?'

'The killer?' she joked. He looked at her, but didn't know her well enough yet to ascertain whether she was joking or not. So he didn't react.

'Of the victim's,' he went on.

'His mobile phone?' she said, thinking out loud.

'Correct, but something else.'

She thought for a moment. 'I don't know,' she said.

'Something big enough you'd need a shed to hide it in,' he went on.

'Oh. Ah, right. His bike. He was on his bike the night he was killed,' she said.

'Exactly.'

'And you think it's in Andy's shed,' she said.

'I do,' he replied. She thought for a moment, trying to figure out whether she'd missed something obvious, before she said anything that might make her look stupid. Although, the fact of the matter was, Cross could make her feel stupid when all she'd said was "Good morning". But she thought everything through and realised that she had a perfectly valid question that she shouldn't be frightened of asking.

'So why don't we just get a warrant to search the shed, get the bike and arrest Swinton?' she asked. He sighed, as he was getting a little weary of explaining this to everyone.

'Because possession of the bike isn't enough. He could say Alex left it there for him to look after.'

'And expect us to believe him?'

'No, but it'd just be another hurdle to cross in court. One we can do without.'

'But together with the van and the damage to the van. I mean, odds are a jury would convict on that alone.' She immediately regretted saying this, as she'd used this exact expression before and been shot down in flames. So she said what he was about to say, before he had the chance. 'But odds are something we can do without.'

'Exactly,' he replied, secretly pleased that some of what he was saying was actually going in. 'It's also an avenue of denial that could cost us a good couple of hours of our window.'

'Okay, you've lost me now,' she said, offering him some crisps, which he refused. She wasn't to know that he never shared things like bags of crisps or nuts. He had to have his own packet.

'The window between arrest and charge. As you know, we only have twenty-four hours before we have to apply for an extension. So every hour counts. The more prepared we are, the less time they can waste. His arguing that Alex had left it there could cost us valuable time.'

It was just after two in the morning when Cross shook her awake.

'Alice, Alice, wake up.' She woke up, not knowing where she was for an instant.

'What's happening?' she asked.

'Over there. Look,' said Cross. The lights had come on in the hall of the Swintons' house. Then a light shone down the alley running alongside the house. Part of Andy's security system, Cross thought. The gate opened and Andy appeared, carrying something wrapped in a builders' dust sheet. It had to be the bike. He put it in the back of his van and got into the driver's seat. Mackenzie looked at Cross, who hadn't moved.

'Aren't you going to arrest him?' she asked.

'No. Follow him.'

She started the car and drove after the van.

'Can I ask you a question?' she said.

'I want to see him dispose of the bike. I want everything. That's the whole point of being cold and uncomfortable in your car for half a night,' he explained.

'That's not what I was going to ask,' she said.

'Oh all right,' he said.

'Was I snoring? When I was asleep. Did I snore?' she asked.

He looked at her, trying to judge something, but he still didn't know her well enough to make a judgement. So he asked,

'Is this a question to which you'd like an honest answer, or would you like me to reassure you?'

'So I was. I knew it.'

'Like a foghorn, actually,' he said matter-of-factly.

They drove on for a while, and then it happened. The car suddenly started shuddering and came to a halt. 'Fuck,' said Mackenzie, as the van disappeared into the distance. 'Shit.' She got out and saw that the back tyre had a flat. 'I'm really, really sorry,' she said, but Cross wasn't listening; he was studying a map on his phone. He then made a note of the time and got out of the car and inspected the tyre.

'Do you have a spare?'

'I think so,' she said.

'You "think so"?' he repeated. 'Is this your car?'

'Yes, of course it is.'

She opened the boot and they found the spare.

'Here, let me,' he said and, taking off his coat, he lifted the spare wheel and jack out of the boot.

'I thought you couldn't drive?' she said.

'Why would an inability to drive preclude my knowing how to change a flat tyre?' he asked. 'Anyway, I can drive. I just choose not to. Do you know where the wheel lock is?' he asked.

'The "wheel lock"?' she said. They found it, eventually, in the glove compartment, hidden amongst various debris. A well-read paperback, hair clips and ties, a few sweets stuck to the side, a couple of CDs and finally, an open packet of condoms. They both saw the condoms and immediately made the decision to pretend they hadn't. Cross set about changing the wheel. As he was about to lift the punctured tyre off the car, the black transit came back down the road towards them. It slowed to a halt. Cross turned away so he couldn't be seen. Mackenzie panicked for a split second, then remembered that Andy had never seen her. He had no idea who she was.

'Are you guys okay?' he asked.

'Yeah, just a flat. Don't worry. My dad's sorting it out,' she said.

'You sure?' he asked.

'Yeah, thanks for stopping though,' she said.

'No problem,' he said, winding his window back up and driving off.

'Blimey, that gave me a scare,' she said, as she took the punctured tyre off Cross. 'Good look for you, though.'

'What?' said Cross, as he looked at his watch and made a note of the time.

'Being my undercover dad,' she said.

Ten minutes later they were driving again, with Cross giving directions from the map on his phone. He'd worked out the speed of the van, the time between their losing it and its return, and calculated where it was most likely their suspect had disposed of Alex's bike. This was at the back of an industrial estate, a couple of miles away, which backed onto a canal. Mackenzie pulled up and they got out. They examined the area, but it was dry. There was no clue, as far as she could see, as to where, or even whether, the van had been here at all. But Cross checked his calculations again and decided this was it. He turned to Mackenzie.

'Do you have an underwater torch?' he asked.

'What? No, why?'

'Well, you'll need it to go in,' he said, indicating the canal, 'and visibility won't be very good. Particularly at this time of night,' he said. She looked at him in disbelief.

'You're joking,' she said, unsure but hopeful.

'I am,' he replied, and walked away quite pleased with himself. She was so used to him always being literal that she still couldn't latch onto his attempts at humour.

Later that morning an irritable DCI Carson arrived at the location. He'd been woken up at five by Cross asking for a diver team, who were now scouring the bed of the canal. Tantalisingly, they had already brought up two bikes, neither of them being the right one.

'Any luck?' Carson asked, as he approached.

'We don't need luck,' replied Cross.

'It would've been a damn sight cheaper to have got a warrant and just pulled this out of his shed,' Carson went on.

'Cheaper, but less clear. This way he gets to pass "Go" and move straight to jail,' replied Cross.

'Do you have any idea how difficult it was to arrange a dive team at this short notice?' Carson asked.

'No,' replied Cross.

'They've had to come from bloody Wiltshire,' Carson went on.

'Another cost-cutting efficiency, no doubt,' said Cross.

'Well, they're here now,' ventured Mackenzie, as if she was trying to make the best of the situation.

'Shouldn't you be in the office?' Carson asked.

'She was here all night, so it seemed only fair that she stayed to see how it all panned out,' Cross replied.

'So why the hell would he kill him?' asked Carson.

'We don't know yet that he did.'

'Yes, but all the evidence is beginning to point very much in his direction,' replied Carson.

'Which is both something and nothing,' said Cross.

Carson decided against pursuing this any further. Ottey then pulled up in her car with a tray of three coffees. She offered one to Cross and Mackenzie, leaving one on the cardboard tray. She saw Carson eyeing it covetously.

'I didn't know you were here,' she said, but he just kept looking at the coffee imploringly. 'No,' she said. 'Absolutely not.' She walked over to a wheelie bin set against the building and threw the tray away. When she turned round, the divers had brought up another bike. This time it was the right one.

'Right, bring him in, and let these boys go home,' said Carson, walking away towards his car as if his work here was done.

'We will. Just as soon as they've found the phone,' replied Cross.

'What? What phone?' said Carson.

'Alex's mobile. The one the text was sent from,' Ottey replied.

'Seriously? What makes you think it's in there? It could be in the house.'

'We don't know. But we might as well check, now that we're here,' she said.

'Okay, well get it done and then bring him in,' he said, getting into his car.

'What else, exactly, did he think we were going to do?' said Ottey. 'He states the obvious then instructs us to do exactly what we're doing, as if it's a brilliantly inspirational piece of leadership,' she moaned. She then sent Mackenzie home to get some sleep, telling her she didn't want to see her in the office till at least two that afternoon.

The search was difficult. Visibility at the bottom of the canal, once the divers had disturbed the silt, was virtually nil, so they had to feel around with their hands. This was not made any easier by the fact that they were wearing thick, protective gloves. But, a couple of hours later, they came up with a smart-phone. It was the latest model, which made Cross think it was Alex's for a few reasons. Its location, obviously. The fact that it was the latest model – Alex liked his tech – and why would someone throw an expensive, practically brand-new phone into a canal unless they didn't want it to be found?

They decided against arresting Andy that afternoon. It wasn't as if he was going anywhere, and Cross needed some sleep. He was fairly sure their suspicion was focused in the right place now. But he wanted to think about his interview strategy and needed to be fresh. Some police thought of an arrest like this as the end of it. That the thing just needed wrapping up. Not so for Cross. This was the vital part of the investigation. The interview was the crucial piece for him. It was just the beginning.

25

Next morning, having ascertained that Andy was still at home, Cross and Ottey arrived at the house in Eastville with a search warrant. Cross could tell that Andy was perturbed by the warrant. He'd had a full day, yesterday, to think that he'd got away with it. That the disposal of the bike early that morning had solved the problem. But the fact that they were back alarmed him, initially, until Cross asked if they could see inside the shed. The man couldn't disguise his momentary relief.

'Sure, of course,' he said, as he got the key and they walked out into the back garden. Mackenzie had asked earlier why they needed to search the shed, when they already had the bike. Ottey explained that it was all part of Cross' strategy. He wanted to build a narrative. Just a couple of days ago Andy wouldn't show them the shed. Cross would relate this narrative in court. It was a small thing, but just another layer of guilt for the jury. More importantly, he was softening Andy up for the interview.

'What do you mean?' Mackenzie asked.

'He wants Andy to think we don't have the bike. He wants him to think he's won this little battle. Build his confidence, so that he can destroy it when he reveals it, at a time of his choosing, and pull the rug from underneath him. Right now, Andy's sure we have nothing and that's exactly what George wants him to think.'

They walked into the back garden. Jean watched from inside the house. They had caught her off guard, Cross thought, as she looked like she wasn't dressed yet. Andy opened the door of the shed and stepped aside so they could look in. It was well organised. Tools hanging off nails on the walls. Everything in its rightful place. Cross turned to Andy, as if he was looking for some explanation.

'Like I told you. My tools,' Andy said.

'Indeed, like you told me,' said Cross. 'One question. Why would you want us to go to the trouble of getting a warrant? Why didn't you just let us have a look? Like you say. It's just your tools.'

'It's a point of principle,' said Andy, locking up. 'There's a line. It's privacy, isn't it?'

Cross thought about this for a minute and then they followed Andy back into the house. Cross looked genuinely thrown. As if he was trying to work something out. 'Did you not like Alex?' he asked.

'Of course. He was fine. Why d'you ask?' said Andy.

'He was murdered. His body wrapped in polythene sheeting and dumped in a row of disused garages,' Cross went on.

'I know. It's terrible.'

'So where do you think privacy and points of principle fit in with a scenario like that? Do you think they're as important as finding his killer?'

'I never said that.'

'No, but your behaviour's rather indicative of it, wouldn't you think?'

'Okay, fine. I should've let you see the shed and I'm sorry. Was there anything else?' Andy asked.

'Yes. DS Ottey?' Cross said, turning to his partner.

'Andy Swinton, I'm arresting you on suspicion of the murder of Alex Paphides,' she said.

'What?' exclaimed Andy, his confidence quickly evaporating.

'What's going on?' said Jean.

'You do not have to say anything. But it may harm your defence if you do not mention, when questioned, something which you later rely on in court. Anything you do say can be given in evidence. Could you turn round please?' she said. He did so, and she cuffed him. Cross turned to Jean.

'Mrs Swinton, we need you to come down to the station as well,' he said.

'What, you arresting me too?' she said, close to tears.

'No, we just want to ask you a few questions and take a statement,' he replied. 'Perhaps you'd like to get dressed.'

'I am fucking dressed, you moron,' she spat.

'If you say so,' he replied.

They had been followed by two police units, so that Jean and Andy could be taken down to the station separately. The presence of two cars outside their house had attracted a certain amount of interest from the neighbours, who were looking out of their windows. Others had been brave enough to venture outside. As they were led to the cars Jean yelled to no-one in particular, 'What are you looking at?' A kid in the street started filming on his phone. 'Oi you! Stop it, you little shit!'

Cross and Ottey got into Ottey's car. 'Last night with Mackenzie, I made a joke. A good one,' he said to her.

'Did she get it?' Ottey asked.

'I'm not sure. I think so. But I didn't check for certain. She should've done. As I said, it was a good one.'

'How did she react?'

'She said "you're joking".'

'And what had you said prior to that?'

'I asked her if she had an underwater torch, because visibility in the canal wouldn't be good at that time of night,' he replied confidently.

'And she said "you're joking"?'

'Yes. She thought I meant she had to go into the canal and find the bike.'

'Okay, so we might need to do a little more work on that. But full marks for trying,' she said.

'Thank you. I thought so too,' he said.

'Thought what?'

'Full marks.'

Mackenzie was looking at Andy, sitting in the interview room, on the monitor in the next-door office. Ottey stopped as she walked by.

'What is it?' she asked.

'He looks so ordinary,' Mackenzie replied.

'They all look ordinary,' said Ottey, 'and, for the most part, they always look vulnerable in there. Except for the career criminals. Don't be taken in by it. You should watch for a bit. This is when George is at his best.'

'How?'

'Quite often, when everyone thinks a case is a slam dunk, and in many situations it is, George just makes the result non-negotiable, inevitable. He makes it watertight, airtight and whatever other tight there is. Most people don't have the patience or the skill. Everyone knows about his conviction rate, but you know what really pleases him?'

'No.'

'The speed of a jury reaching a verdict and speed of conviction. He's days ahead of the rest of us.'

'How do you know that?'

'Oh, because he does his stats, does George. He loves his stats. Be nice to him and he might show you his spreadsheets,' said Ottey, and left. Mackenzie realised that Ottey not only had a seemingly healthy respect for her partner, but also a fair amount of affection.

Even though Jean was not under arrest, Cross interviewed her in much the same way he would have done had she been a suspect. He wanted to interview them both contemporaneously, as he thought any inconsistencies between them would help him steer the investigation, and be more revealing. He began, as he often did, with a dogged, repetitive analysis of the night of the murder. This often softened an interviewee up – frustrated them. Cross was also trying to get them to build up a picture in their minds of the detective in front of them. He wanted them to think they were ahead of him. Were cleverer than him. He wanted them to underestimate him. He basically held one killer question in reserve which, when deployed, generally made their story unravel.

'So let's go over the events of May eighth,' said Cross to Andy, as if he'd never said this before. He had. Several times.

'Haven't we done that already?

'I just want to make sure I've got everything. Where were you?' Cross repeated.

'Like I said before. At home with Jean.' He sighed.

'So you were at home. Who were you with?' Cross asked. Andy looked at Cross and then at his solicitor. Was this man taking the piss? He'd just told him who he was with not five seconds before. His lawyer had experience of Cross and had told Andy, prior to the interview, to be careful and just answer what he was asked, when he was asked it, however many times he was asked it.

'Answer the question,' the lawyer said quietly.

'With Jean,' he said, sighing audibly.

'And what were you doing?' Cross asked.

. . .

'Watching a DVD,' answered Jean in the VA room. She was drinking tea with Cross and Ottey. The atmosphere was more relaxed.

'Which film?'

'That one with Colin Firth,' she said, trying to remember the name.

'*Kingsman*,' said Andy.

'I quite liked that one,' said Cross. 'I saw it in the cinema. I only see films in the cinema. I don't have a television.'

'You've already told me that,' said Andy wearily. This was torture and it had only been going on for an hour.

'I did?' said Cross, quite surprised. He thought for a moment. Played the conversation back in his head, as if to check. 'So I did. I'm sorry. I forget. What did you eat?'

'Chinese takeaway.'

'That's peculiar. You didn't have to think about that. You knew straight away,' he said.

'Good memory.'

'Where did you get the food from?'

'Deliveroo.'

'Which restaurant?'

'You'd have to ask Jean. She ordered it.'

'The Golden Wok,' she said.

'Did Andy leave the house at all that night? After you'd eaten?' Cross asked. She was struggling with these simple questions. He thought part of it was because of the inevitable hangover she was enduring. That would make remembering the events of a couple of nights ago problematic, let alone a couple of weeks ago. But he suspected it was a little more than that. She was having trouble sticking to their script. Their agreed version of what happened that night. Or to be more precise,

Andy's version of the events of that night. It would, undoubtedly, have been him who'd come up with it.

'No, he was there all night,' she replied.

'And did he go to work that night?' he asked.

'I don't know!' she blurted out in frustration. 'Probably. Yes. But I don't know, all right? Can I go now, please?'

'Would you like another coffee? Water maybe?' asked Ottey.

'Call that coffee?' she said, looking at the half finished cup in front of her.

'I know. I could send someone out,' she said.

'You'd do that?' Jean asked.

'Absolutely, you're doing us a favour, being here and helping us. Why wouldn't I do the same?'

'I am, aren't I? Doing you a favour?' Jean said.

'You are,' Ottey replied.

'You could do with remembering that, mate,' she said to Cross.

'DS Cross is very much aware of that. He's just not as good at showing it. Isn't that right, George?' Ottey said.

'How did you find out about Debbie being pregnant?' Cross asked, ignoring them both.

'Cappuccino, two sugars please,' Jean said to her new friend in the room. Ottey got up and left the room to send Mackenzie, who was, quite frankly, relieved to get a break from observing the tedium of Cross' interviewing. If it had been her sitting opposite him, she would have just told him the truth, or anything he wanted her to say, ages ago, so she could have got out of there as soon as possible. When Ottey came back, Jean and Cross were staring at each other. She still hadn't answered his question. Cross waited for Ottey to sit down, then repeated the question.

'How did you find out about Debbie being pregnant?'

'She phoned me.'

'But you said when we first met that you hadn't heard from her for months,' said Cross.

'I said I hadn't seen her.' Cross checked his notes.

'So you did,' he replied. 'Where were you when you received the call?'

'At home, I suppose.'

'You suppose?' he asked.

'All right. I was then.'

'And how did you feel?'

'I already told you that. Do we have to talk about this? I mean I don't have to talk about anything if I don't want, do I? I mean I can just go, right?'

'Yes, whenever you like,' said Ottey.

'So what if I just stand up and go now?'

'You'd miss out on your coffee,' Ottey replied.

'Good point,' said Jean, smiling at her only ally in the room.

When Mackenzie arrived with Jean's coffee, Cross decided it was a good time for a break. So they went back to the interview room. They had left Andy there rather than returning him to the holding cell. This was because Cross wanted him to be aware of the fact that Jean was being interviewed at the same time. To get him concerned about what she might be saying.

Cross sat down and organised his folders on the desk. Then he looked up at Andy.

'Where were you when Debbie told Jean about the pregnancy?' he asked. This caught Andy off guard momentarily. It was a new line of questioning. Did it worry him, Cross was thinking?

'I don't remember,' he replied.

'Really?' said Cross, sounding surprised and a little perplexed.

'Yes, really.'

'Now you see, that seems a little odd to me. You can remember what you ate on a certain night, two weeks ago. What DVD you watched. All pretty trivial stuff, wouldn't you agree?' said Cross.

'I suppose so.'

'And yet, you can't remember something as important as your stepdaughter telling you she's pregnant.' Cross paused, but Andy didn't answer. 'Presumably you'd agree that it is important? A life event. A new family member. Both of you grandparents for the first time.'

'Of course.'

'So let's try again. Where were you?' Cross asked.

'At work, I think,' he replied.

'You "think"? Clearly not memorable then.'

Andy thought for a few seconds then remembered. 'I was at work. I remember it now, because I'd been sent over to Bath for a job. I was on the A4, had to pull over,' he said, as Cross ticked off a question in his file methodically and made some notes.

'And how did you feel about it? Were you happy?'

'Mixed, I suppose. She's so young, and obviously I didn't know how she felt about it, so that was a worry.'

'And you didn't call her,' Cross stated.

Andy thought for a moment, then looked up. 'It wasn't worth it.'

'Why's that?'

'It would have caused too much grief,' he said.

'With Jean?' Cross asked. But Andy didn't answer. There was no need. 'You get on with Debbie, though. Her problems were really with her mother, were they not?'

'Yes.'

'Too similar, maybe?'

'No, not at all. Quite the opposite. She's the most sensible of the three of us.'

'So why did she leave?'

'The drinking. Jean's drinking. It upset Debbie and she started talking to her about it. Asking her mum to stop. It led to terrible rows and she left.'

'What was the breaking point for her? Was there a particular row?'

'Yeah.'

'And what was that about?'

'Well it started out of nothing really. Trouble was, if I'm honest, I'd had a few that night as well. It was a Friday. You know, end of the week. But it's um... I tend to do my drinking with my mates now. Down the pub. Have a few, nothing too much. Then come home, and if she's still up go straight to bed. We're not too good together if we've both had a drink,' he said.

'So the argument, that Friday night. What did it end up being about? What made her leave? Was it about Alex?' Cross asked. Andy looked unsure as to how to answer this.

'It was, wasn't it?' volunteered Ottey.

'Yep. In the end she called him, and he came round and picked her up. That's when Jean said some awful shit. I told her she'd regret it. The girl's sixteen, for God's sake. Sometimes Jean behaves like her older sister, not her mother. It's not right. But it happened.'

'Couldn't you have called Debbie and not told her mother?' said Cross.

'Um, yeah, I suppose so. I don't know. Things have all been so difficult recently.'

'And now you find yourself arrested on suspicion of murder,' said Cross. This brought Andy back to reality with a jolt. Cross often did this. In the middle of an interview that was going quite amicably, non-controversially, he would suddenly remind the suspect why it was they were there. 'Things can't get much more difficult than that,' he pointed out. 'You get on well with Debbie, don't you?'

'Of course I do. She's my daughter.'

'Stepdaughter, in point of fact,' Cross pointed out.

'She's like a daughter to me and she calls me Dad most of the time,' Andy replied.

'I noticed at the restaurant the other day, the closeness of your relationship. She was really pleased to see you. Relieved. She looked like she's been missing you and found your presence there reassuring,' Cross said.

'Thanks. She's a lovely girl.'

'Do you feel badly, that you didn't call her?' Cross asked.

'Okay, so what has this got to do with my being arrested?' Andy asked. Cross never answered these kind of questions from suspects. But it often served as an indication that it was a good time to move the interview on to the next stage. Which he did here.

'As you know, Jean is here, helping us with our enquiries,' said Cross, 'and we're covering much the same ground as we're covering with you. But the thing is, she tells us that you were with her when she took the call from Debbie.' He looked up to see if there was any reaction from Andy. There was none. 'Not on the A4, but with her at home. She's quite sure of it. Can you explain, perhaps? Who's right and who is wrong?'

'She's confusing the time when we spoke about it after. She was upset. She's not thinking straight,' said Andy.

'That's perfectly understandable. She was upset then and she's stressed now. Not exactly the friendliest of environments, police stations, however hard we try to put people at their ease.'

'And, let's face it, she's drunk most of the time, Detective,' Andy went on. 'She doesn't know one day from the next. So it's hardly an earth-shattering revelation that she's got her facts about that wrong.'

'She said you talked about it at length,' Cross went on.

'On the phone,' said Andy.

'That you looked disappointed. That you hugged her.'

'That was when I got home, after work. I hugged her, but I didn't look disappointed. That's her putting what she was thinking onto me.'

'What was she thinking?'

'That history was repeating itself. She had Debbie at the same age and it hasn't done her a power of good.'

'Are you saying she blames Debbie for her present situation?' asked Ottey.

'Yes. She's had a lot of opportunities robbed from her, by being a mum at such a young age,' said Andy.

'Or maybe it was the alcohol that robbed her of those opportunities,' said Cross.

'It's all part of the same thing,' said Andy.

'Oh, so she blames Debbie for her drinking.'

'No.'

'Maybe you do. Do you blame your daughter for your wife's drink problem?' Cross asked.

'Stepdaughter,' Andy corrected him. 'You're just putting words into my mouth now,' said Andy. 'What has any of this got to do with Alex being killed?'

'Well, that's what we're trying to ascertain. But it's quite difficult when neither of you are telling the truth.'

'What are you talking about?'

'You both have different versions of events,' said Cross.

'Like I said. She can't be relied on to remember stuff. You're wasting your time with her. She's a fucking drunk. There, I've said it. Happy now?' Andy said.

'I don't understand the question. Why would your acknowledging your wife being an alcoholic make me happy or otherwise?' asked Cross. Ottey knew that this was a genuine question. Andy didn't.

'Are you trying to be stupid, or does it just come naturally?' said Andy. His lawyer decided to step in at this point.

'I think it might be time for us to take a break,' he said.

'No,' said Cross.

'I beg your pardon?' said the lawyer, but Cross was in no mood to answer. He was more interested in switching things up.

'Can you explain why you have two different versions of...' Cross began, but he was interrupted by an increasingly irritable interviewee.

'Are you not listening? I just said, she can't be relied on,' said Andy.

'Which I'm sure, now that you've made that point on several occasions, the prosecution will make very clear to the jury, if she appears as a witness for the defence,' replied Cross. The lawyer closed his eyes momentarily before Cross continued. 'Two different versions of an event that never actually happened,' he said, and looked up directly at Andy without adding any further elaboration. Andy then looked at his lawyer to see if he could help. But the lawyer was looking at Cross, waiting to hear what was coming next.

'There was no phone call. Debbie never phoned to tell Jean that she was pregnant,' Cross said.

'Yes she did,' said Andy, laughing nervously.

'She did not. She told us herself, did she not, DS Ottey?'

'That's right,' Ottey replied.

'Well, she's obviously forgotten,' said Andy.

'Oh no, Mr Swinton,' said Cross, addressing him by his surname to, subliminally, let him know things were getting more serious – if he hadn't worked it out for himself – with this development. 'She was quite emphatic that she hadn't told you. And bearing in mind how your wife's and your recollection of recent events seems a little hazy, I'm inclined to go with hers.' There was no response from Andy, so Cross went on, 'Debbie never made that call. Why would you and Jean talk about a call that had never occurred?'

'No comment.'

For people who don't understand police interviews, and the techniques they employ, in this case Cross' particular techniques, the "no comment" answer can be seen as a frustrating stonewall. A cul-de-sac of non-cooperation. But for Cross, this was a welcome development. The fact that they'd moved into "no comment" territory showed that they were making progress. That they were now circling the truth in ever-decreasing circles, effectively.

26

Back in the VA room with Jean, Cross asked, 'So how did you really find out about your daughter's pregnancy?'

Jean had to think this one through. She was trying to work out what Andy might have said. Had he agreed that there was never any call? She was confused. Her mouth was dry. She just wanted to go home and curl up on the sofa with a fag and a glass of wine.

'I'd like to go now. I don't feel well,' she said.

'Would you like some water?' Ottey asked.

'No. You can't keep me here, can you? So I'd like to go,' she said.

'We'd prefer you to stay,' said Ottey.

'Well, I'm not going to. You said I was doing you a favour. That I was here helping you. That I could go any time I wanted,' she protested.

'That was before you started lying,' said Cross.

'I've had enough of this,' she said and got up. Cross stood up at the same time.

'Sit down, Mrs Swinton.'

'No, I don't have to. You said. She said. I don't have to be here. Well, you know what? I don't want to, so I'm going to exercise my rights and leave,' she said.

'In that case – Jean Swinton, I'm arresting you on suspicion of perverting the course of justice,' said Cross.

'What?'

Cross and Ottey had let Andy go back to his cell, even though they anticipated it being for only a short amount of time. They had done this so that when he was taken back he would witness Jean being charged at the desk, by the custody sergeant. Which he duly did.

'Jean? Jean, what's going on?' he shouted down the corridor.

'I don't know!' she yelled back tearfully. 'I don't know what's going on. I just want to go home. They won't let me go home, babe!'

'What are they doing?' he asked the officer taking him back to the interview room.

'I've no idea, mate,' was the reply.

Normally it would've been Cross and Ottey retrieving him from his cell, but they knew he might kick off. He didn't, in actual fact. He wasn't that stupid. But, by the time they got into the interview room with him, he was quite agitated. It was like things had moved onto another level. His head was swimming with possibilities. He'd asked to see Cross and Ottey, which was why they were sitting there without his lawyer.

'What's happening to Jean?' he asked, slightly desperately.

'She's being charged,' said Cross as he organised his files.

'With what?' asked Andy.

'I'm afraid I can't divulge that,' Cross replied.

'This has nothing to do with her,' said Andy.

'What hasn't?' Cross asked. 'What hasn't got anything to do with her?'

Andy immediately realised his mistake.

'I'm not going to say anything more till I've talked to my solicitor,' he said. Which was a problem, because the duty solicitor had two other cases in the cells and was involved in a conference with another of them. This wasn't so much a tactic as a fact of life these days. The police lost numerous hours in the twenty-four-hour window – in which they could question suspects, before either charging them or getting an extension from a judge – through doctor's visits for example, but primarily through solicitors having more than one client in the cells. Some wily, tired old hacks often played the "other client" card when they got bored sitting through an endless "no comment" phase of an interview. Or because it amused them to annoy the detectives.

Cross wasn't bothered that the solicitor wasn't available to them at this point, because his suspect was boiling up, and an hour or two in the cell on his own could only enhance Cross' chances of getting to the truth. As they were leaving, Ottey noticed that Andy's breathing had changed. His shoulders were rising on every in-breath. He looked like he was trying to control it. She recognised the signs immediately. It looked like panic, but it wasn't. One of her daughters was asthmatic, and this kind of breathing always indicated that she was about to have an attack.

'Are you okay, Andy?' she asked.

'Yeah, I'm fine,' he replied.

'You don't look it,' she replied.

'It's just an asthma attack,' he said.

'Where's your inhaler?'

'At home.'

'You're an asthmatic?' said Cross. Andy didn't bother to answer.

'Would you like to see a nurse?' Ottey continued.

'No, you're all right. It'll pass.'

'You use a blue?' she asked. He looked up, a little surprised.

'Yeah.' She disappeared and came back with a blue inhaler, which she handed to him.

'I carry a spare for my girl in the bag. Have it. I don't need it back. We have more at home,' she said.

'Thanks.'

While they waited for the solicitor to return, Carson asked them both into his office. He'd got the initial forensic findings from the house. Mackenzie stood in the door. She hadn't actually been asked to the meeting, so she figured that if she was asked to leave, retreating would be less humiliating than if she had to exit the actual room.

'The kitchen is covered in blood; cleaned up, obviously. But it's on the edge of the kitchen counter...' Carson began.

'Where he struck his head?' asked Ottey.

'Yep, and pooled on the floor where he must've fallen.'

'DNA?'

'Too soon, but I'd put money on it being Alex's. Everything points to Swinton.'

They looked at Cross, who didn't seem to be listening. He was deep in thought.

'It certainly looks that way,' agreed Ottey.

'Let's charge him. I'll get on to the CPS. Agreed? George?' Carson asked.

But Cross ignored him, left the room, and said to Mackenzie,

'Alice, can you go and get Debbie? Ask her to come in. I'm sure she'll still be recuperating at the restaurant.' Then he stopped and turned back, looking at Ottey. 'Or should we go there? Will she be up to coming in? We're short of time.'

'Alice could call ahead and ask her if it's okay.'

Debbie arrived an hour and a half later. Helena was with her. Helena's son was dead, her grandchild miscarried, and yet her maternal instinct still prevailed. Whenever Cross came across this with mothers and children in his work, it inevitably made him think about his own mother, and whether somehow she had been lacking in this. He'd read about some women not having a maternal fibre in their bodies. Was his mother like that? He'd actually found himself thinking about it a lot more recently, and had asked his father about it. Raymond was baffled that he should be asking. So he had left it alone. But he was becoming more and more aware that it had become a niggle which needed soothing. He admired Helena's being with Debbie. He thought to himself that maybe, through all this tragedy, Debbie had found a family that would care for her.

They decided to meet with them in the small kitchen area, where they made coffee and tea. There was a vending machine selling snacks to one side. They gave the two women coffee. Cross then got up and went over to the vending machine, found change and bought them each a small packet of short-breads. Helena smiled at the small kindness.

'DS Ottey?' Cross said. He always deferred to her when sensitive information needed imparting to grieving families. In this instance, a grieving family, of which the parents of one member might well be involved in the commission of the crime. No matter how hard he tried, his explanation of the situation always came over as cold and insensitive, which was, more often than not, counter-productive.

'We have both your mother and stepfather in custody.' Ottey let that sink in for a moment.

'Was this because of what happened at the restaurant?' said Debbie, turning to Helena. 'I thought we weren't pressing charges.'

'We aren't,' Helena replied, understanding in that moment the implications of what was going on.

'Your stepfather has been arrested on suspicion of murdering Alex Paphides. Your mother is in custody for perverting the course of justice, but it is possible she might well be an accessory to murder.'

'What?' said Debbie. It might well have occurred to her, when she told them where she thought Alex was going on the night of his death, that they may be involved. But she hadn't thought it through – considered it as a real possibility. Helena just looked at the floor. Cross wondered what was going through her mind, at that moment. He wondered whether she had approved of Alex having a relationship with a girl half his age. If she hadn't approved, or had doubts, what must she be thinking now?

'DS Cross has some questions he'd like to ask, if that's okay.'

'Sure,' Debbie replied.

'Tell me about your stepfather, Andy,' Cross began.

'What about him?'

'How long has he been with your mother?'

'As long as I remember.'

'And you were four when your father left? Is that correct?' Cross was reading the questions off a sheet of paper, and was ticking off each question as she answered them.

'Yep.'

'I don't suppose you can remember a lot about it, can you? Being so young.'

'Not really. Just bits.'

'Which bits, exactly?' he asked.

'Mum was really angry. I remember them burning Dad's clothes in the garden. The smell. They used petrol,' she said. Cross made a note then looked up.

'So, Andy was already around?' he said.

'How do you mean?' Debbie asked.

'When your dad left. Andy was already in the picture. With your mum. Is that why your dad left?'

'What are you talking about?' Debbie asked.

'Did your father leave because your mother was having an affair with Andy?'

'No, he would never have done that. They didn't get together till after he'd gone.'

'But he was there?'

'Well of course he was. What are you on about?'

'Why do you say "of course"? I don't understand,' Cross said.

'Because he's my uncle,' she said. Cross didn't react at all, just wrote it down.

'He's your dad's brother?' he asked.

'Well he's obviously not my mum's, is he? Yes. I thought you guys knew,' said Debbie.

'No, no, not at all. We didn't know.' He was thinking this through. This had to mean something; he just didn't know what it was. Ottey took this as her cue to take the conversation up.

'Do you get on? You and your stepdad?' she asked.

'What was his name? Your dad?' said Cross, interrupting.

'Robbie. Robbie Swinton,' she replied.

'So your stepdad,' said Ottey, continuing. 'You get on?'

'Pretty much. We've had our moments. But he's been good to me. He's the only one who can deal with my mum,' Debbie said.

'How do you mean?'

'He's very calm. Takes whatever shit she throws at him.' Cross looked up at this point, which encouraged her to go on, explain.

'She has problems. Well, you can see that. It's pretty obvious, even though she won't admit it. Mental problems. I think it's probably why my dad left.'

'Okay,' said Ottey, encouraging her to continue.

'And she drinks. She drinks, they argue. She's sorry when she's sober. Doesn't drink for weeks, then makes up for it big time. I can't work out why he stays with her sometimes. It's even worse when he drinks with her and he then loses it. They have big rows and I have to sit upstairs and listen to it. If I try and stop it, I get crap from both of them. So I stopped trying. That's why I left.' Ottey looked at Cross who, she knew, had wanted to lead this interview – he still hadn't shared with her why they'd actually asked Debbie to come in. But he showed no inclination of wanting to ask anything. His look, though,

220

also told her that he didn't want anyone asking anything. He wanted Debbie to go on, in her own time, and talk about whatever was on her mind.

'He's no angel, though. Got a terrible temper. You don't see it very often, but when you do, bloody hell. Like I said, when he's had a skinful as well, the rows are terrible. That sounded bad. It wasn't meant to. But, actually, it is what it is. I'm not worried about getting either of them in trouble.'

'Why do you say that?' asked Cross.

'Well, if you've arrested them... well, you must have your reasons, and if they've done it, I'm not going to protect them. Alex is dead and we...' she looked at Helena, 'want to know who did it. Doesn't matter who it is.'

'So do we, Debbie,' said Ottey.

Cross suddenly got up and turned to the door, about to leave. 'George?' said Ottey. She wasn't asking him where he was going, or what he was doing, just reminding him of something she'd been trying to improve. His social awareness. He stopped and turned round. Ottey looked from him to Debbie.

'Oh yes,' he said. 'Goodbye Debbie, and thank you so much for coming in. I appreciate it very much.' He then turned and left. Ottey thought it sounded like he was reciting from a script. But baby steps.

27

It was Wednesday night, so Cross was due to have dinner with his father on this, their new regular night. He was happy to leave the Swintons in their separate cells overnight. Sometimes, depending entirely on the situation of a case, and the personalities involved, he might go through the night questioning suspects. But he thought that wasn't needed here. But also, even he knew that, had he cancelled his father because of work that night, after the recent problems – his, admittedly – his cancelling would have caused mild uproar. Not with his father, who was always indulgent with his son, but with his partner at work, Ottey. She wouldn't have let it go. She would have got as much mileage out of it as possible, which was to be avoided at all costs. So he'd made a point of telling her where he was going when he left work. She hadn't questioned whether they should leave the Swintons alone, but as he left, he turned and spoke to Mackenzie in a highly unconvincing way that left her completely puzzled and made Ottey grin from ear to ear.

'I'm having dinner with my father tonight. It's Wednesday, I know. But we've changed our regular night to accommodate his new commitment at Aerospace Bristol. Normally I would advocate questioning the Swintons a little further into the night, but I wouldn't want to let my father down. He relies on seeing me regularly for supper.' Then he left. Mission accomplished. Mackenzie turned to Ottey, who then provided a detailed explanation, which Mackenzie actually found quite endearing.

Xiao Bao, at the Chinese takeaway, was also thrown by Cross' arrival for his usual order. He even checked his watch to make sure he hadn't lost a day that week.

'It's Wednesday,' said Xiao Bao as he gave Cross his order.

'Yes,' said Cross, without offering any explanation, and left.

Raymond and he ate in silence, as usual, not even with a recorded *Mastermind* playing on the TV. Cross knew this was because his father was preoccupied with his talk the next evening, and was going over it again and again in his mind. Cross was happy with this, but after he'd cleared up he had a question for his father.

'When your wife left you, how did you feel?' he asked.

'Your mother, you mean?'

'Have you had more than one wife?'

'No, but what do you mean exactly?'

'When she left, how did you feel?'

Raymond thought for a moment. 'Wretched. Miserable. Betrayed.'

'Angry?' Cross asked.

'Of course,' Raymond replied.

'How angry?' Cross asked.

'How do you judge such a thing? I was angry, upset. She was walking out on us. More importantly, abandoning you.'

'Why did she leave?'

'Because she felt it wasn't working. She didn't love me any more,' he said.

'Did she not love me any more?'

'What? Of course she did. You were her son,' Raymond said.

'Then why have I neither seen nor heard from her since?'

'She thought a clean break would be best all round, I seem to remember.'

'"Seem to remember" doesn't sound very convincing, and why wasn't I asked?'

'You were four,' said Raymond.

'A very advanced four. Was there someone else?' Cross asked. Raymond seemed to think about this for a second.

'Why are you suddenly asking? Is it something to do with work?' Raymond asked.

'It is, yes.' Cross saw that his father immediately relaxed, which interested him. He made a mental note of it.

'There wasn't anyone else. I often think it might've been easier if there had been.'

'Why?' Cross asked.

'Because, at least that way, she would've been actually leaving me for someone. For something different. For an alternative she thought would be better. Here there was no alternative. Having nothing was better than having me. That hurt.' This sounded convincing in part, but there was something about it that didn't ring true for Cross. He decided to leave it for another time and continue with his line of thought.

'Did she take everything with her when she left?' he asked.

'No, she left stuff. Books, cooking stuff, some clothes.'

'What did you do with it all?'

'Nothing,' Raymond answered. 'I just left it where it was.'

'You didn't burn her clothes?'

'What? No. Of course not. Why would I do that?'

'Anger. Revenge. I'm not sure. That's why I'm asking.'

'What would be the point of that? What would that achieve? She wasn't coming back, so what would the purpose of that be?'

Cross thought for a moment.

'That is a really good question,' he said, as he left. This was what had bothered him in the meeting with Debbie. The image of Andy and Jean burning her husband's clothes in the garden had troubled him. It would have been different had Jean done it on her own. Wouldn't Andy have said something? She was burning his brother's clothes. Wouldn't he have stopped her, in case he came back for them? Unless, of course, they both knew there was no chance of that ever happening.

'Are you feeling better today, Mr Swinton?' Ottey asked.

'I am. Thanks again for the Ventolin,' he replied.

'You're welcome.'

Andy looked like people often did after a night in the holding cell. Most of them wouldn't have slept very well, naturally. But also Cross felt that for many of them, when they woke up in the morning – if they were guilty of whatever they were being held for – it might have crossed their minds that they were likely to wake up incarcerated like this for some time. It had a sobering – sometimes literally – effect on them. Cross went through his ritual with his folders then looked up.

'How did you find out about your stepdaughter's pregnancy, Mr Swinton?' he asked.

'No comment.'

'But you were aware of her pregnancy?' Cross continued.

'No comment.'

'Well, you were, as you have both told us. So how did you find out?'

'No comment.'

'You see what this looks like, right?' said Ottey. 'It just makes you look like you're frightened of us knowing how you found out. But the fact of the matter is, we've established there was no phone call to tell you about the pregnancy, and yet you knew.' Andy didn't flicker. They'd actually started with Jean that morning, who was quite jittery and bad-tempered. It was quite possible she was entering alcohol withdrawal, Cross thought. She had also, on the advice of her lawyer, gone into the "no comment" phase of her interview. For her it was a relief, as she didn't have to think about anything. She just mumbled it automatically, as soon as the person opposite had stopped talking. At one point, she'd even said it in response to being asked if she would like some water. Cross felt they probably had more chance of progressing the interview by talking to Andy first, then revealing to her what they had uncovered with him. Cross suspected that this would still make no difference, and she would maintain her mumbled "no comments".

'Were you aware that, on the night he was killed, only Alex himself and Debbie knew of the pregnancy?' asked Cross. The solicitor looked up from his notes at this point.

'No comment.'

'And, as we now know that Debbie didn't tell you, there is only one other possibility. Which is that Alex came round that night to tell you. Is that what happened?' Cross went on. The solicitor leant forward and whispered something to Andy. Andy looked back at the detectives.

'Alex told us.'

'When?'

Andy looked as if he wasn't sure what to do next.

'Could we have a brief conference?' asked the solicitor.

'Of course,' said Cross. 'It might help us in the long run, hopefully.'

Carson called them into his office. He wanted to wrap it up and charge, rather than get an extension.

'We're not even sure what we're charging her with right now. We're not sure what we're charging either of them with,' said Cross.

'George, come on. We have Alex's blood in the flat. Swinton dumping the bike. His van in the vicinity of the garage the night of the murder. A witness placing it at the garage. He damages the van, the van has corresponding damage, necessitating its repair, and now it turns out the garage Alex's body was dumped in was rented for years by Debbie Swinton's father's family. It's pretty conclusive.'

'Really?' Cross asked.

'You don't think so?' Carson said.

'I think he's referring to the new info on the garage,' said Ottey.

'Oh right. Yeah, Mackenzie just found out. They ran a repair business out of it, servicing cars, doing MOTs,' Carson said.

'Why wasn't I told?' said Cross.

'I'm not sure but, like I said, conclusive,' said Carson.

'I'm not sure I'd go that far. We know Andy dumped the body, but do we have proof he actually killed Alex? It could be either of them,' said Cross.

'Forensics have matched the roll of plastic in Swinton's van to the plastic the body was in. I've called the CPS and they think we have more than enough to charge him for murder,' said Carson, looking at Cross who didn't respond.

'George?' Carson asked. Cross looked up, and then at the clock on the wall.

'We still have a couple of hours. We might as well use them,' he said.

'Very well,' said Carson. He couldn't really argue with that, and he knew it was often, at this point in a case, that Cross was at his best.

Andy's solicitor read out a statement, confirming that Alex had called in at the house that night. He'd arrived just after eight. He'd wanted to tell them about the pregnancy, before he left for a training trip to Tenerife the next morning. He told them and then left shortly after. Jean and her solicitor corroborated this version of events.

'How did you feel about Debbie being pregnant?' Cross asked Andy, who was a little more confident and relaxed now.

People often felt that when the police didn't immediately challenge their statement – which was often significantly different to the story they'd been propounding up until that point – that the police had, in some way, accepted their version of events. So the interview sometimes had a small window of good-naturedness, until the police produced the next piece of damning evidence.

'Like I said before…' Andy began, sighing.

'When you weren't telling us the truth?' interjected Cross.

'…surprised, to be honest,' Andy continued, ignoring Cross. 'A little disappointed. She's so young. But he seemed like a nice bloke. It was what it was,' he said.

'And how was Alex about it?' Cross asked.

'He seemed genuinely happy. Like he was pleased about it. He told us he wanted to marry her.'

'Why aren't you and Jean married?'

'What?'

'You're not married, even though you call her your wife. Why do you do that?' Cross asked.

'We just never got round to it. We're just as, aren't we?'

'"Just as" what?' Cross asked.

'Just as well married,' Andy answered. 'I mean, it doesn't matter either way, does it?'

'Well, it clearly does matter. As I said, you refer to her as your wife and she calls herself Mrs Swinton. So why didn't you get married? I mean, it's not as if it's difficult,' Cross went on.

'What's this got to do with anything?' Andy asked.

'So Alex left your house shortly after he arrived, fit and well, and looking forward to his training trip to Tenerife?' said Cross, deliberately ignoring the question.

'Yes.' Cross made a note of this.

'Have you and Jean been in touch with Debbie since then?' Cross asked.

'Other than the other day? No,' he replied.

'That's a bit odd, isn't it? You find out she's pregnant and you don't get in touch? Why was that?' Cross asked. Andy didn't answer. 'Was it because you couldn't tell her you knew? Because then, she'd know that Alex had been there that night, and now he was dead. You couldn't afford anyone to know. To have the finger pointed in your direction. What is more, you couldn't rely on Jean to keep it to herself, particularly if she'd been drinking,' Cross said. He'd finished. There was no answer. Cross looked at the man across the table from him. The confidence of just a couple of minutes ago had vanished completely.

'So back to that night. How did Alex get to you?' Cross asked.

'How do you mean?'

'Mode of transport. Car, taxi, bus?'

This should've been an easy question to answer, but Andy seemed to be calculating how to answer it. Finally he said, 'I don't know. I have no idea.'

'Bike perhaps?' Cross asked.

'Maybe,' said Andy.

'I mean, it would make sense, wouldn't it?'

'Like I said. I don't know.'

'You don't know? All right... well I can help you there,' said Cross. 'You see we have him on CCTV leaving the airport where he'd attended a meeting at seven thirty seven. You live a good hour away, which almost accords with what you say. That he arrived around eight. On his bike. Except it was more like eight thirty.'

'I didn't see his bike,' said Andy.

'Really? I find that difficult to believe. I mean he was in his cycling gear. He'd just come from Bristol airport on his bike. Quite a trek, but nothing to him, I suppose. Just a warm-up, really. He was probably wearing his cycling helmet. People tend not to take those off when they call round on someone, till they know they're at home. And he would have walked funnily, because he wears those shoes that clip into the pedals.

Cleats, that's right. So, all in all, I think you should be able to remember if he had his bike with him.'

'Well I don't,' replied Andy tersely.

'I cycle. To and from work mostly,' Cross continued conversationally, 'but I used to take my not very expensive, just functional bike with me into the station. Until I successfully lobbied for a bike shelter to be built. You probably passed it on the way in, on the right. I also take it into my flat when I go home. For the simple reason I don't want it to be stolen. Because it's such a hassle if it is. And Alex had the added consideration that his bike was worth thousands of pounds. Carbon fibre. He wouldn't have left it outside your flat; he would have brought it inside. Unless he didn't come inside? Did he stay outside?' Andy didn't answer. Cross hoped that he was feeling a little cornered. 'Would it help if I showed you a photograph of his bike?' He took a photograph out of his folder. 'Here.'

Andy looked at the photograph. 'The man holding it is the police diver, who got it out of the canal where you had thrown it, by my calculations, at two thirty two yesterday morning,' Cross continued.

'And how exactly can you prove that?' Andy asked.

'I was there. Well, not quite there because I had a puncture. Does that ring a bell? A puncture? Because you stopped to help a damsel in distress, did you not?' Andy looked a little pale. 'Mackenzie?' Cross called out. The door opened and Mackenzie walked in. She was slightly annoyed at her heart beating ten to the dozen, as she played her little part in Cross' arranged theatrics. She'd also never been in the inner sanctum of the interview room, when it was in action.

'Do you remember my "daughter", Andy?' asked Cross.

Swinton said nothing. 'That'll be all, Alice,' said Cross, as he produced an evidence bag from his pocket, containing a mobile phone in an amount of uncooked rice. 'We also found this in the vicinity of the bike, on the bed of the canal. Alex's mobile. The one you used to text Matthew and tell him Alex wouldn't be making the trip. That was a mistake, because it meant that whoever killed him knew about Tenerife. I thought the phone would be quite ruined, but it's amazing. Did you know if you put a wet mobile phone – say you've dropped it in the lavatory or the bath or a swimming pool, you understand what I mean – if you've dropped it in water, you just pop it into a bag of rice like this and...'

But the solicitor had had quite enough by now. 'I think we'll take this opportunity...'

'Oh, I think you should,' said Cross, interrupting him back.

28

The solicitor and Andy returned a little later. Ottey was already there. Cross then appeared and organised his folder and pieces of paper equidistantly on the table. This seemed to take longer than usual. Ottey was watching Andy. He was obviously wound up by having seen it several times now. Once Cross was satisfied, he sat down and looked up expectantly.

'Is that supposed to make me feel nervous or something, or are you just plain weird?' said Andy.

'Mr Swinton...' said the solicitor. Cross just continued to stare at Andy, who exhaled dismissively and looked away. Cross looked at the solicitor, who began reading a prepared statement.

'I was in the vicinity of the canal, on the night in question. I was on twenty-four-hour call and was called out to a...'

'I'm going to stop you there, if I may. The fact is, we're running out of time. Well I am, and so I'd like to move things along. A word of advice, Andy. All this changing what happened, not being able to remember anything, then suddenly having a detailed recollection about the events of that night, or any other night for that matter, doesn't help anyone. It's so much better just to tell the truth because, you see, in these circumstances I will get there in the end. In fact, I believe we already have.'

Andy looked at his solicitor. 'Are you going to finish reading that, or what?'

'Why don't we listen to what the detective has to say?' he replied.

'So, Mr Swinton, here's what you know we know. We have Alex at your house the night of the murder. We have you dumping the aforesaid's bike and mobile phone in the canal, the night before last. What you don't know, and what I'm going to disclose to you now, is that forensics have found blood, the victim's blood, in your kitchen, where you attempted to clear it up.' He looked at Andy, who didn't show a flicker of emotion.

'We have a witness who saw a South West Plumbing van, early on the morning of the ninth, reversing into the garage where Alex's body was dumped, at such speed it damaged the flank of the van. Your van. Which went in for repairs the following day. The paint left on the garage door frame is an exact match for the specific paint used for South West vans. You see, your boss is quite fussy about appearance, as I'm sure you know. The blue paint, on close inspection, has tiny metallic elements to give it a slight sparkle, I suppose you'd call it.' He looked at Ottey for confirmation. She nodded.

'Which makes the paint easily identifiable,' he continued. 'We also have the plastic roll from that van. The plastic you used to wrap Alex's body in and leave in the garage. We know that because you see, when you cut a piece of plastic like that with a knife or scissors, whatever, it doesn't really matter, you leave a unique signature along the cut. The plastic wrapped around the body was cut from that roll. It's a perfect match. So, all in all, that's a pretty convincing case, wouldn't you say? Oh, I forgot to mention the fact that the garage you used had been in Jean's family for years. You knew it was now disused, so you could leave the body there till you'd decided what to do with it. What you weren't to know, was that the demolition would be brought forward, before you had a chance to move it.'

'I'd like to talk to my client,' said the lawyer.

'I think, in truth, we're a little beyond that. Don't you Andy?' said Cross. Andy looked at him. He was cornered by the evidence and he'd had enough of Cross. There was a long pause before he finally spoke.

'It was an accident,' he said.

'Andy Swinton, did you kill Alex Paphides on the night of May eighth?' Cross asked.

'Not intentionally,' he replied.

'Would you like to make a statement now?'

Andy looked at his solicitor, who nodded.

'Yes.'

'Then would you excuse me? An officer will be in to take it. Is there anything you'd like to ask before I go?'

'No.'

'Very well.' Cross then got up and left, followed by Ottey.

'Why didn't you ask him what happened?' she asked.

'It'll go into the statement,' he answered, slightly distracted. She knew something was going on. They always went through a confession after it was made. Particularly Cross, who liked to ensure that the narrative of facts was laid out coherently. But before she could press him any further, Carson walked up to them, extending his hand. Cross didn't take it. No matter how many times this happened, Carson still carried on doing it. Ottey wondered whether it was because he just didn't concentrate; didn't pay attention to what was going on around him.

'Well done,' he said. But Cross was looking far from happy – which Ottey would describe as his default expression. She'd learnt this from numerous enquiries, where she'd asked him if he was all right, only to be greeted by a puzzled reaction and told that he was fine, and that this was how he always looked.

This time, maybe, was different, as the unhappiness was accompanied by a fixed look of concentration. 'What is it?' said Carson. 'It's a result, cut and dried, George.'

'He manifested no sign of relief. No sign of anything. It's as if it's just one more piece of an agreed narrative. For him, it was just a question of when it happened, not if,' said Cross.

'George, come on. Don't do this. Again. Please,' Carson went on.

'We should interview Jean. Tell her Andy's being charged, and that she's being released on police bail.'

'You just don't know when to stop. This is that time, George. Let it go,' said Carson.

'Up until this point they have been each other's alibis. We haven't actually checked this information. We should check South West Plumbing's work roster for that night, and also the mobile phone records of both Andy and Jean,' said Cross, as if he was thinking out loud. Carson was about to remonstrate again, but Cross was already walking off to the custody sergeant, and asking for Jean to be brought to the other interview room. Carson turned to Ottey.

'Josie. Do something,' he pleaded.

'You're the boss,' she replied.

'A concept our friend over there seems to have a little difficulty in grasping at the best of times.'

As soon as they told Jean that they were about to charge Andy, and she would be released on bail until the CPS had decided what to charge her with, she burst into tears.

'So I can go?' she asked. Cross detected an element of disbelief through the tears.

'For the time being,' said Ottey.

'Okay, then I'm assuming we're done here?' said Jean's solicitor.

'Not quite,' said Cross. This time it was the solicitor, not the suspect, who sighed and sank back into her chair. Like a child at school who is told to stay where she is after the end-of-class bell has sounded, because the teacher wants to have a word.

'I'm curious about one thing. We know that Alex came to the house to tell you about the pregnancy. How did he feel about it?' Cross asked.

'How do you mean?'

'Was he happy?'

'I don't know. He just told us,' she said.

'But you must have had a sense of how he felt,' Cross went on.

'He just said he'd do the right thing – whatever that means.'

'Presumably, marry her,' suggested Cross.

'I guess so. Married at sixteen, with a kid at seventeen.' She shook her head.

'Sound familiar?' Cross asked.

'You trying to be funny?'

'How do you feel about your being pregnant at sixteen? In hindsight? How did it affect you?'

'It messed up everything. My parents practically disowned me. It was such a mistake.'

'What was? Getting pregnant?'

'Well, what do you think?' she said.

'I don't know. Which is why I'm asking you.'

'The whole thing was a bit of a fuck-up. It was complicated,' she said.

'But you ended up marrying the father?' he asked.

'Yeah.' She laughed a little mournfully. 'That was the problem.'

'How do you mean?' Cross asked.

'We weren't suited. He was older. You shouldn't get married just because you've been stupid enough to get pregnant. It's not the answer.'

'What is? Termination?'

'Maybe. Or adoption. Funny, isn't it? I can't think of me having an abortion because of Debbie. You know? She might be a little shit a lot of the time, but I still love her. I mean, she's mine. So abortion wouldn't have been the answer for me.' She laughed a bit. 'But then thinking about it, I can't talk about adoption either, with her. Now I know her.'

'Much easier to talk about those things before,' Cross suggested.

'What do you mean?'

'Much easier to talk about a termination or adoption, before the baby is born.'

'I guess so,' she said. Ottey could see where this was going, which was just as well, as Cross looked at her in that way that said "you take over". He must've felt it might be a better conversation between two women.

'Is that what happened when Alex came round?' Ottey asked.

'What?' Jean asked.

'He didn't actually want the baby, did he?' she said.

'What? No, I just told you, he said he wanted to marry her. Have the baby,' she said.

'I don't think that's true, is it Jean? He wanted her to have an abortion. That's why he hadn't even told his mother. Because he didn't want to be talked out of it,' Ottey said.

'No,' said Jean. 'You've got that arse over tit. He was all for it; it was...' but she stopped.

'It was what? Jean?'

'Nothing. Can I go now?'

'She's telling the truth,' said Cross.

'Thank you,' said Jean.

'To an extent,' Cross went on. 'Alex did want the baby. He wanted to look after Debbie, in a way that her own family hadn't.'

'What's that supposed to mean?'

'Or, more accurately, in a way that her mother hadn't. It was Debbie who didn't want the baby, wasn't it Jean?' But she didn't answer. 'You see, what puzzled me about all of this, Josie, is why would Alex bother to go and tell Jean and Andy that Debbie was having a baby? Debbie had left home. Things weren't good. He hadn't told his own family, who were much more supportive as a whole. Much tighter. So why go and tell Debbie's parents, if she was just going to go ahead with having the child? There was no urgency. He didn't have to go then. Unless, of course, Debbie had decided she didn't want the baby. She wanted to get rid of it. I should imagine by termination. Because she knew that as her pregnancy became more obvious, there was no way on this earth that Helena, a proud and fiercely protective matriarch, would let her put the baby up for adoption. Abortion was the only way. Is that closer to the truth, Jean?'

She thought for a moment and then began to speak, but without looking at either of the two officers.

'He blamed me. He said she didn't want it because of me. Because of what had happened to me, being a mum so young. She didn't want that happening to her.'

'Had you been drinking when he came round?'

'What do you think?' she said.

'You had a row,' Cross said.

'He said it was my fault. That Debbie was killing his baby because of me. He got more and more angry. It was my fault, because I had been such a shit mother. Because I hadn't been a mother at all.'

There was a knock at the door, and Mackenzie entered with a piece of paper, which she handed to Cross.

'For the tape, Police Staff Officer Alice Mackenzie entered the room and has now left,' said Ottey. Cross looked at the paper, and if it was in any way relevant or of interest to the case, he didn't show it.

'What happened then?' asked Cross. She thought for a minute.

'Andy got involved. He said Alex had no right to come into his house and speak to me in that way.'

'How did you feel about what Alex was saying? About the baby?'

'I thought he was wrong. I thought Debbie was right to want an abortion,' she said. 'I told him he couldn't see it now, but it would be better in the end. Debbie was right. She didn't want her life ruined in the way she'd ruined mine.'

Ottey couldn't help herself at this point. 'You're honestly saying, you think that Debbie ruined your life?'

'Look at me? I never had a chance. Any hopes I had were taken away from me by her.'

'Are you serious?' said Ottey.

'Josie...' said Cross, his usual role with her reversed somewhat. Cautioning her to keep her feelings to herself.

'It's the truth,' said Jean.

'How did Alex react to this?'

'He said it was bullshit.' She started to cry. 'He said I would've ended up a hopeless drunk, whether or not I'd had her, and he'd told Debbie that. But she didn't believe him, and that's why she was going to get rid of it.'

'Why was he there, though? He didn't just come round to have it out with you and Andy, did he?'

'He wanted me to talk to her and tell her not to do it. I said I didn't think she would listen to me. But then I said that I wouldn't talk to her, because I thought what she was doing was right. I thought she should get rid of it. That's when it really kicked off. Andy stepped in. It was so quick. They grabbed each other and started fighting, then suddenly they both fell over, with Andy on top of him. He cracked his head open on the edge of the kitchen countertop. It made a horrible noise. There was blood everywhere. I went to get some kitchen roll, but when I got back, Andy said he was dead.' She stopped and looked up at Cross. He'd seen this before. She was trying to work out whether he believed her. He just looked back at her. 'That's what happened,' she said. He thought she said it, not with a certainty that she'd remembered that night clearly, but that she'd remembered her script perfectly. 'That's what he must've told you.'

'He's making his statement now,' said Cross.

'Well it'll be in there, just like I told you,' she said.

'Oh I'm sure it will. As long as he remembers the story as well as you did. Doesn't leave anything out,' Cross said.

'What do you mean?' said Jean.

'I think there's some truth in it. Mainly the fight and his skull's fatal connection with the edge of the kitchen surface,' he replied.

'Yeah, like I said,' she replied.

'But not Andy's role in all of it,' he said. He picked up the piece of paper Mackenzie had brought in, and looked at it for a few moments, as if it was the first time he'd seen it. He then gave it to Ottey who, after a few seconds, looked a little surprised. She looked up at Jean, as she put the paper back on the table.

'What?' said Jean.

'I have a copy of your phone records here, and Andy's. Also, Andy's hours for the last month, at South West Plumbing,' said Cross.

'So?'

'Andy wasn't with you that night.'

'Yes he was. I just told you that and so did he,' she protested.

'Let me rephrase that. He was there, but not till later. Much later. He was on a night shift.'

'What are you talking about?'

'Your phone records show that you placed seven calls to

him from your mobile, between eight forty-nine and ten fifty-three, when he eventually picked up.' He looked at her for a reaction. But there was none. 'He wasn't there when Alex died. Your argument with Alex escalated. He was furious that you agreed that Debbie should have an abortion, as she was planning. And he blamed you. That's why he'd come to the house in the first place – to tell you she was planning an abortion and to ask for your help. You refused. What happened? Why did you hit him?'

'It was self-defence,' she said.

'How?'

'He came for me. He lunged at me. It was self-defence,' she repeated.

'I don't think he came for you. I think you may have thought that,' said Cross.

'What are you talking about? He threw himself at me,' she said.

'I think we both know what happened and I think you know this, having had the time to think about it. You were arguing; he moved towards you – maybe to make a point, maybe to plead with you to see sense, and he lost his balance. He was wearing bicycle cleats. Very easy to lose your balance wearing those. I know that, because I tried them once without success, it has to be said, and anyway I decided that taking cycling seriously wasn't for me. It wasn't without its attractions, but I didn't really see the point. I'm very much an A to B cyclist. The journey has to have a point. A utilitarian cyclist, I suppose you could call it.' He stopped. She was looking at him like he was mad. He was accusing her of killing someone, and was banging on about cycling. 'You may or may not have thought he was coming for you, but in any event, you hit him, as you say, with the ashtray and he fell, cracking his head, fatally, in the process. Those, I think, are the only two truthful things about your version of events.'

He paused, giving her the opportunity to say something,

contradict him, even. She turned to her solicitor for some sort of help, but none was forthcoming.

'It must've been awful. You panicked. Couldn't get hold of Andy. You had to sit there with a corpse in your room till he got home. But then he sorted it out, didn't he? As he always does.'

29

Jean was eventually charged with manslaughter, on the instructions of the CPS. Andy was charged with perverting the course of justice and preventing the lawful and decent burial of Alex. The team were going over to the pub to celebrate. Cross, of course, didn't join them. Carson came into his office with Ottey and three glasses of single malt whisky. He gave one to Ottey and the other to Cross who, as usual, left it on the desk untouched. Ottey didn't know why Carson bothered with this new ritual, but again put it down to his having watched too many American cop shows on TV. She had convinced herself that he probably didn't even like whisky, but possibly only because the thought amused her. She'd seen him in the office open his bottom drawer, pull out the bottle of Scotch, get two glasses in the other hand – it had to be one hand – with a gunslinger's dexterity and pour a thumb each for himself and whoever he was trying to impress. If he wanted to get down and dirty he would dispense with the glasses and grab the nearest two coffee mugs – for more gritty effect, she thought. Depending whether he was in an episode of *Midsomer Murders* or *The Shield*.

In truth, when Cross came up with a turnaround in a case

like this, Carson always wanted a debrief. He genuinely thought at times, though he would never say it to George, that he was learning at the feet of a master. Odd, eccentric and infuriating, but a master of detection nonetheless.

'So come on. What was the clue? What made you go in that direction?' he asked, like some sort of superfan.

'He didn't display any signs of anxiety for himself, only when Jean was mentioned. He's spent years apologising for her. Like the other day at the restaurant. Despite everything, he loves her. It still could have been him, but we'd been working on the principle that they were each other's alibis. Checking the phone records, his worksheet would have been done earlier, but hadn't because of this. So it was worth checking. But it was the reason Alex had gone there in the first place. Why go there at all? It had to be because Debbie didn't want the baby and he either thought Jean, as her mother, could persuade her...'

'He obviously didn't know her that well,' said Ottey.

'That's true,' Cross replied. 'Or he wanted to express his anger at Jean.'

'Well, good result as ever. Cheers,' said Carson, raising his glass to Cross, then, realising his mistake, to Ottey. He downed the drink and got up. 'Good work; mañana,' he said and left. Ottey got up herself, and poured Cross' whisky into her glass. He looked at her.

'I'm going to chuck it. Don't worry. Mother of two, dear. Homework and dinner to be done. Problems listened to and solved, or just arguments to be had and resolved,' she reassured him.

'Have the interview transcripts been done?' he asked.

'Probably not all of them. Why?'

'I just want to go over some things.'

'Can't it wait?'

'No.'

'Well, if they're not done, you could always work off the tapes. If you're that desperate.'

244

She left and found Mackenzie packing up for the day.

'What's he doing?' Mackenzie asked.

'Crossing all the t's and dotting all the i's,' Ottey replied.

'Have we missed something?'

'Oh you can be sure about that,' said Ottey, smiling.

She was smiling a little less when she got a call from Cross at six forty-five the next morning.

'I need an excavation team,' he said.

'What?' she replied.

'I need an excavation team.'

'Where are you?'

'At the office,' he replied.

'Have you been there all night?' she asked.

'Yes. Can you call Carson for me?' he asked.

'Why can't you call him?'

'Because the chances of him getting me a forensic excavation team when, one, he thinks the case is closed, which it is by the way...'

'Then what do you need an excavation team for?' she asked.

'...and two,' he said, completely ignoring her, 'he still hasn't forgiven me for calling him at five the other morning.'

She agreed to make the call and meet Cross at the dump site. She had no problem calling Carson. Her only regret was not to have been there to see his face. Hearing that, despite the fact that the case was closed, Cross was now asking for an excavation team would, without question, send him into a cheek-inflating, blood-vessel-bursting paroxysm of frustration. This would be compounded by the fact that she was unable to explain the purpose of Cross' request. When it came to it, there was such a long silence on the other end of the phone that she thought he must've either cut the call off, or just fallen back to sleep.

Ottey got the girls off to school and went straight to the

garages. The first person she saw was Morgan, the contractor. 'Good morning,' she said.

'Well, it was till you lot showed up,' he replied.

A large white tent had been erected over the demolished remains of the garage where Alex's body had been found. Cross was standing outside, observing. As were several people on the balconies of the flats overlooking, including Cross' witness, smoking as usual and watering her plants.

'How was last night?' Ottey asked Cross.

'What do you mean?' he said, puzzled.

'It was Thursday; your dad was giving his first talk. Didn't you go?'

'Of course not,' he replied.

'Why?' she said, surprised.

'Because I'd already heard it several times. I didn't need to hear it again, and anyway I was working.'

'I can't believe you didn't go.'

'At the risk of repeating myself, I'd already heard the talk, several times.'

'That's not the point. You should've gone to support him. He would've really appreciated that.'

'If he'd wanted me to go there, he would've asked. But he didn't.'

She was about to continue when Carson arrived.

'Would someone mind telling me why we are here, at the scene of a crime, no not even a crime scene, a dump site which was involved in a crime we have already solved?'

'Because I think we're about to find it is also a crime scene,' Cross replied.

'What?'

'Why did they burn Robbie's clothes?' Cross asked.

'I don't know. Who the hell is Robbie?'

'Jean's first husband. Debbie said that Andy and her mother burnt her father's clothes after he left. She remembers the smell of petrol. She remembers her mother being very angry, and she's always assumed that she was angry about her father leaving them. But why did he leave his clothes? Why didn't he take everything with him?'

'Maybe he was coming back and she did it to piss him off. Or he left in a rush,' said Carson.

'Both possible, but both equally as unlikely,' Cross replied. 'I've had a sense of unease...'

'Do you mean a gut instinct?' Ottey asked mischievously, knowing how dismissive he was of them.

'I do not. I mean a sense of unease, brought on by the discovery that Andy and Robert...' He turned to Carson, as if he believed his boss needed everything explaining to him, several times. '...Jean's first husband, were brothers and that he'd brought up his brother's daughter as his own. I checked hospital records, and around the time before Robert disappeared, Jean was in casualty several times with bruising to her face and other injuries consistent with domestic abuse. Then I began to wonder why they hadn't got married, even though Andy referred to Jean as his wife. But you can't get married if you haven't been divorced. But no-one would know, as her name hadn't changed. It was still Mrs Swinton.'

At this point, one of the forensic team came out of the tent and showed them a photo on his camera. At the bottom of the hole they were digging, there was part of a skeleton – an arm and a hand.

'Is that a body?' asked Carson.

'If I'm right, it's Robbie Swinton,' said Cross.

'Fuuuck,' said Carson.

'You can't declare someone dead without informing the authorities that he's missing. Which would then bring up a load of questions it would be better not to have to face,' Cross went on.

'So...?' asked Carson, trying to make it sound like he was trying to figure out where Cross was going, even though he was clueless.

'Robbie was killed by his brother Andy, to protect Jean and her baby,' Cross went on. Carson turned to him. 'Their baby, in point of fact,' Cross concluded.

'What?' said Carson, who was beginning to wish he'd just had a coffee and gone straight to the office.

'I think we'll find that Andy Swinton is Debbie's father. It's why he's so protective of her. Treats her like his own. Because she is his. I had my suspicions, but it wasn't till his asthma attack in custody that I began to think it was a real possibility.' He paused, as he thought both Ottey and Carson needed a moment to take this all in and process it. 'I think, on balance, they probably told Robbie the truth about the child's paternity. The child he had brought up for four years, believing it to be his own, and it was too much for him. The entire marriage was a sham. If they'd told him the truth right at the beginning, maybe this wouldn't have happened. I think there was a fight and Andy killed him. Jean has covered for him for the last twelve years, and now it was his turn to cover for her. You can understand it, I suppose. He hadn't paid for his brother's death, so he was determined, if they were found out, to pay for Alex's. Even though he hadn't done it.'

'Okay,' said Ottey. 'I get all of that. But how did you know he was here? Robbie?'

'Because the witness on the balcony,' – they all looked up and there she was, watching them, and she gave them a wave – 'told me the history of the garages. A couple of car mechanics used to work out of the garages till about twenty years ago, and one of them had an inspection pit. One of the mechanics was a friend of her mother's. She remembers the pit really well. After the garages closed the kids used to play in the pit. The garage with the pit being the garage belonging to Jean's father. But then I remembered that the inspection pit was no longer there. Why would you go to all the trouble of filling the pit up? You'd just leave it, wouldn't you? Unless you had something to hide in it. Like a body.'

He then turned and walked away. He was quite exhausted. Not just because he'd been up for thirty-six hours, but because cases like this really took it out of him. Part of his drive to solve cases was an inbuilt intolerance of things being wrong. He had to get them sorted out before he could relax. It wasn't so much about justice, as a need for things to be right. To be just as they should be. Until they were, he found it appallingly stressful. So, more than feeling vindicated, or successful, he just felt immensely relieved, plain and simple.

THE END

Read on for an exclusive preview of the third thrilling mystery for DS Cross…

THE PATIENT
CHAPTER 1

C ross was unlocking his bike in the shelter outside the Major Crime Unit in Bristol when he heard a noise behind him. He turned, expecting to see maybe a stray cat or dog, but instead found a woman crouching in the corner of the racks, eating a sandwich. He'd seen this woman before. She had been sitting in the reception of the MCU for the past three days. On one occasion he'd seen her talking to the desk sergeant. She had seemed quite calm, gently spoken, as if whatever it was she was there for was being dealt with. She was well-dressed in a middle class, fairly affluent way. She didn't seem to be creating a fuss or making a nuisance of herself.

After three days of passing her Cross had determined to talk to her and find out what the issue was. But she wasn't in reception as he left that day, so he assumed that whatever she had been there for had been dealt with. Her presence in the bike shelter obviously contradicted this. She had left the building, yes, but she hadn't left, per se. His previous curiosity was now doubled by her apparent dogged determination not to leave. She was bedraggled, her hair and clothes wet from the incessant rain they'd had that afternoon. "Wet rain" was how his work partner DS Josie Ottey had once described it. When he'd asked her whether rain was not, by its very nature, always wet, she explained that she meant the kind of rain that fell in large voluminous drops. Drops so large they were almost impossible to avoid, as if there was a giant leaky tap in the sky.

The woman's dishevelled appearance wasn't helped by the fact that she had tied the plastic carrier bag in which she had brought her lunch round her head as a makeshift rain-proof scarf. She had brought her lunch with her every day for the past few days. She'd planned her visits and was organised; obviously anticipating a lengthy wait, he remembered thinking. He had also noticed that she made her sandwiches with baguettes, not sliced white bread. He took this as a further sign of her being middle class, though he was sure that Ottey would call him a snob for such an observation. She looked like she was in her late sixties.

He stopped unlocking his bike when he saw her. She said nothing; nor did he. He was never very good at initiating conversation unless he was conducting an interview, in which case he realised it was a fundamental requirement. However, it occurred to him that in this instance, as he had been intending to talk to this woman when she was inside anyway, he probably shouldn't wait for her to speak first.

'What are you doing in here?' he asked.

'Keeping out of the rain,' she replied, quietly.

'Wouldn't that have been more efficiently achieved if you'd stayed inside?' It wasn't an unreasonable question, he thought.

'They asked me to leave,' she said.

'Why?'

'Because they obviously think I'm a nuisance and don't want to have to deal with me.'

'Well, that would be because this isn't actually a police station. A police station has to deal with everyone. I can tell you where the nearest one is,' he replied.

'I've already been there. I've been to all the local police

stations and they sent me here. Now they've sent me away as well.'

'Why?' he asked.

'"Why" what?'

'Have you been to all the neighbouring police stations?'

'And who are you exactly?' she asked.

Cross thought this was a perfectly legitimate question. 'I'm DS George Cross of the Major Crime Unit,' he replied.

'Oh good. You're just the person I need to talk to then. My name is Sandra Wilson and my daughter has been murdered,' she said matter-of-factly.

Why this had been of no interest to all the desk sergeants in the area was exactly what intrigued Cross and led to him inviting her back into the building to his office. It was possible she had mental health issues, he thought; though if she had, she was hiding it well.

As they walked into the MCU reception police staffer Alice Mackenzie was leaving, her day finished. 'Goodnight, DS Cross,' she said politely.

'Towel,' he replied.

Mackenzie stopped in her tracks, swivelled round and said to his disappearing back, 'What?'

'Towel,' Cross repeated.

She looked at the woman walking up the stairs with Cross and saw that she was soaking wet. She sighed and went back into the building in search of a towel. She had become used to his often peremptory-sounding instructions by now and didn't take offence – most of the time. She couldn't help smiling, though, as she heard the desk sergeant calling after Cross futilely. He was presumably wondering what Cross was doing taking the woman who'd been sitting in reception for the last three days, and who he himself had escorted off the premises at lunch time, back into the building. This was classic Cross. He was Marmite to most of his colleagues at the MCU. They either liked him or loathed him. There was no in between. He often came across as rude, difficult or plain obtuse. But it wasn't intentional. George Cross was on the spectrum which sometimes made him a little challenging to work with. But it was also his gift. It was what made him an extraordinary detective.

Cross took his time going through the slim file of documents Sandra Wilson had given him. Mackenzie had decided to invite herself to the meeting, if indeed that was what it was, as she'd said that it might make Sandra feel "more comfortable". Cross wasn't entirely sure why this was but was too tired to take her up on it. For her part Mackenzie had quietly congratulated herself on being a little more assertive with Cross recently and proving her value to him since she'd joined the force the year before. Despite her initial qualms, she was loving the job more and more each day. She was also beginning to see where she could be of use to Cross, which helped; making others at their ease with him was one of those occasions – unless, of course, she had determined that a degree of discomfort was what Cross wanted from his interlocutor. She made small talk with Sandra as Cross concentrated on the file. He finally looked up and cut across their conversation completely, as if it wasn't even taking place.

'The coroner has determined that your daughter died on June 17th of this year from an accidental overdose. There was an autopsy, and the toxicology report clearly confirms his finding. Your daughter Felicity...'

'Flick,' Sandra interrupted. 'We called her Flick.'

'Your daughter Flick had a long, troubled history of drug abuse. Several unsuccessful stays in rehab. There's a detailed statement from her psychologist...'

'Dr Sutton,' Sandra volunteered.

'...saying that she had been a suicide risk in the past. It all points to a tragic death, Mrs Wilson – self-inflicted, whether deliberately or not. Anyone reading this report would come to the same, inevitable conclusion. Which is, I imagine, the reaction you received from the various police stations you've visited.'

'She did not kill herself, deliberately or otherwise,' Sandra said.

'Sometimes these things are hard to accept, particularly for a mother,' said Mackenzie.

'I'm telling you, she didn't kill herself. She was murdered,' Sandra reiterated.

Cross wondered about this woman's conviction for a moment. She was obviously determined, as evidenced by her presence in their reception for the last three days, as well as her apparent refusal to take the verdict of the coroner and the subsequent reactions of the police as final. 'Why would anyone want to murder your daughter?' He asked.

'I have no idea,' she replied.

Cross went back to the report, turning the pages slowly.

'Nothing was taken; there was no evidence of there being a break-in. Indeed there is no evidence of anyone else having been with your daughter at the time of, or immediately prior to, her death. What makes you so convinced, in complete contradiction to the facts such as they are, that she was murdered?'

'I knew my daughter,' was the reply.

Cross said nothing. He'd heard this kind of intuitive, emotionally based statement thousands of times before from relatives, friends, family who couldn't accept what they were being told: that their son was a killer, a rapist, a thief or, as in this case, dead. A refusal to believe what was evident and right in front of them was understandable but, in his opinion, equally frustrating. Sandra was an obvious case of this. He regretted having brought her back into the building. The facts were plain to him. Suicide or accident.

'Many people think they know those close to them, only to find out that something was being hidden from them all those years. Do you know anyone who might have wished your daughter harm?' he asked.

'I knew everything about my daughter. Everything. And I am telling you. She was killed,' she said, ignoring his question.

Cross was never impressed by people's instinctive convictions about things. He dealt in evidence. Facts. There was nothing in this situation that made him think that the grief-stricken woman in front of him was right about her daughter. He went back to the coroner's report to ensure that he hadn't missed anything. He read it again. Twice. This took a further twenty minutes, during which he didn't look up.

Mackenzie filled the silence by making small talk with Sandra. She was pleased she'd stayed, because even though Cross may not have valued her presence there, she was sure Sandra would have derived some comfort from it and it might be of use in the long run. She had discovered in her time at the MCU that she could be useful sometimes as a point of contact for people during an enquiry. She thought of herself as a conduit between them and Cross.

Cross looked up, pushed the file across his desk back to Sandra and stood up, hoping to indicate that the meeting was over.

'Mrs Wilson, there is really nothing I can add to the information you have been provided with. It seems quite clear to me that your daughter died from a heroin overdose, accidental or otherwise. Nothing in there indicates any other possibility.' He looked at her with a neutral expression which he hoped would go some way to persuading her that he was telling the truth. He then remembered what Ottey had told him to say in such circumstances and so added, 'I'm sorry for your loss.'

The woman got up, obviously very disappointed, but she smiled in a dignified manner and put the file back into her handbag. She then said, 'Thank you for your time, Detective Sergeant.'

'I'll show you out,' said Mackenzie. 'Where are you off to now? Do you need transport?'

'No, you're very kind. I'll take the bus. I'm picking up my granddaughter from a neighbour who's been looking after her.'

'How old is she?' Mackenzie asked.

'Just two; she's Flick's child,' Sandra replied as Mackenzie closed the door behind them.

Cross thought for a moment then immediately strode over and reopened the door.

'Your daughter had a small child?' he asked.

Mackenzie and Sandra stopped and turned.

'Yes, Daisy,' Sandra said.

Cross did not speak for a moment but was thinking as he stared at the carpet.

'Where was this child when your daughter overdosed?' he asked.

'In the flat with her. In her bedroom,' Sandra replied.

'The child was in the flat?' he asked again.

'Yes. Flick would've just put her down for the night. She was very big on routine. Daisy went to bed at seven every night, tears or not.'

Cross thought about this.

'So she puts the child down and then injects herself,' he said slowly, as if asking himself.

Mackenzie thought she detected a tone of disbelief in his voice, but with him it was always so difficult to know.

'Exactly,' said Sandra.

Mackenzie showed Sandra out of the building ten minutes later. Sandra was happy to leave, as Cross had promised to look into a couple of things. She, in return, had promised not to come back to the MCU until he'd called her with some more information.

Mackenzie went back to Cross' office but he'd gone. He

often did this, she had noticed, when he didn't want to discuss something, or wanted to avoid confrontation. Sometimes it was when he simply wanted to have time to think on his own. He would then leave the office by the back stairs, and have to walk round the entire building, on this occasion in the rain, to get to his bike. She toyed with the idea of running down and intercepting him, but decided against it.

What she didn't know was that it wasn't her Cross was avoiding. It was his boss DCI Carson, who he knew was still in the building, as he'd seen his car outside in its parking bay when he'd gone to get his bike. He knew that Carson would have been informed by the desk sergeant, who didn't like Cross and had no time for his "weirdness", that the woman Carson had asked to be removed from reception had now been taken back into the building by DS Cross. Cross had neither the time nor the patience for issuing unnecessary explanations to his superior that night.

His interest in Flick's death had been piqued by the obvious lack of logic in the process of her overdose. He found it hard to believe that Flick, either about to relapse or kill herself, would not make arrangements for her child. Her infant. If she had been wanting another drug-induced trance – which he thought unlikely in the context of her recent behaviour – or wanted to kill herself, she surely wouldn't have done it with the child in the next room. That seemed out of place to him. What alerted him even more was the fact that the child hadn't featured at all in the inquest. That indicated a lack of thoroughness to Cross, and more often than not such an approach led to a mistake. He'd give it more thought in the morning. Right now he needed his bed.

ABOUT THE AUTHOR

Tim Sullivan is an acclaimed screenwriter, whose credits include *A Handful of Dust*, starring Kristen Scott Thomas, *Where Angels Fear to Tread*, starring Helen Mirren and Helena Bonham Carter, *Jack and Sarah* (which he also directed), starring Richard E Grant, Judi Dench and Ian McKellen and *Letters to Juliet*, with Amanda Seyfried. He is also a television director whose credits include *Sherlock Holmes* and *Cold Feet*. He has written extensively in Hollywood in both live action and animation, working with Ron Howard, Scott Rudin and with Jeffrey Katzenberg on the fourth *Shrek* movie. He has now embarked on a series of crime novels featuring the eccentric and socially-awkward, but brilliantly persistent DS George Cross. *The Dentist* is the first in the series, followed by *The Cyclist*. Tim lives in North London with his wife, Rachel Purnell, the Emmy award-winning producer of *The Barefoot Contessa* and *Pioneer Woman*.

ACKNOWLEDGEMENTS

As ever thanks to James Maw my editor. Sandy Crole for his meticulous notes. Sue Davison for her proof-reading skills. Jason Bartholomew my literary agent. Laura and Anna at Head of Zeus. Finally, Rachel for everything – hopefully when she sees this she'll understand that I actually do work upstairs.